THE PALE APE AND OTHER PULSES

Also by M.P. Shiel,
published by Tartarus Press
The Purple Cloud
Prince Zaleski

The Pale Ape
And Other Pulses

by

M.P. Shiel

Tartarus Press

The Pale Ape and Other Pulses
by M.P. Shiel
The Pale Ape was first published by T. Werner Laurie, 1911
This edition is published by Tartarus Press, MMVI at Coverley House,
Carlton-in-Coverdale, Leyburn,
North Yorkshire, DL8 4AY
All stories copyright © The Estate of M.P. Shiel.
'Introduction' by Brian Stableford is copyright © B. Stableford.
This edition copyright © Tartarus Press.

ISBN
1 87262198 8
978-1-872621-98-2

This edition is made possible by the kindness of Javier Marias (Xavier of Redonda), the executor and holder of the Estate of M.P. Shiel.
The publishers would like to express their thanks to King Xavier, Brian Stableford, David Fletcher, Mark Valentine and the Redondan Cultural Foundation.

This edition of
The Pale Ape
is limited to 300 copies

Maestro de las Reales Prensas en Lengua Inglesa.

Contents

Introduction *by* Brian Stableford v

The Pale Ape 1
The Case of Euphemia Raphash 15
Cummings King Monk 29
A Bundle of Letters 103
Huguenin's Wife 117
Many a Tear 129
The House of Sounds 141
The Spectre-Ship 171
The Great King 189
The Bride 199

THE DURANCE OF DECADENCE
An introduction to
THE PALE APE AND OTHER PULSES
by Brian Stableford

Fifteen years separated the publication of M.P. Shiel's first collection of miscellaneous short stories, *Shapes in the Fire* (1896) from *The Pale Ape and Other Pulses*, which was published by T. Werner Laurie in 1911. A great deal had changed in the interim, not only in Shiel's life and career but in the literary marketplace that provided its context. Some of those changes are mapped in the contents of this second collection, which draws its material from the entire span of the interim period.

Like its immediate predecessor, which chronicled the extraordinary adventures of *Prince Zaleski* (1895), *Shapes in the Fire* had been planned as a book publication to be issued by John Lane, the most important promoter of the English Decadent Movement. None of the stories in it had been published in periodicals, all of them having been designed as ornately-stylised works of a much more highbrow stripe than the common fare of middlebrow magazines. It would not have occurred to Shiel to republish therein such early magazine stories as 'Guy Harkaway's Substitute' (1893) and 'The Eagle's Crag' (1894). When the market for that kind of book disappeared, however—which happened almost immediately after the publication of *Shapes in the Fire*—Shiel had no alternative but to consider the possibility of adapting his future short fiction into formats in which it might obtain magazine publication, while retaining the possibility of eventual collection in book form.

The earliest of the stories included in *The Pale Ape and Other Pulses* to see publication, 'Huguenin's Wife,' appeared in the April 1895 issue of *The Pall Mall Magazine*. *Shapes in the Fire* had not yet appeared, although the collection had presumably been submitted to its publisher beforehand, and 'Huguenin's Wife' had been published before the fate of the short-lived English Decadent Movement was sealed by the backlash generated by the conviction and imprisonment of Oscar Wilde. In another and kinder world Shiel might have been able to place more stories as exotic as 'Huguenin's Wife' in the magazines, at least for a while, but that possibility vanished along with the possibility of publishing more books like *Shapes in the Fire*.

'The Case of Euphemia Raphash,' which appeared in the 1895 Christmas supplement of *Chapman's Magazine*, might well have been written, and perhaps accepted for publication, before Wilde's downfall, but 'The Spectre-Ship,' which was published in *Cassell's Magazine* in September 1896, was almost certainly written afterwards. It is possible that one or two of the stories published for the first time in *The Pale Ape and Other Pulses* had also been written before the end of 1895, but had failed to find publication then—'The Great King' is the most likely candidate—but whether that is true or not, all the materials in the collection reflect, in one way or another, the fact that English Decadent prose suffered a drastic decline in fashion in 1896, from which it never recovered. Publishers in all sectors of the marketplace became less sympathetic to it, if not actively antipathetic; in seeking to distance themselves —publicly, at least—from Wilde's supposed moral decadence, they began to distance themselves from everything he had stood for, including the exuberant flamboyance and exoticism of his literary style and ironic wit.

Oscar Wilde's fall was not the only cause that his arch-enemy, the Marquess of Queensberry, had reason to celebrate in 1895. As well as pursuing Wilde for the supposed ruination of his younger son, Lord Alfred Douglas, Queensberry had also been waging a campaign of hatred against the man he considered responsible for the ruination and suicide of his elder son, Lord Drumlanrig: Lord Rosebery. Queensberry was never likely to bring Rosebery down in the way that he brought down Wilde, because Rosebery was more highly placed in the peerage and had the additional advantage of being the prime minister, but circumstances beyond either man's control contrived to bring down Rosebery's government in 1895 and put an effective end to his political career.

The Durance of Decadence

The cloak of secrecy and subtle deceit with which Shiel cloaked his private life makes it difficult to be certain, but it seems likely that his acquaintance with Oscar Wilde was relatively slight. He probably knew Rosebery much better, having moved in the social circle of the higher echelons of the Liberal party for some years, but how intimate their acquaintance was remains a matter for speculation. The principal crack in Shiel's discretion regarding this association was the heavily disguised dialogue on aesthetic and philosophical matters contained in *Shapes in the Fire*, 'Premier and Maker,' in which a writer whose fictitious name borrows aspects of both Shiel's and Wilde's conducts an animated discussion with an unnamed prime minister very obviously modelled on Rosebery.

The extent to which Shiel distanced himself from all that Wilde and Rosebery stood for can be gauged by a dialogue contained in the present collection, which plays a similar role to the one contained in *Shapes in the Fire*: the middle section of 'Cummings King Monk,' subtitled 'He defines "Greatness of Mind" '. Both Wilde and Rosebery are included among the names of those to whom Monk—here engaged in a dialogue whose first person narrator is addressed as 'Shiel'—denies true greatness of mind, finding evidence of a fatal mediocrity in both. Rosebery's supposed flaws are not discussed in detail, but seem to be primarily political—Shiel, as a committed socialist, had moved considerably to the left of orthodox Liberal politics—while Wilde is condemned for his superficiality, for being a poseur in life and literature alike. Shiel's commitment to the Decadent style, and to its appropriate literary deployment, was always more earnest and intense than Wilde's.

The discussion between Shiel and his imaginary *alter ego*—a kind of über-Shiel—regarding greatness of mind is bound to seem slightly odd to a modern reader because its main specimen of examination is Cardinal John Henry Newman, a man still famous at the time—although he had died in 1890—but now a more obscure figure. Newman was the most famous Victorian convert from the Anglican Church to Catholicism, who subsequently argued theological matters with the zeal that is typical of converts anxious to justify what might otherwise seem a kind of treason. Shiel's interest in Newman might conceivably have sprung from a brief dalliance with the idea of making a similar conversion himself; his own father had been an Anglican minister, and he spent a great deal of time in Paris, where he must have become acutely aware of the fact that the author of the paradigm example of Decadent prose fiction, Joris-Karl Huysmans, had made a very public reinvestment in the Catholic faith. Huysmans had recommended such an investment in the final page of his 'Decadent Bible,' *À rebours*, on the archetypally perverse grounds that its creed and ceremonies were such a spectacular tissue of lies and impostures. The fact that Huysmans had entered a monastic order may well have something to do with the fact that Shiel's first fantastic projection of his own personality, Prince Zaleski—whose lifestyle is even more flamboyant than that of Jean Des Esseintes, the hero of *À rebours*—had been replaced by a 'King Monk'.

Cummings King Monk is so merciless in his analysis of Cardinal Newman's intellect that he not only denies him the greatness of mind widely credited to him in the Victorian era but diminishes him to the level of a 'savage'. That is not quite the unalloyed insult that it seems, since Monk also establishes that Socrates and Plato—the inventor and populariser of the very dialogue form he is employing—were also 'savages,' as was Jesus himself; Newman is, however, held to have far less excuse than they, for they knew nothing of the modern science whose intellectual mastery is the key to greatness of mind, while Newman had wilfully ignored it.

Monk inevitably has difficulty in finding anyone, even among his contemporaries, who meets all of his criteria of greatness of mind, but his rankings are interesting, particularly his judgment of two of Shiel's fellow socialist writers, George Bernard Shaw and H.G. Wells. Shaw is held to fall shorter of the ideal by a more considerable margin than Wells, the great pioneer of scientific romance. Shiel wrote several novels allied to the latter genre, although the best and most famous of his futuristic fantasies, *The Purple Cloud* had been as much a religious fantasy as a scientific romance. Whenever Shiel discussed the future of religion and the philosophy of faith in his fiction—as he often did, from *The Purple Cloud* (1901) and *The Last Miracle* (1906) to *The Young Men are Coming!* (1937), he did so in terms that attempted to replace the moral teachings of the Old and New Testament with a faith accommodated to the discoveries of modern science, which was therefore compatible with Monk's definition of 'greatness of mind'.

Any comparison of Cummings King Monk with Prince Zaleski is bound to find the former a less colourful figure, Both characters are, in essence, derivatives of Edgar Allan Poe's fantastic self-projection C. Auguste Dupin (and thus may be ranked as kissing cousins of Arthur Conan Doyle's Sherlock Holmes) and both retain the key features of their original model, but they develop those features in somewhat different directions. Zaleski is Dupin taken to Decadent extremes of which even Jean Des Esseintes only dreamed, drowning in the bizarrerie of his surroundings and languishing in a drug-assisted phantasmagoria. Monk, though even richer than Zaleski, chooses to live far more modestly, exercising his exotic tastes with much greater restraint. Monk is also more active than Zaleski. Although Zaleski had been prepared to go out into the world to admonish the members of the Society of Sparta for employing murderous means to their idealistic ends, Monk is not only prepared to mount the large-scale social experiment outlined in 'He Meddles with Women' but also to take the good fight much more aggressively to the self-described 'exact scientist' featured in 'He Wakes an Echo'.

Monk has disciplined himself to an extent that Zaleski never would have done, although he is still an ultimate *amateur* who regards crime-fighting merely as a means of alleviating his *ennui*. He is not much interested in crimes as puzzles; his fascination with social deviance cuts deeper than that, and he sees that it is problematic in more ways than one. In that respect, he is very much in the mainstream of Shiel's evolving literary work, of which *The Pale Ape and Other Pulses* provides a fascinating cross-section.

Although 'Huguenin's Wife' would have slotted very well into *Shapes in the Fire*, being as conspicuously Decadent an *hommage* to Poe as 'Xélucha' and 'Tulsah,' the other stories in the present collection make manifest efforts to move away from the aesthetic philosophy of the earlier collection, in much the same direction that Cummings King Monk followed in subjecting Prince Zaleski to a thorough rehabilitation. 'The Case of Euphemia Raphash' is a crime story cast more obviously in the Holmesian mode than any of Zaleski's adventures, although it is far more interested in crime as a product of abnormal psychology than as a threat to social order. Indeed, the notion on which its plot hinges—that of multiple personality—was to become something of an *idée fixe* of Shiel's in the years following its publication. The first short story he published in 1896, 'Wayward Love,' may have been omitted from this collection because its theme also hinges on dramatic personality transformation, but that did not prevent Shiel from including 'A Bundle of Letters,' which is a wry inversion of the same theme in the context of a popular love story. Nor did it prevent him from including 'The Pale Ape' and 'The Bride,' both of which similarly revolve around issues of confused identity, one objective and one subjective.

There is nothing very surprising about Shiel's use of fantastic projections of himself in literary dialogues that extrapolate his own internal disputes, nor in his continual dabbling with the melodramatics of multiple personality and secret identity—these are methods and preoccupations to which many writers have been exceedingly prone—but it is worth noting that Shiel's interest was considerably more focused than the average. When he had imagined himself, allegorically, as an alloy of Adam and Job in *The Purple Cloud*, he objectified the contrary impulses at war within himself as 'the black' and 'the white,' although they do not reflect any simple contrast between good and evil. The same complexity—or, at least, obliquity—is evident in the various stories in this collection in which characters provide the focal points for internal motivational warfare. By comparison with orthodox fantasies of multiple personality modelled on Robert Louis Stevenson's Dr Jekyll and Mr Hyde, Shiel's are far more peculiar, in moral as well as psychosexual and psychosomatic terms.

The other elements of Shiel's work that continue their trajectories in this collection include his use and development of the *conte cruel*, which is the typical form of Decadent short fiction. Shiel had always cleaved closer to Poesque models of the *conte cruel* than many of the French writers who took over its evolution—including the Comte de Villiers de l'Isle Adam, who gave the subgenre its name. Such archetypal Shielian examples as 'Huguenin's Wife' and 'The Spectre-Ship' are tales of relentlessly-unfolding doom of which Poe would surely have approved wholeheartedly, although the latter is marked by a distinct move towards literary naturalism in spite of its exotic setting. While

'Huguenin's Wife' draws upon the mythical past, 'The Spectre-Ship' is set in a clearly-defined historical context that forbids the kind of casual supernatural intrusion employed in the earlier story; here, the hand of fate works its will just as inexorably, but also more ironically, working through the power of the imagination rather than literal manifestation.

In the context of this shift 'The Bride,' which first appeared in *The English Illustrated Magazine* in 1902, and 'Many a Tear,' which first appeared in the U.S. version of *Pearson's Magazine* in 1908, offer interesting examples of the mutation of the format. 'The Bride' is far the more Poesque of the two in every respect but its setting, which transposes a formula designed for use in exotic contexts into the formulaic setting of contemporary 'shopgirl romances'—a transposition that few writers would have found comfortable, although Shiel was never afraid of calculated oddity. The result is an evident anomaly, but the mundanity of the setting adds an extra ironic edge to the conclusion that some readers will find uniquely delicious. 'Many a Tear,' by contrast, is not at all Poesque, being solidly cast in the kind of determinedly naturalistic frame that eventually gave rise to 'dirty realism' and *noir* fiction, providing a harrowing account of everyday human cruelty whose moral indignation is deftly muted.

The development of these two stories mirrors a drastic shift in the pattern of demand to which the middlebrow magazines of the early twentieth century were responding. The 1890s had been an era of experimentation, when editors would try anything, but after 1900—by which time Decadent excess had already taken one mortal body-blow—the results of those experiments were generally held to have been firmly established by experience. It became a matter of editorial dogma that what the public wanted to read were crime stories and domestic dramas that held closely to the fundamental story-arcs now typical of those genres: in the former instance, crimes committed were solved and expiated; in the latter, relationships hazarded on the basis of natural affection ultimately triumphed over social barriers inhibiting their consummation.

Neither of these formulas held any significant attraction for Shiel—whose foremost literary interest was always in their subversion by *conte cruel* assumptions and their perversion by the divers operations of abnormal psychology—but he had perforce to operate in a context of demand in which they had become familiar and in which they set the standards of thematic and stylistic normality. There is a sense in which the whole contents of *The Pale Ape and Other Pulses* show Shiel wrestling with that fact of literary life, as heroically as he could. He never gave in to the extent of producing pastiches of conventional popular fiction in large quantity, but he did find a certain fascination in various patterns of compromise. 'A Bundle of Letters' is as close as he came to attempting a conventional 'happy ending,' and the conspicuous half-heartedness of the attempt may have prevented the story from selling to the popular magazines that must have been its envisaged market.

Of the other stories in the collection that had not been previously published in 1911, 'The Great King' is the most conspicuous example of a story that was unrepentantly ill-fitted to the new publishing regime. Although its setting is only a little more exotic than that of 'The Spectre-Ship,' it is as firmly committed to the conventions of the mythical, rather than the historical, past as 'Huguenin's Wife'. Its plot is, in effect, much the same as that of 'The Bride,' and fits much more comfortably into its quasi-Biblical milieu than it does into the subrealm of the shopgirl romance, but it is the sort of neat fit of which the popular magazines had become very suspicious. 'The House of Sounds' is even more flamboyantly Poesque than 'The Great King'—it is a calculated exaggeration to an imaginative ultimate of 'The Fall of the House of Usher'—but is somewhat less extreme in its exaggeration than the story of which it is a new version, which had appeared in *Shapes in the Fire* as 'Vaila'.

'The House of Sounds' might have been written as a stylistic experiment, when Shiel had decided that he ought to tone down the Decadent features of his prose and personality alike—which he must have done sincerely rather than as an exercise in cosmetic diplomacy—but it was more probably a straightforward exercise in abridgement written in response to some editorial offer that never came to fruition. At any rate, Shiel evidently came to prefer the second version, for that was the one he reprinted several times over. Some of the changes are purely cosmetic; for instance, the alienist in the story—who is evidently modelled on Jean-Martin Charcot, professor of neurology at the Sorbonne—is named Carot rather than Corot, presumably to avoid confusion with the painter, and the island of Vaila becomes Rayba. Others are more substantial; a considerable section is lopped out of the alienist's commentary on a hypersensitive patient, which carefully likens his malady to the extraordinary apprehension of the Supreme Being, and two sections from Harfager's crucial discourse relating to life's endurance beyond the cessation of breathing are omitted.

Some readers (I am one) do not consider these material cuts to be to the story's advantage, but there is undoubtedly a logical rationale in their making. They tighten up the story-line, and make the story more reader-friendly, reducing the exoticism of the prose by cutting out many terms borrowed from other languages and exotic spellings—the long passage represented as a quote from Hugh Gascoigne's *Chronicle of Norse Families* uses more conventional spelling in this version than the earlier one, and many other (though by no means all) esoteric terms employed in the story are removed or modified. The continuity of the climax is improved by the excision of a brief passage in which the narrator is seized by the intoxication of the storm, although the cost of greater consistency is the loss of the story's most high-flown speech, in which the narrator judges the house to be 'jaunting on the scoriac tempests and reeling bullions of hell!'

'The House of Sounds' makes an interesting pair with the third section of 'Cummings King Monk,' which also describes a labyrinthine house in the grip of terminal decay. The references in the former story suggesting that Shiel was familiar with the work of Charcot imply that he might also have heard rumour of the ideas of Sigmund Freud relating to the symbolism of dreams, but even if he had not, his reading of 'The Fall of the House of Usher' would have familiarised him with the notion of a house mirroring and incarnating the psychology of its owner. There is no shortage of such symbolic edifices in Gothic fiction, and new ones were being produced by Shiel's contemporaries—William Hope Hodgson's *The House on the Borderland* appeared three years before *The Pale Ape and Other Pulses*—but Shiel's dark, twisted and decaying houses trembling on the brink of annihilation are more extreme mirrors of more elaborate hysteria than any others of their kind.

The Pale Ape and Other Pulses

The not-so-stately homes featured in 'The Pale Ape' and 'The Case of Euphemia Raphash' are markedly less exotic than those featured in 'He Wakes an Echo' and 'The House of Sounds,' but their membership of the same symbolic subspecies is unmistakable. The edifices similarly displayed in 'Huguenin's Wife' and 'The Great King' are not houses in quite the same sense, but they too are elaborations of the human psyche, which pay due heed to its innate complexity and perversity. Whether they are fallen already, doomed to fall or capable of some semblance of survival, all these houses are balefully lit and direly uncomfortable to inhabit. They are all subject to unnatural vibrations, born of the storms which—by virtue of the conventional literary inversion of the pathetic fallacy—inevitably reflect the emotional turbulence of their inhabitants.

For all his hectic and inveterate extravagance, Shiel was not a man to use words carelessly, and he must have been sensible of the implications of calling the items in *The Pale Ape and Other Pulses* something other than 'stories' or tales'. He probably had in mind the obsolete significance of the term that is defined in Webster's dictionary as 'a stroke; an impact; also an attack' as well as the figurative meaning that refers to an 'underlying sentiment, opinion, drift, or the like' discoverable by skill in perception. The whole point of *contes cruels* is that they are strokes or impacts—attacks, even—that aspire to perceive something underlying, unacknowledged if not properly hidden. In this sense, 'pulses' is as good a word for them as any, and it is in this sense rather than in terms of regular rhythm that *The Pale Ape and Other Pulses* is a striking, as well as a heartfelt, book.

THE PALE APE

'A big thing of a Pig.'—ARISTOPHANES.

Yesterday again I stood and looked at Hargen Hall from the lake; and it is this that has brought me to write of my life in it. Wintry winds were whistling through the withered bracken and the branches, whirling withered birch-leaves about the south quadrangle; and no birds sang.

When I first entered it I was a girl, one might say—gay enough; but now I have known what one never forgets; and the days and the hairs grow grey together.

Five titled names among my friends gained me an entrance to Hargen in the fall of the year '08. I arrived on the evening of 10th November, and shall never forget the strangeness of the impression made on my mind that night: for even ere I rounded into sight of the house, the sound of the waters far off filled me with me a feeling of the eerily dreary—the house being almost surrounded with mountain and cliff, down which a series of cascades shower; and that night I had some difficulty in catching quite everything that was said to me, though in two or three days, maybe, my ear became used to the tumult.

It was four days before I met Sir Philip Lister himself—Davenport, the old butler, told me that his master was 'indisposed'—but Sir Philip sent me a polite missive inviting me to take things carelessly a little: so I spent the first days in learning my pupil's moods, and in roaming over the place, from 'Queen Elizabeth's Room'—behind the bed still hung a velvet shield broidered with the royal arms in white wire—to the apes and the cascades. A sense of forlornness pervaded it all, for scarcely ten of us were in all the desert of that place, with an occasional glimpse of two or three gardeners, or a groom. The kitchen was now a panelled hall like a chapel, with windows of painted glass containing the six coats-of-arms of the Lister-Lynns, a hall in whose vastness the cook and her assistant looked awfully forlorn and small; and hardly even a housemaid ever now entered all that part of the east wing which had been singed by a fire fifty-five years since.

It was on the fourth forenoon, a day of 'the Indian summer,' that my pupil took me to see the apes. There were three of them—two chimpanzees, one gibbon—in three rooms of wire-netting close to the east line of cliffs, i.e., about six hundred yards from the house. There, chuckling and chattering in the shadow of chestnuts, they lived their lives, anon speculating like philosophers upon their knots, or hearkening to the waters which chanted near in their ears. And there was a *fourth* room of netting in the row, but empty; as to which my pupil said to me:

'The one that used to be in this fourth room was huge, Miss Newnes, and had a pale face. He died some time before I came to Hargen: but his ghost walks when the moon is at the full.'

'Now Esmé,' I muttered. (Her name was Esmé Martagon, daughter of the Marquis de Martagon and of Margaret Lister, Sir Philip's sister; the child being at this time twelve years of age, and an orphan—a rather pretty elf with ebon curls, but as changeable as the shapes of mercury, now bursting with alacrity, and now cursed with black turns of sadness.)

'But if I have seen it?' she gravely replied, gazing up at me with her great eyes.

'The ghost of an ape, Esmé,' I muttered.

For answer, flying off into vivacity, she cried to me: 'Come, you shall hear it!'—and she led the way northward through the park, until we walked down a dark path tremulous with spray, where one of the smaller waterfalls came down. By stepping on the tops of rocks in its froth, one could get, in the rear of the torrent, into a grot, where the greenery grew very vigorous and gay from the perpetual spray; and when I had followed Esmé's career into this hollow in the rock, she hollaed into my ear in opposition to the tons of thunder sounding down: 'Now, listen a little: this one is named "The Ape".'

The Pale Ape

For some minutes—three to six—I heard nothing but the burden of the cascade's murmur, and was now about to say something sceptical, when there sounded what I am bound to say affected me in a rather startling way—a sound very sharp and energetic—the *chuckle, chuckle* of a monkey—most pressing, most imperative, in its summons to the attention. It was over in a moment; but presently came again: and in the course of half an hour's listening it came altogether five times, not quite at regular intervals, but still with a kind of periodicity: and I concluded that some small cause, perhaps only a condition of the wind, acted ever and anon to modify the cataract's tract, and produce this curious cackling.

My pupil hollaed to me: 'And if you kept on waiting to hear, and listening to it, do you know what would happen to you, Miss Newnes?'—and when I asked what, she called: 'You would go stark mad!'

'Not I,' I said.

One of the shadows darkened the child's face; and presently she remarked: 'I should, I know. Three of the ladies of the Listers, and one of the Lynns, have—among them my mother's mother. It is in the blood, I think.'

I started!—for I now suddenly believed her. Indeed, to my consciousness, there was something ironic in the torrent's chuckle, and at once, taking the child's hand, I said: 'Come.'

Later in the day when we were together in what is called 'the Great Hall,' Esmé, ever sage beyond her age, again spoke of the chuckling cascade, begging me not to mention, or show it to her Cousin Huggins when he came: for a young man of this name, who had hardly been at Hargen since he was six, was coming from India in some months, and was expected to spend a month with us.

It was that night that, for the first time, I saw Sir Philip Lister: for he dined with Esmé and Mrs Wiseman and me in the main building dining-room, the old Davenport waiting upon us in state with his silent footsteps, we five making a pretty insignificant group in that great room, whose array of windows have a south aspect upon the south quadrangle. It has (or had) tapestry all round, and rows of Jacobean carving-tables, which give the room an air of very gloomy state; and a wood-fire bickered on the iron-work fire-back, under whose oak over-mantel Sir Philip sat with

The Pale Ape and Other Pulses

Esmé and me ten minutes then took himself away into his own sequestered nook of the house.

Two days after this he again had dinner with us, and again the day after that; but that third time the child, in one of her chatterbox fits, chanced to observe that 'Uncle Philip is lending his presence since Miss Newnes has come'—and like a bird that shies Sir Philip showed himself no more to us for many days.

I regretted this, for his presence interested me, his manners were in such a high degree grave, dignified, and gracious. He was big, and, if not handsome, interesting to the eye—quaint, one might say—his face smooth like an actor's, his hair longer than usual, with great owl-eyes, whose glowering underlook was thronged, to my thinking, with mysteries of sorrow—something shifting, though, uncandidly shy, in them. His age I guessed to be about forty-five.

He was engaged in the writing of what I heard was 'a great work,' six volumes long, on 'The Old Kingdom' (fourth of sixth dynasty of Egyptian Kings), and lived a life of such privacy, that it was three weeks ere I met him afresh. Meantime, Esmé and I entered upon the course of our adventurous studies—'adventurous,' for never for two hours together was my pupil the same girl. Esmé had fits of headache; and she had fits of reading, when she feasted upon volumes with a hungry vulture's greed; and she had fits of indolence, dormouse torpors, fits of crying, dark-minded lamentations, fits of flightiness, of crazy dissipation, of craving for—wine. As for her knowledge, it was astonishing in such a child, and she anon plied me with queries to which I could find no reply.

On a forenoon in the fourth week, when she was feeling out of sorts, we were sauntering in the park, when, for once, I saw Sir Philip out of doors. We came upon him with his face against the ape-house netting, gazing in at the gibbon—so eagerly, that we were near him ere he seemed to hear us. When he suddenly saw us, he stood struck into a posture as of suspense, but presently was very affable in his reserved manner, and conversed with me some minutes about the apes and their various traits. They had the names of Egyptian kings, the chimpanzees being Pepy II and Khety, and the gibbon Sety I; and at the gibbon Sir Philip shook his finger, saying with a playful solemnity: *'That fellow! That fellow!'*—I had no idea what he meant.

The Pale Ape

Suddenly, in the midst of our talk, he—with a certain awkwardness of his lids—proposed a picnic-luncheon out of doors to which Esmé and I readily assented. But three minutes afterwards he started, furtively murmuring the words: 'I must be getting back to work,' and was gone—to my astonishment!

After this he again made himself very scarce for three weeks. Esmé and I, meantime, got into the habit of spending our hours of labour in the great hall, sitting on a day-bed that lay in the solar-room gallery there—the gallery from which of old one gazed down upon the retainers at table below; and those days of my life, that I whiled away in that place, are to me at present days touched with much strangeness and a tone of Utopia. But the great place was quite plain and empty—a plain ceiling, plain white walls, oak-panelled half-way up: only, as it was lighted by fourteen great windows with shields of painted glass, when the sun glowed through them, it transfigured that old room into glory-land. . . . But it is gone from me now like a dream, and I shall not see it again.

It was on the Thursday afternoon of my thirteenth week at Hargen that I received from Sir Philip Lister a singular missive: he had injured his thumb, he said, and wished to know if I would 'kindly write from his dictation.' But what, then, I asked myself, was to become of Esmé meantime? I did not wish to leave the child! However, I could not say no: and so entered that day the sacred den. He, with his fingers in a sling, instantly jumped up with a gush of apologies, showering upon me a thousand thanks that were at once gushing and shy, till the shyness triumphed, and he was suddenly silent and done. Then, I sitting at an old abbey-table, he on an old farm-house settle, he dictated to me with his eyes closed, in a low tone, all about Khufu, and Khafra, and the things of 'the Pyramid Age,' until I had the impression that he was himself something Egyptian and most ancient, and I with him, and in which age of the world we were I was not at some moments certain. In the midst of the dictating he all at once pressed his left palm upon his forehead, as if tired or muddled, his eyes tight shut; and, jumping up, he muttered to me, 'thank you! thank you!' offering me his hand. Some of his actions had a wonderful swiftness and suddenness; and that hand of his which I touched was as chill as snow: so that I made haste from him.

The Pale Ape and Other Pulses

That night I retired, as usual, soon after eleven to my room, which was in a rather remote and lonely region of the house; and was soon asleep. Two hours later I awoke terrified—I could not quite tell why—but so terrified, that I found myself sitting up in bed—with a singular sound, or the memory or dream of a singular sound, lingering about my ears: and I was trembling, my brow was wet with sweat. Through my two windows, which stood open, shone the full moon's light, lying over the floor, lighting the stamp-work tapestry on my right; and I could hear the night-breeze breathing drearily through the leaves of the cedar, some of whose branches, held up with chains, brushed my panes. For some minutes I sat so, hearing my heart beating in my ears, the breezes shivering through the tree, the streams showering, the soundlessness of the house and hour, and as conscious of some living spirit hovering round me as though I saw it. If it had lasted long, I must have lost consciousness, or else cast off the oppression of it with a shriek: but presently something reached my ear—a chuckle, a little giggle of glee, just distinct enough to convince me that it was due to no lunacy of my ear: and immediately, with a creeping in my hair, but a species of rage and desperation elevating me, I was out of bed, and at one of the windows: for just after the chuckle a sharp rush through the leafage of the cedar seemed to reach me, and I rushed to see.

What I saw made me faint—whether instantly or after some seconds I cannot say: I know that when I came to my senses I was seated on the floor with my forehead leaning on my old oak chair, and the tower-clock was now sounding the hour of three. But however soon I may have swooned after seeing it, it was not so instantly that I could have the slightest doubt as to the actualness of what my eyes saw. For though the moonlight left the interior regions of the tree's leafage in some obscurity, I was sure that some brute of the ape species with a pale face was hanging there in the cedar—hanging head-downward among the network of chains and branches in such a way as to see into my chamber; and I have an impression of hearing—either before I fell, or through my swoon afterwards—a succession of chucklings; and then a voice somewhere remonstrating, pleading, commanding, in a secret species of shout; and then a strangled outcry of horror, of anguish, somewhere, all mingled with a dream of the chuckle of the chuckling stream.

But the strongest of my impressions was undoubtedly that drowning outcry of horror—an impression so strong, that I could hardly believe it to be a dream, or all a dream. This cry was somehow connected in my mind from the first with old Davenport; and this feeling was confirmed in me when Davenport was nowhere to be seen the next day, nor for four days after. Mrs Wiseman, the housekeeper, who for days was pale, and occasionally fell into a vacant staring, told me that Davenport was 'suffering'. She asked me no questions as to the night, but I twice caught her eye piercingly bent upon me with a meaning of inquiry, of anxiety, in it; and the same thing was true of Sir Philip when, three days later, he appeared towards evening: for he took my hand with a tender solicitude, and a lingering look of question in his gaze. As for Davenport, when I next saw him it was under a tree in the park, where he sat like a convalescent, in his flesh that pathetic pallor of the flesh of aged people who have passed through an illness; and the wrappings round his neck could not wholly hide from my eyes that his throat had been most brutally bruised.

During those days it was as if a blow had fallen upon Hargen. Esmé no longer laughed, and a lower tone of talk overtook us all. It was obvious that each held the consciousness of a secret which none dared breathe to another; and in vain I consumed days of musing in seeking to see into the meaning of these things. For my part, I was ailing, nor could quite hide it. I had the thought of moving out of my room, which I now shrank from entering even in the day-time, but did not care to show so openly that I was afraid. Through the nights I burned a light, but slept with my nerves awake. Not that I was ever of a very nervous temperament, I think: but terror infected me like a sickness in those days; the stare of eyes of affright in the night was ever present in my imagination; and Hargen soon grew to be to my haunted heart the very home of gloom. Then one day, on a sudden, all this trouble of mind rushed away from me like a shadow; and my being galloped into a mood of gladness in which gloom was abolished, and I forgot to be appalled in the dark.

I will tell of it very briefly. It happened that one afternoon when Esmé and I were sitting listlessly in that solar-room gallery, an open grammar lying idle between us, suddenly behind us, there rose out of the floor, as it seemed, a young man who clapped his fingers over Esmé's eyes, smiling with me the while. 'Cousin Huggins!' the child cried out—much surprised, for Huggins Lister was not expected at Hargen for some days yet. He caught her up in his big arms, and bussed her like a gun, for he was a being made all of ardours and horse-play: and then he looked into my eyes, and I looked into his eyes.

It was as if I had always known him—long before I was born; and what hurried me more into the sort of maelstrom in which I was now caught was the circumstance, that on the day after that first day Esmé took a chill, remained in bed, and I was all alone with Huggins Lister in that wilderness of Hargen. The young man was, or pretended to be, interested in old things, and would have me show him all the cassone and old needlework, the Spanish glasses giving their glints of gold, the old girandoles with their amorini. He dined with me, we two alone, and Mrs Wiseman: for Sir Philip more than ever kept himself to himself. Only, on the fourth evening when Huggins Lister and I were walking in the park, Sir Philip suddenly appeared before us, walking with precipitate steps the other way; did not pause, nor utter a sound, as he passed by us with a bowed brow, his hat raised; but when he had gone some way beyond us, he stopped, and—shook his finger at us! was going, too, I am sure, to venture to say something, but failed; and suddenly was gone on his way again. I remember being very offended at the moment: but a moment more, God forgive me, had forgotten that Sir Philip Lister lived.

I showed the young man the apes, and the Queen's Room, and the cascades, save one, and the ivory inlay of the two Spanish chests, and the Tudor fireplaces, and what was in 'the long gallery'; and still he wished to see things. And just under the window that lights the great staircase, there stands on the landing a sedan-chair painted with glaring variegations, the window-glass casting the gauds of the six coats-of-arms of the Lister-Lynns upon the already gaudy chair: in which chair he got me to sit—it was high noon, on the open stair, but we were as solitary there as if night veiled us in a monastery; and, indeed, all that waste of Hargen seemed but made to beguile and mislead our feet to our fate— he got me to sit in it, I say, and then, having me well in his bondage in the sedan-chair, began to sob to me with passion; and when I hid away my face for pity of him there in his passion on his knees, and dashed one wild tear from my eyes, the young man ravished my lips with his lips, there in the chair on the stair that day. I could not help it, for in respect of me Huggins Lister came, and saw, and conquered! and I was as one drugged with honey-dew, and dancing drugged, in Huggins Lister's hands.

Also, the young man persuaded like a hurricane! and hurried me as madly into marriage as those sand-forms of the sand-storm which madly waltz into oneness. Within six months, he said, he would arrange everything so as to proclaim the marriage; but meantime it must be secret, and must be immediate! Against this tyranny I made a feint of resistance; but half-heartedly; and it availed me nothing: indeed, he was dear to me, and near, and had me all in the hollow of his hand and heart. And so one forenoon I stole out of Hargen gates, and met him at a house in St Arvens townlet, the place of our marriage; but, as we were passing out, married, from the door of the house, my heart bounded into my mouth to see Sir Philip Lister walking hardly ten yards away. Yes, he who never left home was there before my eyes in the broad light in St Arvens street with his oak-stick—walking away from us, indeed, seeming unaware of our presence: yet I have an impression, too, of his head half-turned toward us a moment, of a face ashen with agitation: and my heart, for all its warmth, shivered as with a mortal chill in me.

My reeling feet led me back to Hargen in a kind of dream, a wedded wife, as wild with thoughts as with wine that day, for I was my beloved's, and he was mine: and in what way I spent that day I could not say, since I was new in heaven, and can but remember my fruitless efforts to hide from Esmé's eyes the state of my mind: for she had lately risen from her ailment, and I made a pretence of study with her, and I was severe with my dear, denying him my presence until the evening; and even then retired betimes, leaving him sighing.

My chamber-door I barricaded with a chair—a bridal childishness, since, to secure the room, I should have locked it. And I lay awake for a long hour, looking at the luminosity of the full moon, until, wearied out by the reel of my day's dream, I fell into a brief sleep.

From this a roar awoke me: and may a sound like that sound never more come to me to summon me with its trump. I understood that some soul was in *extremis,* and out of the deeps of grief and horror was horridly appealing to his God; and, finding myself on the ground, I knelt one wild second, crying aloud: 'Almighty God, guard my love from harm in this house of horror.' A moment more I had thrown a gown round me, and was gone out of the door.

As I ran along the corridor, trying to strike a light to the candle that I carried, there seemed to reach my ear from somewhere a chuckle very hushed and low, like the jackal chattering over its carrion; and my fingers were so shaken by this thing, that they failed to bring the match into relation with the candle's wick. When the heat reached my hand I dashed down the match. Still running, I lit another—or half lit it: for in the instant when the match fused at the scratch, I saw—or in some manner knew—that some mad and monstrous animal was with me; at the same moment the match went out, or was puffed out; and a thing most chilly cold touched my skin. I felt pain then, the pain of the awe of the darkness; and I stood palsied. But within some seconds, I think, I was rushing afresh toward the corridor-end, without the candlestick now, which had dropped from me; so that I could not see that the portal at the end, which I expected to be open as usual, was shut; and I rushed with a shock upon it. It was not only shut, but locked!—finding which, I, standing there, piled the passion of my whole soul into cry on cry, crying 'Huggins! Sir Philip! Davenport! Huggins!' then I stood, hearing the streams murmuring as through eternity in the silence of the night, and the strong knocking of my heart against my side—but no reply to my calls.

This was not very astonishing, as my room was in such a solitary part of the mansion: and I stood imprisoned, suffering, expecting every second the coming upon me of that which would strike me dead with fright. The stillness lasted half a minute, perhaps, and then I became aware of a sound outside the door, a bumping going down the stairs in a regular way, like something massive being dragged down, with bump, bump, bump: and such was the solemnity and mystery of this thing to me in my solitude there in that gruesome gloom, that to linger any longer there in my pain soon grew to be impossible to me; and before I knew what I was doing I was out of a window, moving along a ledge fifty feet aloft toward the next window. The ledge was scarcely more than a foot wide, I think, and how I dared it, and why I did not fall, I can't now say. With my nose close to the wall—conscious all the time of drizzle tossed by high winds, conscious of the night full of a wild light, though the moon was quite hidden—I stepped flutteringly along over thin snow in dizzy suspense, keeping my sob until I should reach the next window: and there, as I leapt, I gave it vent, and fainted at my safety. I did not cease to hear, though, the bumping sound going down; and when it got to the bottom, something in me gave me the dauntlessness of heart to go after it.

Down I crept, haltingly, crouching, stair by stair. Halfway down I seemed to hear something being dragged over the floor below. I went on down. The sound had now gone out through a doorway, and I knew which doorway; but as I followed that way, my bare toes struck upon something cold, and I dropped upon my hands over it. I moaned then for pity of myself, because it was dark, and because I did so suffer. But I was conscious, as I dropped, of a rattle of matches, for I still had the match-box in my hand, without knowing that I had it: and the desire took me to strike a light. It was some time, though, before I would, or could, and when I eventually ventured, I saw the sight of the body of the old butler in his night-attire lying wildly before me on the floor: and I knew by a look that was in his eyes that they were for ever sightless.

At the same moment I was aware of the slamming of a door some way off; and again I knew which door—the little side-portal by the kitchen-entrance, leading out northward into the park—and again something gave vigour to my knees, and lifted my feet, to go to see. I made my way to the little portal; opened it slowly; my soles were out on the snow. And before me on the short gravel-path going north into the park I distinctly saw the pale ape, bearing a body against his breast. A moment later he laid down his heavy load, and bent over it; and when I saw him horribly muttering over it, something in me stooped, took up a stone, and threw it at the brute.

It went straight to his head.

After some seconds the creature raised himself slowly, and raced with reeling feet into the darkness of the park.

I staggered then to the body, and saw that it was Huggins Lister strangled; and on the body of my beloved my senses left me.

It was ten in the day before I knew anything more; and then I lay on a bed, on one side of it Esmé, on the other side Mrs Wiseman.

The latter had a fixed stare; and from the manner in which Esmé was smiling, with her face held sideward, while she persistently counted on her fingers, I could make out that the child was now insane.

I lay still, I said nothing; little I cared.

Presently a girl named Bertha entered to murmur the words: 'He isn't found yet'; and from some words murmured in reply by Mrs Wiseman, I gathered that Sir Philip Lister had disappeared.

Little I cared, I lay still and sullen, with closed lids.

Near noon again came the news that the men seeking for Sir Philip Lister could even yet discover no trace of him; but at about five in the evening he was found dying in the hollow of the rock that lies behind the cascade that they call 'The Ape,' and was brought to the Hall.

Very soon afterwards Mrs Wiseman, who had then left my side, flew in again to me with crying eyes, imploring me to try and go for a moment to the dying man, who was hungering to have one sight of me; and I let her throw some clothes over me, and was led by her to the death-bed.

By this time I knew—for Mrs Wiseman during the day had revealed it to me in a flood of tears—that Sir Philip Lister's mother had too much listened to the chuckling cascade, and so had borne him the being he was—a being capable at any agitation of shedding his human nature to resume the nature of the brute, and hurling away human raiment with his human nature in the murderous turbulence of his nocturnal revels—he who in my eyes had been so perfect in gentleness, so shy, so staid! But none the less I shuddered to the soul when he touched my hand to pant at me through the death-ruckle rolling in his throat: 'I have loved you well'—a shudder which perhaps saved me from death or from madness, for I had lapsed that day into a mad apathy. It was nearly night then, and the light in there was very dreary; but I could still see that the hair which overgrew the ogre's frame was considerably more than an inch deep—greenish, and gross as the gorilla's. It clasped him round the throat and round the wrists in lines perfectly defined, like a perfect coat of fur that he wore; and it did not thin, but continued no less thick where it abruptly ended than everywhere else.

But he had 'loved me well,' and I him now—for if he had been perniciously jealous, it was for love of me that he had been jealous; and in dying he looked into my eyes with human eyes, kindly, mildly, looking 'I have loved you well'; and when with his last strength he pointed to where the pebble I had flung had sunk into his skull, then I lifted my voice and wept to God because of him, and myself, and Hargen Hall and all, not caring any longer if my face was buried in the horror of his hairy breast. And so he died, and Huggins Lister, and I was left alive.

THE CASE OF EUPHEMIA RAPHASH

'Man's goings are of God: how can a man, then,
understand his own way?'—PROVERBS.

'Oh, Mr Parker, he is coming at last, sir!' the housekeeper said; and I: 'God! the doctor?'

'The Doctor, sir,' she said—'saw him myself—he is on foot—must have passed through the north-park gates, and is at this moment coming up the drive!'

I ran to the lawn; saw him slowly coming in the old frockcoat of flimsy stuff, his gaze on the ground.

'Ah, Parker,'—he glanced up and held out a limp hand—'Well, I hope.'

'*I* am well enough, thanks, Doctor.'

'But why the accented *I*? My sister, Parker?'

I was astounded! 'You have not, then, heard?' I asked.

'I have heard nothing.'

'In heaven's name! In what land have you, then, been?'

'Parker, in a land fairly far away.'

I said nothing more, nor he. He felt fear—fear to ask the question which I felt fear too answer; and we moved together into the gloomy home, an ancient place in ruins, the home of a race most ancient; till in the room we called 'study' he seated himself on our sofa, and with complete composure said: 'Now, Parker—my sister.'

'Miss Euphemia, Doctor, is no more.'

His face was stone; after a minute I distinctly heard him murmur: 'I thought as much. So it happened once before.'

What had? Heaven knew! I only added: 'Three weeks ago, Doctor.'

'Of what?'
'She was—'
'Say it.'
'Doctor, she was—'
'Oh, say it, man—she was murdered.'
'Doctor; she was murdered.'

I see him again now—spare and pigmy, grand in forehead, which at the top bristled with a scrub of iron-grey; yellow shaven face; and those eyes, grey, so unquiet, never an instant still, a name high in the eye of the world among the hierophants of learning. During the fifteen years of my secretaryship, we had produced ten books, every one monumental in its way. His energies, in fact, might be called vast—though I don't say steady, or at least not steady so far as I was concerned: for anon, perhaps in the midst of some work, he would suddenly vanish from Raphash, without warning, nor at such times did I ever know whether it was some Old Dynasty 'find' that had enticed him overseas, or excavations at Mycenae, or at Khorsabad, or at Balbec: I knew only that he was gone, and that in due course he would as quietly be back again at his labours.

An old 'lady-housekeeper' and myself, besides the Doctor and Miss Euphemia, were the only inmates of the old place, for we occupied only an insignificant nook of the ground-floor of one of the wings. Never a visitor broke in upon our solitude, except one man, whose calls always corresponded with the Doctor's absences. The lengthy *tête-a-têtes* of this gentleman with Miss Euphemia led me to suspect an ancient flame, to which the Doctor had had objections.

Miss Euphemia was a lady of forty-five years, taller than her brother, but remarkably like him. She, too, had become learned by dint of reading the Doctor's books. I cannot now say how it was, for they hardly ever exchanged a word, but I had arrived at the certainty that each of these lives was as necessary to the other as the air it breathed.

Yet for three weeks the newspapers had been discussing her disappearance, and he knew nothing of the matter! He looked at me through half-closed lids, and said, with that dryness of tone which was his: 'Tell me the circumstances.'

The Case of Euphemia Raphash

I answered: 'I was away in London on business connected with your Shropshire seat, and can only repeat the depositions of Mrs Grant. Miss Raphash had, strange to say, been persuaded to attend the funeral of a lady, known to her in youth, at Ringlethorpe; and, staying afterwards with the mourning friends, did not return till midnight. She wore, it seems, some of the old jewels. By one o'clock, however, the house was in darkness; and it was an hour later that a shriek reached Mrs Grant's ears. She managed to light a candle, and had opened her door, when she saw a man rushing towards her with some singular weapon in his hand which flashed in the half-dark—a little man, she thinks. She had but time to slam her door, when he dashed himself frantically against it, whereupon she fancies she heard the angry remonstrance of another man. Here, however, her evidence is vague; some hours later when she woke to consciousness, she rushed to Miss Raphash's room, and found it empty.'

'Of the jewels?'

'Of Miss Raphash herself.'

'And the jewels?'

'They lay on the dressing-table where they had been placed, untouched.'

'Clearly the murderer was not a burglar.'

'Clearly he *was*. He, or they, took other things, valuables from your room and mine to the amount of four hundred pounds.'

'But some of these have been traced?'

'Not one. Some have been found—none traced.'

'Where found?'

'In a clump of bushes immediately beneath the balcony of the south wing.'

'They were singular burglars. And my sister's body was found—'

'Nowhere.'

'It was buried in the park.'

'Quite certainly not. The park has been subjected to too minute a scrutiny for that.'

'It was burned.'

'Not in the house, and again not in the grounds. It was for some ghastly reason conveyed away.'

'It is not *now* in the house, for instance?'

'No—if the most recondite search in the darkest recesses of the mansion are of any value.'

'There were blood-stains?'

'A few on the bed.'

'No clue?'

'One. It would seem that the assassin, or one of them, before gaining entrance, drew off his boots, and, on running away, left them, for some undreamable reason, behind him:'

'It is very simple. He went in a pair of yours or mine.'

'No. Had his foot, as measured by his boot, been one-third as small, it could never have been forced into a boot of yours or mine.'

"Yet Mrs Grant says he was a small man; it is peculiar he should have so huge a foot.'

'It seems clear that there were more than one.'

'Yet I incline to the one-man theory: for through some failure of courage or memory, one might have left the jewels but hardly two. Mrs Grant, being distracted, may have mistaken his stature; and in the course of my anthropological experience, I have even come across that very discrepancy between man and foot—the survival of a simian trait.'

'There is another point,' I said, 'the boots were found to be odd.'

'But that is a clue!' he said. 'I have the man in my grasp. Have you now told me everything?'

'Except that a gentleman had called to see Miss Raphash that afternoon.'

'Ah—what sort of man?'

'Tall, black-dressed, middle-aged, with side-whiskers. I have seen him here when you have been away. Mrs Grant says that Miss Raphash spoke to him with some show of anger, though no phrases could be made out.'

'Ah!' said the Doctor, and resumed a restless walk.

'It is not impossible,' he remarked after a while, 'that deeps, dark to the eye of a policeman, may become visible to the eye of a thinker. Let us go over the house.'

Science had habituated the Doctor to labour without the stimulus of expectancy, and in this search we spent hours in the vastnesses of the house, the stillness of wings which perhaps no

The Case of Euphemia Raphash

step had set barking with echoes for centuries, down in the vaults. We came at length to a room on the second floor of the south wing overlooking a patch of shrubbery—a room very damp and gloomy, its arras rotted to grey shreds. The Doctor had used it as a depository of bones, embrya in formalin, fossils, implements of stone, and bronze. Along one side was a chest, which, as well as a recess behind a panel in the wall, contained piles of bones, all labelled.

The lock of the door was of special construction, and the Doctor had the key ever about him. I could not therefore but smile, when on entering, I said to him: 'Here, at least, our search is fantastic.'

He glanced at me, and passed in doggedly to a gloaming where the light that struggled through the grime of the window-glass hardly lit bits of armour, or grave-stones of Etruria showing in the gloom grey freckles of fungus, a dank dust covering everything.

'Someone has been here,' said the Doctor.

'Doctor!'

'The catch of the window seems awry; notice the dust on the floor.'

'But it is impossible, it is impossible,' I answered.

He opened the window. Below was the balcony of the first floor of that wing, from which a rain-spout ran up; and it was among the bushes of the shrubbery just under the balcony that the stolen valuables had been discovered.

'He climbed up, you see, by the spout,' said the Doctor, the feat seems superhuman: but there is the spout, and here the turned window-catch. We must confront phenomena as we find them.'

'But at least, Doctor, he did not climb up with a dead body in his arms?'

'No; you are right.'

'And he did not enter by the door.'

'No.'

'Then our search here is absurd.'

'Doubtless. You might look behind the panelling.' I looked, and saw only the bones of old bodies.

'She is not *in here* now?' he said, and tapped the oaken chest with his knuckles.

I smiled. 'No, Doctor, not in there. The man does not live who could open with a key *that* lid.'

'Come, then, Parker. Come—we shall find her.'

We moved out, and he locked its old solitude within the room once more.

☙

Men of great intellects undertake tasks which, from their very largeness, seem simply pig-headed or silly to men of smaller gauge. The region of the impossible, indeed, is the real sphere-of-action of genius. But, on the other hand, the crowd may be excused if, in such cases, they become incredulous, resentful, nay, cachinatory.

And, I confess, it was not without resentment that I listened to Doctor Raphash when he said to me: 'Let us find *him,* Parker, the murderer of my sister, the secreter of her body. This is a task which we must not relegate to the intellects of the recognised authorities. Let us hunt *him* down—and, *after* that, we shall resume our studies.'

But his method, at least, was singular. To acquire personal intimacy with a whole class of individuals is an undertaking which, if possible, is the tallest order! But this was his notion; and in a few months we had learned a new language, become denizens of a new world—the language and the world of the East of London. Our dress was the dress of the navvy; our habits those of the ne'er-do-well.

And now were revealed to me the deeps in Doctor Raphash's character. The intensity of his hatred of an unknown man! 'Let us hunt *him* down;' he said, and his life became the incarnation of that sentence—a fury bordering on lunacy behind the scientist calm; the avenging angel *without* the flaming sword.

Days and nights we spent in public-houses, gambling-hells, cells of pawnbrokers, with roughs at slum-corners, crowds at music-hall doors. We were pals of rascals who related to each other without secrecy or shame their achievements in every species of felony. In the mornings we parted; to compare late at night notes of the day's haps. Then far into the morning I would hear the slow cheetah-step of that divine patience stealing to and fro in

The Case of Euphemia Raphash

his chamber near mine. This, and a heightened glare in his eyes, were all the indication he gave of the mania flaming in his heart.

One day I heard something. It was in a gin-palace where two women, dissolute pigs, gossiped upon their pots.

'And how about your old man, then?' I heard.

'Oh, he must fish for hisself, he must. I took his boots to the pawn this morning, and they wouldn't take them.'

'Ain't they no good?'

'They're good enough, but they're odd.'

'Go on!'

'I near tore his eyes out over them same boots. I buys my lord a seven-and-eleven pair in the summer and sends him hop-picking in them; lo and behold! two months ago he turns up with his own boot on the right foot and somebody else's on the other.'

'And what account did he give of hisself?'

'There's where the provoking part of it comes in. Every time I asks him, it's "Drop it, mate." He was on the job, you may bet, got into some scrape, and now dursn't say nothink about it.'

I need not mention the steps by which, in half an hour, I had become the bosom friend of these two women. The time, place, and circumstances of the boots profoundly impressed me, and when I separated from them I doubted not that the name and address I had obtained were those of the man we wanted. When Doctor Raphash got back haggard to our garret that night, I pressed his hand.

'You have news for me, Parker.'

I told him the incident.

'Let us go,' he said.

'You look tired tonight; tomorrow perhaps—'

'Not at all! Tonight, man—*now*—is the time to find what we seek'—and he stamped on the floor.

I glanced, startled, at him, for the action was like a sign of the break-up of that serenity which characterised him.

We passed out, I with a revolver. When, by way of a labyrinth of streets, we reached the address, the Doctor at last spoke, saying: 'There is no light, you see: he is, probably, still out. Suppose you wait till he comes; then speak; take him under the lamp there, see the boots, and ask him to drink with you. I, waiting at yonder corner, will then join you.'

Flakes of snow were floating downwards, while I strolled sentry-wise, and the Doctor crouched at his post. From a Swedish church near I heard the strokes of twelve, and at the same moment a working-man approached me.

'Cold tonight, mate,' I said carelessly.

'Ah, that it is,' he answered.

His teeth chattered—his cheeks wore a blue hue. Turned-up coat collar, and pocketed paws, and forward pose, spoke of his Polar unrepose.

'You look frozen. Come and have a drink along wi' me.'

'I could do with one, mate. Not tasted grub this blessed day.'

'What—broke?'

'Dead broke!'

'Come along then—the Brown Bear.'

He followed me. Under the lamp I stopped.

'Like the Brown Bear? If not—?'

The light fell upon him, and a sense of contempt and disappointment overcame me at the sight of his weak face, sheepish eyes. But there at any rate, were the fellows of the two odd boots which I had handed over to the authorities. The Doctor had been slowly approaching us, and was now in the middle of the road when Hardy, glancing, saw him.

The change in the man's face was sudden and wonderful: his eyes stared, he clung to a railing; then, suddenly taking to his heels, fled, as for life, down a side-street.

The Doctor followed, and then I. And now powers of physique, as unexpected as previously depths of soul in my old friend, stood revealed to me. He distanced me. His feet grew winged. Hardy, indeed, had an advantage in his knowledge of the intricate streets down which he dodged and sometimes for a moment disappeared; but the Doctor slowly won upon him, 'hunting him down,' till suddenly, Hardy dashed into a cul-de-sac, of which the house at the end was empty, every window broken. If the fugitive, then, could gain an entrance there, his escape by the back was safe, and I guessed that this was the house for which he had all along been making. And, in fact, on reaching it, Hardy dashed down the area-steps to a basement below the street-level.

'Shoot!' cried the Doctor, looking back at me: 'shoot with the revolver!'

The Case of Euphemia Raphash

This I was far from willing to do, but it was already too late: for Hardy had disappeared. A minute afterwards we, too, had darted down the steps, and through a door sped into a cellar of which the ground was powdery dust, covering our ankles. There seemed no other means of egress, and I was looking about for Hardy, when the door banged suddenly behind us, and a bar clanged down into a staple outside.

That the man had entered the cellar was certain, also that he had had some means of leaving it other than the door. But here our knowledge ended. The blackness was Erebus itself; clouds of dust rose at our every step and choked us; and soon the intensity of the cold, after our race, made speech nearly impossible. I groped round the walls, shot off my revolver, but the flash revealed nothing but a portion of unhewn wall and low ceiling; I howled at the door; but the neighbouring houses were ruins—an echo answered me.

Towards morning I received, I confess, a thrilling experience of horror from Doctor Raphash. That he was not himself, that he suffered more than I, had become apparent. Once or twice only had he spoken through the night, seated in the dust in a corner, his knees bent up, his head buried in his arms. By palpation I knew him to be in this position.

Once I said in alarm: 'Doctor, do not sleep! This cold—'

The Doctor laughed aloud. 'No, no,' he said bitterly; 'no sleep; little fear of that tonight.'

I walked for warmth to and fro, treading warily on the dust. Then a groan drew me to him, and my cold fingers touched his forehead with the sensation of contact with something hot.

'You are suffering terribly,' I said.

'Leave me alone, Parker!'

An hour, and I knew that he was stalking fast up and down all the length of the cellar; swiftly! filling it with a continuous smoke of dust: and long I stood mute, noting his faint sounds on the ground as he came, losing them, following in fancy the growth of his cloudy progress, guessing that now he was here, now yonder. His mutterings guided me. He seemed to forget my presence.

When the air finally became unbreathable, I moved to go to him, and in this act my head came in contact with something, which on catching I found to be a rope hanging down. Unable to divine its purpose, I succeeded after many efforts in climbing it, my head struck the ceiling, and feeling round with my hand, I encountered what seemed the panels of a trap-door. The means of Hardy's escape now flashed upon me. I pushed with my knuckles, and some light entered. In another minute I was free on the other side—it was already day.

A strange, pale face peered up at me, rolling wild eyes. When I had drawn him up, together we passed out to the street.

Here he suddenly seized my hand.

'Parker!'—his pantings came in gasps—'be a gadfly in your tenacity, as you love me, man! Hunt him down! Goodbye. . . . Madman! do not follow!'

And before my brain could wake from its depth of stupor, he had dashed furiously down the road, and vanished into a passing cab.

ဆ

After Dr Raphash's mysterious desertion of our quest when success seemed near, I merely returned to the Towers, and waited. I now, in fact, considered my duty done when I had described to the authorities the fellow with the odd boots, who at this time was in hiding.

It was a month afterwards that I remarked one evening, as I was walking about the grounds, that a man, hearing my approaching footsteps, had ducked his head from me in a clump of bushes—the very bushes, by the way, in which the stolen things had been discovered.

I was accompanied by a mastiff: so, on coming close to the spot, I said aloud: 'Do not run, simply rise, and hold your hands over your head. I happen to be armed—and you see the dog.'

The crack of a gun would have much less astonished me than the hang-dog air with which he rose before me. I recognised instantly the insipid face of Hardy.

'No offence, master,' he said, touching his hat, trembling like aspen.

'We have met before, Hardy.'

He scrutinised my face, but shook his head.

The Case of Euphemia Raphash

'You know me better'n I know you, sir.'

'Well, Charles, you must come with me,' I said, and led him by the arm into a room of the house, instructing Mrs Grant at the entrance to send for a couple of the rather distant local police. I then closed the door, and proceeded to examine my prisoner. The creature wept!

'Now, Hardy,' I said, 'dry your tears, and tell me how you came to be in those bushes tonight.'

'I was looking for the rings and things. It was hunger drove me—they've been hunting me like an animal for the last month, and I give myself up.'

'What rings?'

'The rings I dropped in those bushes. I thought that, anyway, one of them might by chance be left there still.'

'You admit the burglary, then?'

'Yes, master, I admit it. It was my first, and it will be my last. I haven't had a moment's peace since. I even put up a rope in an old cellar to hang myself, only I'm a coward—'

'And you admit the murder?'

'Murder, master?' he cried with a scared face. 'Why, it wasn't me as did the murder, it was one of the other two, and didn't I nearly drop dead with fright when I see it done?'

'There were, then, two others?'

'Yes, sir, a working-man such as myself, and an old gent.'

'Tell me about it.'

'I and a mate of mine, sir, came down hop-picking—one of your wild chaps, and hops was too slow for *him*; so he says to me as how some of these country-houses was mere child's play, with plenty to be got, and not much danger, so one night here we stood behind a shed, waiting till the old lady was well asleep, when all of a sudden, as if he'd sprung out of the ground, this old gent stood between us. I started running; he looked like a spirit to me; but Jim, he stands his ground, whistles to me, and when I come up, he ses, "'Ere's a lark, Charlie," ses he, "old chap's on the job hisself!" "Partnership's a leaky ship, Jim," ses I; but he only ses, "Oh, bother, live and let live." Well, I and Jim get our boots off, we all get inside, and no sooner inside, than the old cove takes the lead, showing the way, telling us what to do, me and Jim doing everything he tells us, nat'ral like. He knew every crick of the place! and first he takes us into a room, and ses he, quite wild like, "Plunder now! raven and harry! to your souls' content!" Then he reaches down a case from a shelf, and takes out a strange, shiny knife, locks the case again—I believe he had keys to every lock in the place and rushes out of the room into the one opposite. "Queer chap, that," ses Jim, looking queery hisself, "gives me the shivers," and before I could tell him I felt sure the dove was a devil or a ghost, we hear a struggle going on in the opposite room—someone gasping—then a great shriek which I ain't ever going to forget. Immediately after, out he flies with his wild eyes, and dashes hisself on the other old woman's door yonder. Jim, with the cold sweats on him, he plucks up courage to reason with him a bit, but no go, the old cove spurts back to the murdered lady, and dashes out again with her in his arms, a gash showing all across her chest, her grey hair trailing on the ground. And now he comes up to us, and, lofty like, ses he, "Marshal yourselves before me—march! march! and I will show you where treasures lie thick for yer 'arvesting!' and he makes us walk before him across the building into the other wing and up two stairs, till we come to a room with a lot of bones—and, there, Great God! Hide me! there-*there he is!* He'll kill me, as he killed my mate—he'll kill you, too—'

He stared wildly about, rushed behind my chair, and crouched down there, the man's shriek of panic horror thrilling me through, as the ponderous door swung slowly open on its hinges, and Dr Raphash calmly walked into the room.

'Well, Parker,' he said in the old cold tone, 'here I am again, you see. But whom have we . . . the murderer caught!' and triumph lighted his eyes as they rested on Hardy, who, pallid and panting, at present lay propped upon the tapestry.

'Yes, the murderer!' gasped Hardy, 'but that's not me! Oh, there's plenty of proofs, if it comes to that! That coat's the very one you had on—have you washed the blood off the sleeve yet?'

Dr Raphash sat down, barely smiling, examining the face of Hardy. Presently he looked at his arm.

'Remarkable thing,' he said, talking to himself: 'I *have* noticed a stain on my sleeve; it cannot be blood; Parker, see.'

But, as for me, a mist hung before me: I could see nothing.

'It *is* blood,' continued Hardy, gaining courage from the Doctor's calm—'you know it is, or perhaps you were too mad that night to know anything. Who but a madman would have carried the lady's body all the way to that old chest; and didn't you chase Jim round and round the room and stab him like a dog, because you said one body wasn't enough to fill the chest? And if I hadn't slipped down to the balcony by the spout, wouldn't you have killed me, too? and didn't you look out of the window and tell me to prepare myself because you was coming, and didn't I have to jump from the balcony to the ground, rolling over, and dropping all the things I had? and didn't I just have time to draw on two of the boots, and they odd, when you ran down and started after me?'

I was looking at Dr Raphash: during this categorical charge, no sound had issued from his lips; but gradually a pallor as of death had overspread his face, whose muscles became tense and fixed; his head tumbled forward, his legs stretched rigidly from his body, the stony glare in his eyes giving to his face an aspect of rhadamanthine grimness ghastly to see.

I ran and grasped the clammy fingers in mine; but he did not recognise me. So he remained for several minutes, no breath breaking the stillness there.

Then, still rigid in all his limbs, he raised his head, and let it drop heavily back over the back of the chair; and, with this action, there burst from his blanched lips—higher and higher, peal on peal, in shrillest staccato—carillons of laughter.

With creeping flesh, I seized Hardy by the arm, rushed—faint—from the room, and locked the door upon the ruin within.

ಸಿ

In this way Dr Arnot Raphash hunted down the murderer of his sister; and so, with him, fell the Jewish House of Raphash in the county of Kent.;

Some days later I received a letter, of which the following are extracts:

'. . . . When I tell you that I am the proprietor of the private asylum from which this letter is dated, and a cousin of Dr Raphash, you will at once conjecture that his (to you) strange absences from home always corresponded with his voluntary sojourns in my establishment. He well knew the warning symptoms—head-pains, a high temperature, etc—and he usually had two or three days grace before the definite onset of the malady. Sometimes, again, the attack was more sudden, especially when preceded by any excitement; thus, when he reached my establishment a month ago he was already mad, and I at once divined some violent agitation. . . . His first paroxysm occurred at the age of thirty when he destroyed a just-married wife by cyanide-vapour poison . . . In the sane state he had no recollection of his insane acts, which were distinguished by a mania to kill, directed mainly against those for whom he most cared. He never knew anything of his wife's doom, for he was at once placed under my care, and on returning to the Towers found her already interred. . . . When he was leaving me 'cured' after his sister's death, I deemed it prudent to tell him nothing of that death, preferring that the journey to the Towers should intervene before the shock of the news dropped upon his newly restored powers: hence his ignorance of this thing. . . . You have probably seen me on my visits to Miss Raphash when the Doctor was away from home, my object being to give her those minute reports of her brother's progress which alone could console her. On the very day of her tragedy I had a rather angry argument with her regarding the good of putting her idol into irons, she deprecating, I insisting. Unfortunately, I permitted her to influence me, and her death was the consequence, for it is now beyond all doubt that the Doctor escaped from my establishment that night, though how he contrived to pass out of the house and grounds and then into them again without detection is still unexplained; but then to his cunning there were no bounds . . . I need only add that I shall soon have the pleasure of telling you of the death of Dr Raphash; for the end cannot be delayed. . . .'

CUMMINGS KING MONK

I
HE MEDDLES WITH WOMEN

'Apple tarts! Apple tarts!'—HEINE

I once had occasion to hire a first floor in Bloomsbury, in one of those houses where the first floor is respectable, and the others but shabby genteel. It was there that I first saw Cummings King Monk, who occupied the top floor.

Without knowing his name, I would occasionally meet him on the stairs; but his name came out one day when I asked a servant who was carrying up a tray of letters if all those were for one person, and her answer was: 'They are for Mr Monk: every post brings him sixty or seventy.'

I thought to myself: 'Either this man is a begging-letter writer on a big scale, or a personage of great importance in the world,' for I could see that the envelopes bore the crests of courts and clubs, and though some were but illiterately scribbled, on one I noticed the well-known autograph of an English Prince.

The only other fact which I then knew about Monk was the fury with which he flew up and down stairs, three at a time. But soon afterwards it happened that I had invited two ladies to a 'first night,' could not obtain tickets, and was at a loss, when Monk one afternoon stopped me, saying that he had desired my acquaintance, had a box for the 'first night,' and was I disposed to take it?

Afterwards he sent me down an invitation to dinner, and when I replied that it was impossible that evening, it was then that I first came into contact with this man's control over his fellow-creatures; for he sent me down a second note, informing me that De R—— had promised to make a third in our party, and concluded with the words: 'Do not try to resist that inducement, since you will fail.'

It was quite true: and I remember being struck by his knowledge of my passion for a particular art, for this particular artist, and the self-sure manner in which he had adapted the special bait to my special nature.

Monk strongly resembled the late Prince Consort—medium height, a figure lithe, slight, a browned countenance crowned by a brow livid-white and high, his hair curling forward in two curls about his ears in a quaint way; in one of the ears being a gold button, worn, I believe, for a weakness of the eyes. His manners were of an extreme feverishness, his speech keen, frequently even furious and voluminous.

I cannot refrain from mentioning an incident of that Café Royal dinner of ours.

De R—— wished to hear a certain 'star,' and Monk proposed that we should all go; we none of us, however, remembered which was the music-hall, the waiter was absent, no newspaper visible; but suddenly Monk said: 'There is an old Major with a paper; we'll get that.'

'But—he is reading it!' I said.

'He is reading one column, yes—has already read it thrice—' and he rose at once and stepped towards the Major, passing behind him, his eyes meanwhile peering into the paper. He then said: 'May I ask, sir, if your paper contains a graphic account of the grand charge of which we are all talking?'

'Why, yes,' the Major answered; 'are you interested?'

'Acutely. It is a former servant of mine who has done the deed.'

'What, Mackay? Is that so? Is it not a thrilling piece of work? If you were to read this description in *The Evening*—'

'But I could hardly deprive you—'

'Do not mention it,' and as Monk was half-way back to our table, the Major called after him: 'The Ensign Eversleigh who led the charge is—*my son!*'

All Monk said to us in explanation of his rape of the paper was that he had known that the Major was perusing something which touched his self-love: 'He is quite happy now,' he added, 'in picturing to himself my rapture as I read.'

Well, within a year I had gathered a good many facts concerning Monk—such as that he was of noble rank, had some Hebrew blood, and was among the six or seven wealthiest men. Fortune, he told me, had made of him a target, and from his youth, had gunned him with gold, the estate of three millions left him in tail by his father forming a trifling item in the river of his revenues, the bulk being derived from a great-uncle of his mother, a Nurnberg Jew, who had invested his fortune for accumulation, designating as his heir a child to be born who should fulfil all the conditions fulfilled by Monk.

He was frequently to be met in the queerest dens, had a liking for Cockneyland, and in his pockets keys to five or six lodgings, into which he might dive and disappear.

As to the tone of his mind, I can describe it best by saying that Monk was a conjuror from his cradle, his conjuror's tools being now philosophic concepts, and now human beings.

This has been said of other men, of Richelieu, Bismarck; but Richelieu, Bismarck, were conjurors by a figure of speech, not like the mummer I knew as Monk, who was anon a conjuror playing exactly with the self-consciousness, in the manner, and with the airs, of a paid conjuror, and in general with some recklessness of the cost or consequences of his play.

I will adduce an instance, it being understood and when I was not present, I had the facts from Monk himself.

Once when I dropped in upon him in a garret in a 'court', he then bending over a pigmy grate reading Greek, 'Bully of you to come,' he broke out at once. 'What do you think, now, of this man Orpheus? A musician who could play so sweet as to make trees jig!'

'Wasn't Orpheus rather a sun-myth?' I asked, sitting on the one chair, Monk being on the rug.

'Or he might quite well have been a man with headaches,' he said, 'who, if he didn't make trees jig, did do other similar things. Rather fascinating! And why? Because men guess that there are powers latent within their own brows boundlessly greater than they have ever been trained to show, and that here or there a man may have breathed by whom they were actually shown.'

'We must have degenerated,' I said. 'Instead of Orpheus and his womenfolk swarming after his music, we have Kubelik and bouquets—'

Monk smiled with, 'You jest as to "degenerated", and you talk of women swarming! Why—'

He stopped.

'Well?' I said.

'Stop—let me see. Could I? Would you like to see, my friend, a swarm, all women, raging through London after one solitary male?'

He uttered it with a sudden flush! And I believe in that minute had schemed each detail of some whim which now filled him.

He clapped on his cleft felt hat, caught my arm, saying, 'Let's have some lunch. See if I don't show you something soon. . . .'

∞

That evening a mysterious circumstance which created a sensation occurred at a ball of Lady Tw——, in Park Lane, I myself being as puzzled as anybody when I heard of it, although it certainly occurred to me that this might be but the first act in Monk's new comedy.

At this ball the Princess W—— of B——, in the oddest manner, lost her wedding-ring—a ring having an enormous fancy-value, owing to the fact that it had long been the badge of marriage in that family. On its surface was a scratch, cross-shaped.

The Princess W—— happened at the instant to be in conversation with the French Ambassador, two Countesses, Cummings King Monk, and a Reichs-Fürst. Early in the morning it was, they standing on a balcony hanging over a back garden with some lanterns, only one electric jet in the leafy ceiling relieving the shadow; and the conversation had turned on the wedding-ring.

'Prince Henry,' the Princess said, 'regards it with a sort of awe, like some genie ring.'

'By it's magic he hold the Princess W——,' observed the Ambassador.

'But one wonders whether its binding virtue lasts after so many bindings,' said a Countess; 'like those electric belts which run down—'

'I fancy it holds my husband indifferently well,' muttered the Princess with a shrug.

'A ring, the symbol of eternity, must be unaffected by time,' observed Monk.

'Or improved by it,' added the Ambassador, 'like wine: for both bind friendship, and open a lady's tenderness.'

'I must see the famous ring some day,' said Monk.

'You would like—?' asked the Princess. 'Then why not now?'

'You're glove—'

'Doesn't matter. Though there is really nothing to *see* . . .'

Talking still, she drew off her glove; and, talking still, half-averted, held out the little hand sideways, her finger-tips resting on Monk's left hand, three of the fingers being now encrusted with a crowd of rings.

Monk bent over the hand, and touching a spot of the Princess's third finger with his own right forefinger, muttered: 'This middle one must be it by the Ungar *mode*,' but immediately added, 'No, this is not it. *Which* is it?'

The Princess, turning, bent to show him. 'This one,' she said; and then immediately, 'why, no; where is it?'

She bent lower, and now went pale.

Where was it? It had vanished. She moved, all flurried, hurried into a room where there was light, the others following. She drew off the other glove, doubting her left hand and her right; then looked blankly about.

'It is not here.'

'This is most strange!'

'It is incredible.'

'But it is impossible!'

'How could you lose it?'

'It is not here.'

'Are you sure?'

'It was just here.'

'Where?'

'Where this ring now is.'

'How remarkable!'

'But I don't remember this ring! Is it mine?'
'It must be.'
'I suppose so. I was dressed so hurriedly—'
'Have you had off the wedding-ring today?'
'Yes—once.'
'Then, perhaps—'
'No, I am sure that I put it on again.'
'Ah, in that case— But may you not have put on the other ring, thinking it somehow the wedding-ring?'
'I can't think that.'
'Then, it is an amazing thing!'

The hostess came up. The alarm spread. The mystery was of such a kind that no mind could begin to divine it.

Monk found an opportunity to breathe at the Princess's ear:

'I hope you are not going to distress yourself. I even assure you that it must be found. Then your pleasure will more than repay you. . . .' But she was not to be comforted.

The next day the ring was the theme of the papers, which announced a reward of five thousand pounds for its recovery.

It may be said at once that the loss of this ring was due to Monk; and by nine-thirty that morning he was engaged in the second act of his drama, being then in an office in Hatton garden, before him a portly Jew, to whom he was saying: 'Now, look you, I am interested in this affair, Bernstein—have guaranteed the Princess that the ring shall be found, and so on. But, you see, it has nothing to identify it, except two scratches; and now that this reward is out, what is to prevent all England from buying wedding-rings, scratching crosses on them, and presenting them as the real ring. Think of the bother of it! We can't have that, you know.'

'Oh, I follow you, Mr Monk,' lisped Bernstein, rubbing his plump palms, 'and I take it that you want me to—'

'Yes, to get out a circular quick—you are in such close touch with the trade—let no wedding-ring be sold, in London, anyway, for two days. You will undertake a three-and-half per cent reimbursement on profits for every ring refused to be sold by the retailer, and I reimburse you at four—Oh, look at the oil of gladness on his face now! But, hullo! I don't see that nephew of yours anywhere.'

'You don't want to insult a man, Mr Monk, I'm sure,' was Bernstein's answer to this.

'Insult? What, because he got those six months, you mean? But where's the good of playing the Pharisee before a man like me? I bet if Sam were to come to you with one of his fetching schemes in an hour's time, you'd finance him! And who could blame you?'

'Well, he knows his way about, and that's the truth, does Sam,' said Bernstein, softening. 'But still—don't mention the gaol-bird's name to me, sir, I beg!'

'So where's he now?'

'Oh, shamming sick at one of the hospitals, I believe.'

'Which one?'

'St Thomas's.'

'I think I shall look up the poor devil, Bernstein, and give him a job. Be prompt, now, about stopping sale of rings,' and he rushed out to his cab, calling out, 'St Thomas's Hospital!'—Sam Bernstein being the next pawn in this game. And presently Monk was sitting by a bedside in the 'Caroline' ward, saying to Sam, 'Well, Sam Bernstein, shamming sick again?'

'Anything for a quiet life, Mr Monk,' answered Sam on his elbow, adding: 'To what may I owe the favour of this visit, sir?'

His eyes examined Monk—a wizened wight, true Cockney, true Jew, true criminal, impishly shrewd of face, with fleshly lips, and matted black locks hanging about his pallid countenance; while a rattle in his chest showed that his illness was not wholly a sham.

'The favour of my visit?' said Monk. 'Why not drop that whine? Your uncle was just telling me that you are down in the world—'

'Moy loif, been to my uncle so early in the morning, Mt Monk?'

'And have some move on, of course—you suspicious wretch. You might guess why I went— Or haven't you heard of the robbery?'

Sam's interest instantly quickened. He sat up.

'Robbery?'

'Well, the Princess W—— lost her wedding-ring last night, and there's a reward of five thousand—'

'Moy loif!'

'I happen to be interested, so hurried to your uncle Bernstein to get him to stop sale of wedding-rings for a day or two.'

'Stop sale—what's the deal, Mr Monk?'

'Why, where are your wits?' asked Monk. 'The lost ring has only two scratches to identify it; anybody could counterfeit it—provided he could get a ring to buy.'

Sam lay back, pondering this, not a wrinkle on his forehead, but his eyes as alive as lightning.

And the tempter went on: 'Another thing—the Princess says she lost the ring last night, because she missed it last night; but, of course, it may have been lost five years ago. A married woman isn't always looking at her ring—knows it is there all right—doesn't trouble. So that, suppose Mrs Brown or Mrs Jones has a wedding-ring with some scratch on it, the first thing she will think is that hers may be the very Princess's ring, stolen long ago, and bought by Jones for her. Then, of course, she presents her ring as the lost one.'

Sam was all interest now; he muttered half to himself, 'No fear about women parting with their wedding-rings for any money—bad luck! But *the husbands* might be got at, though. Only I don't quite see where a deal would come in— '

The tempter smiled, saying, 'True, the husbands; *they'd* part with their wives' wedding-rings for five thousand pounds lightly enough. And that's why I'm afraid of someone or other perpetrating a big fraud on those same husbands this day.'

'Fraud?' muttered Sam with irritation; 'strike me silly! I don't see through the game.'

'Why, it stares you in the face,' said Monk. 'Well, you wouldn't do such a thing yourself—I'll tell you. First of all, where do you suppose the Princess's ring is at this moment?'

Sam's lips twitched. 'Where, sir?'

'On her finger, I imagine—though I have a reason of my own for not giving her the hint for some days.'

'Finger?'

'Who could get it off, without her knowing—except her husband? And he's in France. I'd almost swear that someone had a motive for changing her wedding-ring into another kind of ring while it was on her finger.'

'But—how?' Sam's stare was like a cat's over a mouse-hole

'Why, where *are* your wits today?' asked Monk. 'What's simpler than to clap upon a wedding-ring a row of stones like this'—he exhibited from his purse a curve of turquoises, the big one containing a pigmy magnet and piston of soft iron to create a vacuum—'any goldsmith's 'prentice could make you one in an hour. And now do you see how the husbands of half England could be swindled in this affair? But it doesn't concern you, Sam Bernstein. What I came to tell you is that, if you care to do some copying for me, I can give you a job.'

A change had passed over Sam's face; for where the deal came in he could see, and, for an instant could not conceal an aspect of keenness as of the cat wriggling to spring; but then said wearily, 'I am feeling so bad, Mr Monk, of late. Copying, I don't think, wouldn't hardly suit me, though sorry I am—'

'Then—I'm off,' Monk said, rising. 'You are very independent, my friend. I suppose it's because you know that Uncle Bernstein will receive you with open arms, the first good thing you have to put before him what?' and he was gone.

He was probably no sooner out than Bernstein bounded from bed; and the same hour had claimed a Briton's liberty, and was out, bound for his Uncle Bernstein's.

All that day he was blissfully busy, like a liberated being revelling in its own element once more; his consumption vanished; he had talks with his uncle in which they bent together, with magnifiers imbedded in their eye-sockets, over little curves of turquoises; he visited his acquaintances, and they sat gravely together in cabinet-councils; he hired in haste three offices—in Westminster, in Bishopsgate, and in Whitechapel—and in each he had carpenters hammering; he left at newspaper offices this advertisement: 'Whoever is the happy possessor of a wedding-ring with a scratch should bring it to one of the three following addresses for identification. Five thousand pounds reward.'

Before nightfall London began to feel the influence of his energies—and to respond to it. By the next morning there was trouble.

I, personally, came into contact with the results of Mr Sam Bernstein's activities several times that day—without any suspicion of their significance. First, in passing out in the morning, I was asked by my housekeeper if I had happened to see anything of a ring. 'It is nonsense asking, I know,' she added.

'No,' I said, 'what kind of ring?'

'My wedding-ring! It hasn't been off my finger this five-and-twenty years'—and, in truth, I could see the pale place on her finger where the ring had pressed it.

'It's the queerest thing!' she cried out. 'I could almost take my oath that it was on my finger last night; yet this morning when I woke it was gone!'

And again, about 3 p.m., at Oxford Circus, I witnessed the meeting of two girls, from one of whom, in the act of shaking hands, burst the words, 'Where's your wedding-ring?'

'My dear, it's lost! But how quick you notice!'

'Haven't I cause?' said the first. 'Both Maude Wilson and my Kit lost theirs during the night; and now yours, too!'

The very expression of mystification kept their lips agape. I, for my part, somehow had a thought of Monk, and the women-crowds of Orpheus; but it was but momentary, since it was not possible to conceive how *he* could have a hand in this.

And again at Clapham that night, while writing a post card in a stationer's shop, I noticed that the woman of the establishment was looking about, under the counter, everywhere, with a face of worry. So I asked if she had lost anything.

'My wedding-ring!' leapt from her lips.

She had missed it from her finger that morning about nine.

This miracle so pricked my wonderment that I went hunting for Monk that night at several of his haunts, but failed to find him. It was not till the next morning that I first saw Mr Sam Bernstein's advertisement: 'Whoever is the happy possessor of a wedding-ring should bring it to one of the following addresses . . .' but this brought no light to my mind, since at the time I was ignorant even of the existence of Sam.

Anyhow, those 'three addresses' were during three days besieged by a crowd, all males, from morning to night; for the reward was five thousand pounds, and at the advertisement of Bernstein, who was assumed to be some authorised agent of the Princess, fevered became the agitation, each of not less than twenty thousand London men conceiving the hope that Chance might pick *him* out as the possessor of the lost ring. Some, acting in bad faith, rushed to jeweller after jeweller, but failed to obtain a wedding-ring to scratch, since Monk had stopped their sale; others, acting in good faith, imagined a scratch on their wife's ring, and believed it not impossible that it might prove to be the Princess's, lost perhaps long previously; and all, in the end, by one means or another—during sleep, by some ruse or scheme—got hold of their helpmeet's pledge of wedlock, to wend hopefully with it to those addresses of Bernstein's advertisement; but everyone went away with a face fretted with perplexity and dismay.

Bernstein's three offices had all been partitioned into compartments, each to hold one man only in its dingy cell, Sam or one of his gang standing behind the rude counter, leaning over a huge ledger on whose leaves lay strewn jewels and rings—none of them wedding-rings; nor did Sam look up from his writing when Brown entered from the queue outside; he said only, 'Fill up this form,' and 'Name, please.' Brown gave his name, meantime depositing his ring among the others on the ledger, which completely covered the strip of counter.

'Address, please.'

It was given, the shopman wrote it in the ledger, and now straightened himself up to ask: 'Where's the ring?'

'There,' said Brown, with a hovering finger.

'*Where?*'

'Why, didn't I put it there?'

'I don't see it.'

Brown's fingers began to fumble in his pockets.

'Hurry up, please,' says the shopman, who, while Brown had been preoccupied between writing and answering, had by the motion of a finger-tip pushed a concave of jewels to stick to the convex of Brown's ring.

And after one minute's contention Brown was both believing the incredible, and disbelieving all things: he had lost the ring on his way—his eyes were a lie—the universe was lunatic. He went away with a bowed brow of worry, moody, mute, still fumbling in his waistcoat, boring his way through the waiting multitude straining for admittance. It was Sam Bernstein's 'deal.' By the end of the second day he owned a sum of thirty thousand pounds sterling in wedding-rings.

He took the precaution, however, in view of the Law, to attach for the present to every ring a ticket, bearing the name and address of its owner.

But on the third day there was a hitch, when one of his customers—a man with a Yankee beard and a sombrero—happened to step into the very cell where Sam himself bent over the ledger.

'Name, please,' said Sam to him.

'John P. Wood.'

'Address.'

'No 9, Keppel Street.'

Sam wrote it, and straightened himself.

'Where is the ring?'

'*There!*' answered the man, and pointed definitely.

At once Bernstein lost his nerve, turning ashen.

'But that's not a wedding-ring, my good man, can't you see?' he whined with reproach. 'It belongs—'

'To *me*, and it is a wedding-ring, Sam, with some stones stuck on it.'

Upon which the man made a snatch at Sam's beard, pulling it off, at the same time pulling off his own. And Sam staggered; his twitching lips wished to spit out, 'Mr *Monk!*' but could utter nothing.

'So this is the use you make of my chance chat with you, you jackal!' said Monk. 'Quick, Sam—quick, lad—three years for this, unless you hand over to me each and all of those rings within the half-hour! The books first!'

Sam had collapsed; and presently was accompanying Monk in a cab to his other offices, which Monk left bearing several cash-boxes crammed with ticketed rings.

A thundering banging made by somebody in distracted haste sounded at my door that night about nine. When I looked out in wonder, Monk shouted irritably from below: 'Come quick!—never mind about hats!'

I bounded down, and was away with him, he quite breathless, red with ecstasy, and, as we dived into a cab, cries he to the driver: 'Five pounds to get us to the Mansion House within seven minutes!'

In the cab he showed me an advertisement, inserted by himself in the papers that day: 'Let lady who has lost wedding-ring meet advertiser before Mansion House at nine sharp this evening. She will recover, free of cost. Husband, show this to your wife.'

But we were late, and all the time he held watch on palm, as up Holborn we dashed at a gallop and we had hardly got to St Martin's, when we saw that something had thrown the traffic into one mass of confusion, no passage anywhere, cabmen fiercely vociferating, policemen fretfully busy.

'Come—can't wait!' muttered Monk to me, jumping out, and away he dashed, forgetting to pay, dashed back again in a passion of haste, and we were off anew on foot, up Cheapside, dodging amid the wheels of the long block of vehicles in the middle of the street—for the pavements were thronged—dodging with a breakneck precipitancy, but hampered, like ship-shadows dodging through billows. And all the while I knew not at all what the to-do was about! But suddenly saw—for all that space between the Mansion House, the Stock Exchange and the Bank was one sea of people; and away down each street leading from the space one could perceive vistas of people teeming; and they were nearly all women, some twenty thousand, come to meet Cummings Monk.

By the largeness of the thing, all the oddity of it, my consciousness was somehow utterly bewildered. The air was full of tongues and rumours—but sounding in a tone quite *outré*. High, unusual with crowds. I remember that in the midst of my bewilderment of mind, a singular giddiness, a quite wild kind of gaiety, somehow struck me, for something electric was about, some bacchic influence, emanating from the crowd. I saw it in the face of Monk, from whom I had got somewhat separated; I saw it on the faces of the scores of constables. Monk was then in the centre of a number of inspectors and constables, some of whom evidently knew him, explaining something to them, and I saw him hand round something—money possibly—whereupon the officers separated, and went disseminating some message among the ladies. At the same time Monk bored his way to a four-wheeler near the Exchange, and standing erect on the seat, began some harangue, which my ear could not exactly catch, though I understood that he was assuring them that their rings were in his hands, and that, given the chance, he would deliver them up that very day.

Then, as he leapt down and moved, there were shooting fingers at him, shouts of 'That's he! that's he!' and I heard one woman say earnestly to another: 'Whatever you do, don't let him out of your sight this night!'

Monk now started out on a deliberate walk down Cheapside, where the crowd was thinner, and where the police had by now organised a pathway between the vehicles down the middle of the street; whereupon some few of the ladies came after Monk, and soon there ensued a definite movement, a large tendency flowing after him, then a march, a rolling Rhone, the mass of an army's tramp. By the time we were at Bennet's Clock, a decided tide of life was on the move, Cummings Monk the moon that moved it. I forced my way towards him.

Suddenly, coming from Lime Street, a company of lads who had some tin fifes and a drum, crossed Monk's path; and at once he pounced upon the drummer, whispered doubtless some one of his wizard words, quickly had the drum hanging round his own throat, and began to batter at it.

'Follow the music!'—backward he flung this howl; and soon in the mass of the crowd there arose a rumour of *Follow the music!* while on by St Martin's, down Holborn, the host flowed after the rattle of his ran-tan, four work-girls going ahead of him whirling in dance, hurling jests at the multitude, on each side of Monk a policeman, one of them—a plump lump—stepping in a rhythmic way with a swinging head, solemn!—as ridiculous a thing, I think, as I ever saw; and anon, far-repeated in the rear would arise the cry and rumour of '*Follow the music!*'

Monk spoke to me without ceasing in a species of shout. Here and now he was happy, in contact with humanity, warm, nourished, gushing with comradeship, nor have I ever known him so blushing with gaiety, or glib with wit, and ever his mass of femaledom, flanked by policemen, teemed far-reaching after him, drawn by his nimble drumsticks' rumbling—on down Oxford Street, to Southampton Row, and thence up into Russell Square. Here Monk leapt up the door-steps of his house near a corner, so hard-pressed from behind, that he had hardly time to fumble in his key, slip within, and slam the door. Outside there were cries, a crush, one woman fainted: and without delay the square was flooded and a-sound.

When he appeared on the balcony, wearing still his little split-hat and his drum stuck on his stomach, someone holding a lamp by him, he was recognised with a great, vague tumult and movement of the women like wind within the woods. He came to the rail, leant his fists on it, and presently the sounding square stilled down a little around him.

'Ladies!' he shouted, 'you now see where I live—my bachelor home! Let that for tonight satisfy you, since it is impossible with my own hands to distribute your rings among you in a moment. Thousands of you, ladies! Imagine the nature of my sensations at this moment! My heart cannot count you—you embarrass me—I am become the paragon of patriarchs and sultans. And henceforth my prayer shall be, 'Thy Lesbos come!' For don't you know that ancient lists of names, such as biblical lists, show that the earth in the bigness of her early vigour turned out more men than women? then as many women? and now more women? So we need but go on to behold this globe one blessed Lesbos; and may you and I then be here again. But what I have to tell you in all seriousness is that your rings are safe. I have here behind me an army of clerks directing envelopes, and every one of you may be certain of having back her own identical ring tomorrow first thing (Vast Applause), accompanied for all your trouble and travel by a little half-sovereign: I have only, then, to thank each of you most heartily for coming to meet me, to ask you to disperse like good girls, and to wish you a sincere—Good night.' He stepped backward, bowing, amid a shouting of bravos, and shower of flowers rent from many a breast.

It may be added that the Princess W—— got that same day an anonymous letter, telling her that a little tug would get off the row of stones from her wedding ring.

II
HE DEFINES 'GREATNESS OF MIND'

'Come, now, and let us reason together.' —ISAIAH.

'This indeed appears to me to be a beautiful thing, if someone is able to instruct men, like Gorgias the Leontine, and Hippias and Elian: for each of these, in the cities which he visits, has the power of persuading the young men, who give him money, and thanks besides, for his instruction.' —SOCRATES.

On a night in December when Monk dined with me, he wore a shade over his eyes, and was quiet and subdued—a mood in which I liked him best, since then instruction was sure to come for me from his strong forehead. But in dining I happened to make some remark as to Cardinal Newman, to which my friend answered: 'Well, but Newman was a savage': whereupon I could not but exclaim against the use of such a word to designate such a personage. Monk, however, it turned out, had not used the word as some loose semi-expression of a moment's sentiment, but strictly, as a term in a scientific proposition; and he replied to me: 'Since you deny that Newman was a savage, it is for you to tell me what you say that a savage is.'

As we had just then risen from dinner, I took a dictionary, and read out to him: 'Savage—a human being uncivilised: one of a brutal, unfeeling disposition.'

This caused Monk to laugh! and he said: 'But are not dictionaries made by leisured gentlemen in a state of hibernation? especially that one which you have in your hand, in which, if you look out "high," you will find "not low," and if you then with anxiety look out "low," you will find "not high." Is that inspired to define a savage as "one of a brutal disposition" when tribes assuredly savage have been known for mildness? the Caribs, for instance? "the mild-eyed, melancholy Lotus-eaters"?'

'No,' I answered; 'but there remains the other definition: "a human being uncivilised".'

'Notice the poetical position of "uncivilised"!' he laughed. . . . 'So, then, that is your definition? . . . "a savage is an uncivilised adult"? Very good. But as to the ex-Sultan of Turkey, now: was he a civilised person, or an uncivilised?'

'Uncivilised,' I answered after some thought.

'A savage, then?'

'Well, yes.'

'And as to a navvy of Whitechapel who can't read: a civilised person or an uncivilised?'

'Uncivilised.'

'A savage, then?'

'I suppose that I must say so.'

'But as to Plato of Athens,' he said: civilised or uncivilised?'

'Civilised, certainly,' I answered.

'Not a savage?'

'No.'

'Was Cato the Younger?'

'No.'

'Is Mr Bernard Shaw?'

'No.'

'Was Julius Caesar?'

'No.'

'Was Dante?'

'No.'

'Was Milton?'

'No.'

'But,' he said, 'the difference betwixt a savage and one not a savage must be considerable: what, then, is it which makes so much difference betwixt Plato and the Sultan that Plato was not a savage, but the Sultan is one?'

'This,' I answered: 'that Plato represented the utmost culture of his age—mental, moral, sociable, physical; but the Sultan has not attained the utmost culture of his age, at any rate, moral: for he encourages massacres, and is dubbed Abdul the Damned.'

'So, then,' said Monk, 'a person who has not attained the utmost culture of his age—mental, moral, sociable, physical—is an uncivilised person, or savage?'

'Yes,' I answered, 'more or less.'

'Well,' he said, 'we have come to something now! for first you defined "savage" as "an uncivilised" person, and now you define "uncivilised" person: he is a person who has not attained the utmost culture of his age in those four respects. Now, Plato did, perhaps: so I understand now why you say that Plato was not a savage, but the Sultan is one. But as to Lord Rosebery: is he one?'

'No,' I answered.

'Yet,' said Monk, 'Lord R—— has not attained the physical culture of Maude Allan, the utmost of his age: is not his lordship, therefore, a savage?'

'No,' I said: 'it appears that I must leave out the physical: civilisation, I now say, is in respect only of mental, moral and sociable culture.'

'Well!' said Monk: 'but it is not to be supposed that Lord Rosebery has attained the moral culture of a Sister Agnes Jones or a Newman, the utmost of his age, nor quite the sociable culture of an *exquis* like Oscar Wilde, the utmost of his age; and Carlyle, we know, could be something of a boor. Are not his lordship, then, and Carlyle, savages?'

'No, no,' I answered: 'I see that I must leave out the moral and the sociable, as the physical; and the mental remains: so I say that "a savage is a person who has not attained the utmost mental culture of his age".'

'But in that case,' said Monk, 'the Sultan may not be a savage, though he encourages massacres.'

'Well, but he is one,' I insisted, 'everybody calls him so: for, obviously, one must have *some* moral culture, or one is a savage.'

'But how much moral culture?' asked Monk: 'as much as Lord Rosebery? or less? or more?'

'About as much as Lord Rosebery,' I answered: 'that is to say, the average moral culture of his age.'

'Very good,' said Monk, 'I mark that much. But as to Carlyle, now: if, instead of being merely rather Presbyterian, he had eaten like Johnson, nor ever washed himself, would he not have been savage?'

'Yes,' I answered, 'for one, obviously, must have *some* sociable and physical culture, in order not to be savage.'

'But how much sociable and physical culture? As much as Carlyle? or less? or more?'

'About as much as Carlyle: that is to say, the average sociable and physical culture of his age.'

'Quite so,' he said: 'but as you have now made some changes, you had better define "savage" afresh, so that we may understand where we are.'

'Well,' I said, 'we appear to have reached to this: that "a savage is a person who has not attained the utmost mental, and the average moral, sociable and physical culture of his age".'

'But,' said Monk, 'just think: is Rosebery's "mental culture"—whatever that means—equal to Spencer's, the utmost of his age? You will not say so. Yet his lordship is not, because of that, a savage?'

'No,' I said, 'for Spencer's culture, if higher, is not immensely the higher: and a somewhat lower culture does not justify so lush an adjective as "savage".'

'Then,' said Monk, 'you should pack that into your definition: for we wish to be exact.'

'A savage, then,' I said, 'is a person who is *far* from having attained the *utmost* mental, and the *average* moral, sociable and physical culture of his age.'

'Good,' said Monk: 'I now love our definition better, and by still bungling about it we may get it on its legs in the end. But I am still somewhat against it. What, for example, does *culture* mean? I am never quite certain and clear: it is such a pliant kind of word, except when applied to plants and land. So, for my sake, could you not find some other word than "culture"?'

'What other word?' I said: ' "refinement"? "attainment"? I don't know.'

'But,' said Monk, 'what is the *note of* culture? in what respect does a cultured rose specifically differ from an uncultured? a cultured muscle, a cultured skull, from an uncultured?'

'The cultured is always the larger,' I answered.

'Or at all events,' he said, 'can we not always say that it is somehow "the more developed"?'

'We can,' I answered.

'So let us say "development" instead of "culture",' said he.

'All right,' I answered.

'Or, instead of "development," shall we not say "evolution," Shiel? since the two mean one thing?'

'Since that pleases you,' I said, 'we shall say "evolution".'

'So what now is a savage?' he demanded.

'A savage,' I answered, 'is "a person who is *far* from having attained the utmost mental, and the *average* moral, sociable and physical *evolution* of his age." '

'But of *his* age!' exclaimed Monk, 'surely that is a slip of your tongue. Was there not, then, an age when all mankind were naked savages?'

'Why, yes,' I answered.

'And was not any one of those savages, though he had attained the utmost evolution of *his* age, still a savage in *your* view?'

'Yes, of course,' I answered; 'I see that I must change the definition yet again, and give it as, "a savage is a person who is far from having attained the utmost mental, and the average moral, sociable and physical evolution of the most evolved age, i.e., of this age." '

'Well,' said Monk: 'But tell me: is it not odd that in order not to be savage a man must approach to the "utmost" mental evolution of this age, but need only approach to the "average" moral, sociable and physical evolution? Yet moral evolution, for example, is a most important matter, is it not? How, then, is this?'

'I don't know how it is,' I answered, 'but it does seem to be so: for we have already seen that Lord Rosebery is not a savage, even though his moral evolution may be far from the utmost, inasmuch as his mental evolution is not far.'

'Yes,' said Monk, 'I don't deny that it is so; I only say that it seems strange, and inquired the reason, though I can see that the reason is suggested in our definition itself by the words "this age".'

'In what way?' I asked.

'Tell me,' he said: 'is not a savage a relative? A Bushman is not a savage to a Bushman, but he is one to a Basuto? and a Basuto is one to you?'

'Yes.'

'And a cart-horse is not a savage to a carthorse, but he is one to an Ascot-horse, no doubt? and a donkey to a cart-horse, no doubt? As, then, animals ascend a definite step in development, those on the steps just below get the name of 'savage,': so, given a condition of things in which no evolution was going on, a savage would not occur, for, that there may be worse, there must be better. But with respect to the moral, sociable and physical among men, there has been no evolution during ages, meaning that ages since particular standards and averages were reached in these respects which remain much the same, and may so remain for ages more. St John, for example, was hardly less holy than Newman, nor St Catherine than Sister Dora; Alcibiades was probably quite as die-away a cock as Oscar Wilde; and an Olympiad champion as fit as Jackson—some think fitter. In holiness, then, in sociableness, and in physical fitness, a particular average and a particular ideal were attained in antiquity which have remained practically fixed, so that no modern man even aspires to be holier, politer, or fitter than the holiest, politest, or fittest of those times. Since, then, in these respects, there has been little or no evolution, there has been little savagery; for the savagery of some is relative to the evolution of others. The mass of men have settled down at a not very variable average of moral, sociable and physical evolution, and only when some rare fish tumbles well below this average do we dub him a savage, as you dubbed the Sultan. And not only is this average and this ideal fixed and oldish, it is practically universal on the earth. I assume that a Yogi, or a mahatma, is as holy as Newman; a mandarin can be quite as exquisite as Oscar Wilde; and a Japanese champion has matched Hackenschmidt. So, in these respects, there has been no breezy pioneering and large-minded Alp-climbing by any regiment of the army of man, leaving the less adventurous regiments in the rear in the morass of savagery; and the pioneers toward the ideal are so scanty, that in the eyes of the mass a kind of fantasticality even attaches to a mahatma, a Wilde, or a Hackenschmidt. But with respect to mental development, is not the case different? Are we not better than our fathers, Shiel, and the Chinese?'

'Yes,' I said, 'that is very much so. But still, Monk, I am not quite enlightened as to why it is that a man is not a savage who is far from the highest, say, moral evolution, though he has the average: for evolution is evolution: and if a mahatma is a savage who is far from the mental evolution of Lord Rosebery, then, Lord R. should be a savage compared with a mahatma, because far from the moral evolution of a mahatma.'

'But,' said Monk, 'do you say that Lord R. is a savage compared with a race-horse, because he is far from being able to run so fast?'

'No: there is no comparison.'

'But do you say that a cart-horse is a savage, compared with a race-horse because he is far from being able to run so fast?'

'Yes.'

'But do you say that a race-horse is a savage compared with a mine-horse, because he is far from being able to see so well in the dark?'

'Certainly not.'

'And do you not refuse to say this because you understand that the evolution of a horse is specially in the direction of running? not specially in the direction of seeing in the dark?'

'Yes.'

'But the evolution of a man is not specially in the direction of running? but of something else?'

'Yes.'

'In the direction of what else is it?' he asked.

'In the directions,' I replied, 'of thinking, of being holy, of being polite, and of being fit.'

'But,' said Monk, 'in the directions of being holy, of being polite, and of being fit, no modern man has evolved beyond Hebrews and Greeks, nor even beyond people grossly savage: I know, for instance, an old negress in the Indies who is as holy as Sister Dora; and as regards the growing lad, we know that he is sometimes no more holy, polite, or fit at fifteen than he was at nine. In these respects, I say, evolution nods; there has been no evolution for long. Yet man has been rapidly evolving. In what direction, then, specially, is the evolving of man?'

'In the direction of thinking,' I answered.

'Just as the evolving of horses is in the direction of running, Shiel?'

'So it certainly seems to be,' I observed.

'Man, then,' said Monk, 'is an animal formed to think always more wondrously as horses to run always more wondrously. He is, moreover, an animal formed to be holy, to be sociable, and to be fit, but not somehow specially formed for these things, but for thinking, as horses may very conveniently haul carts, and see in the dark, but are hardly somehow specially formed for these ruts, but for running. So Lord Rosebery is no savage for being far from having the holiness of a mahatma and the muscle of a Sandow, since holiness and muscle are not somehow in the special footpath of man's evolution, but thinking, and since the most evolved men are hardly the holiest, most sociable, or fittest, but the most thoughtful. In this respect, then, I think, your definition stands solid: that "a savage is a person who is far from having attained the *utmost* mental, and the *average* moral, sociable and physical evolution of this age." However, in other respects the definition does not stand so satisfactory: it is negative, for instance, giving what a savage is not, not what he is. But it should not be difficult to you to pull it into a positive definition.'

'Well,' I said, 'since "a person who is far from having attained the highest mental evolution of our age" is a person of primitive mind, I now define a savage as "a person of primitive mind, or one who is far from having attained the average moral, sociable, and physical evolution of the historic ages".'

'But *primitive mind* is so vague,' replied Monk.

'Let us say, then, an undeveloped, an unevolved mind,' I said.

'But "unevolved" is again negative,' he objected.

'What, then, shall I say, Monk?'

'But what,' he said, is an *unevolved* person? What were you and I twenty years ere we evolved into what we are?'

'By Zeus, Monk, we were children,' I answered.

'Shall we not, then, Shiel, define a savage as "a person of childish mind as compared with the most evolved minds, or one who is far from having attained the average moral, sociable, and physical evolution of the historic ages"?'

'We will,' I answered: 'though "childish" itself seems vague, if not so vague as my "primitive".'

'Yes, "childish," too, is vague,' he answered; 'but will not all its vagueness vanish the moment we recall to mind the known notes of a child's mind?'

'Let us, then, recall these notes to mind,' I said.

'We will,' he said; 'and is not the chief of them a certain *skittishness,* levity, irrelevance? due to an unconsciousness of facts? a certain kicking-up of the heels, for one's own part, at the vague universe? seen in the filly, the kid, the kitten? in the grown cat also? the grown horse in spring? the gorilla? and in the black of the Congo who cocks a battered top-hat on his head, and, naked else, rakishly promenades, so arranged, to parade his charm?'

'Yes,' I said, 'there is that skittishness in children.'

'But how as to credulity?' he next said. 'Is not this another note of a child's mind?'

'Very much so,' I answered.

'Will not a child catch at almost any statement made to it, and rest upon that as upon a prop, to prop its wee weak top? just as in learning to walk it catches hold of the first thing? Or as a fledgling flutters down upon the first shrub? But when it has evolved to the Harrow age, it is already much more sceptical? and will ask questions if any strange thing be told it?'

'That is quite true,' I said.

'Do you say, then, that scepticism is the bloom of mental evolution, as pear-trees are sure to bear pear-blooms?'

'From this of the growing child it must be recognised to be very much so,' I replied.

'But as to the other known notes of a child's mind,' said Monk, 'is not *over-belief* one of them?'

'Over-belief?' I said. 'Is not that credulity?'

'But a very special example of it,' he answered. 'Credulity is a weak-minded leaning upon the statements of others, as upon a crutch, or prop; but over-belief is a weak-minded leaning upon the adumbrations and presentations of one's own brain. When in the West Indies seven months since, I met many instances of it among the infantiles there. For example, funerals there are on foot, and after a time the funeral-train naturally becomes a little flurried, the driver of the coffin-cart shakes his reins a little, and the pace quickens; well, at such a moment one mourner will remark to another, "Ah, poor thing, ain't she (the corpse) eager to get home?" "True, true," will be the answer, "she's hurrying home, she's hurrying home." Or take this: One dark night a ship-of-war, cruising off the north coast of St Lucia, flashed its searchlight ashore, striking terror into the natives, and the workers in a certain "boiling-house" (where sugar is boiled) were bounding frantically about, very like a troop of ecstatic baboons, when a son of the "overseer" flew to howl in at the door, "*Pa*! Ma tell you come home quick, let's all die together!" To this, however, the stout old overseer answered, "Boy, go back home and tell your mother dere's plenty of time before morning. It's only the antichrist; for the Word of God say the sea has got to burn up first." Now, this is not story, but history; and think of the whole cloud-town of belief, its streets and squares laid out, springing up at the apparition of a ship's flashlight; the very succession of events on Judgment Day, now come, established in the otherwise blank consciousness, like a photo flashed over it by the fancy, and weakly accepted by it as authentic. And is not this a chief note of a child's mind?'

'It is so,' I assented.

'But how as to stubbornness?' he said: 'is not this another one of them?'

'Stubbornness?,' I said.

'Yes, for do we not know of "the strength of childhood's impressions?" and how a mind which does not much evolve with time, but continues childish, clings to its initial beliefs with a stubbornness of the crab's claw, equal to the indifference with which it received them? and so all round resembling the crab's claw? which troubles not about what it grips, but, having gripped something, hugs it grimly? You who have not visited negroes can't even conceive the really infinite scorn with which a Catholic negro regards a Methodist, and a Methodist a Catholic. It would be in vain for the Methodist to attempt to convince the Catholic of the simplest fact, or the Catholic the Methodist, for the acceptance of first impressions has been so perfect that anyone who, in any respect, has received a different impression seems merely weak-headed to him. This stubbornness, then, you will say, is a chief note of a child's mind.'

'This, too,' I assented.

'So, then,' said Monk, 'our definition is no longer vague? but we can say with conviction that "a savage is a person of comparatively skittish, credulous, over-believing, stubborn mind—in a word, of childish mind—or one who is far from having attained the average moral, sociable, and physical evolution of the historic ages"?'

'We can say this with conviction,' I said.

'Then,' he said, 'let us test by the definition as it now stands the judgments which you have pronounced upon particular persons. The Sultan of Turkey, for instance: is he still a savage?'

'Yes,' I said, 'for is he not far below the average moral evolution of the historic ages, since he encourages massacres?'

'Well, let that be so,' he said. 'But as to Julius Caesar; is he still not a savage?'

'Caesar was a great mind,' I said. 'A great mind cannot be a savage mind.'

'I fully agree with you in that,' answered Monk, 'for a great mind is certainly a strong mind; and we have seen that a savage mind is a childish, i.e., a weak mind, trying to think like the wee weak knees of children trying to toddle. But are you sure, my friend, that Julius Caesar was a great mind?'

'Are not you?' I said. 'Is not Caesar recognised as the greatest mind of antiquity—a general, an architect, a statesman, and other things?'

'He may have been so,' answered Monk, 'but mark that it is not antiquity that is now calling him "a great mind," but *you*; and this, I confess, seems to me undignified of you. Is it not, then, a fact that "au royaume des aveugles les borgnes sont rois"? I, for my, part, understand that there is scarce at this moment an English schoolboy who is not a greater general, a greater architect, a greater statesman, a greater mind than Caesar. Does it seem to you that I should undertake a long and a difficult thing, if I undertook to prove this to you?

'By Zeus, Monk, it does seem so to me,' I said.

'Yet I think not,' said Monk. 'Let us, then, see. But to begin, let us get to an agreement as to what a great mind is. What *is* it?'

'One that is least like a savage's or child's mind,' I said.

'Precisely so,' he said; 'least like the child's, the savage's, the gibbon's, the bee's, the amoeba's mind. The mind, then, that is more *mindly*, so to say, than other minds, in which the quality of *mindliness* is more evolved? But now, what is the special trait of Mind, from the mind of plants to the mind of man?'

'Consciousness,' I said.

'And consciousness is a perception of facts?' he asked.

'Yes,' I said.

'And since greatness of mind is a great evolution of the quality of mindliness, and the trait of mindliness in consciousness, and consciousness is a perception of facts, does greatness of mind, then, consist in a great faculty of perceiving facts?'

'It does,' I agreed.

'And in nothing else?'

'No, there is nothing else,' I said, 'inasmuch as all the modes of Mind are modes of consciousness.'

'Let us, then, be convinced of this thing,' said Monk, 'that greatness of mind consists in a great faculty of perceiving facts, and in nothing else; so that, if Napoleon was a great general, his greatness consisted in this—that he, facing the opposing general, more perceived the facts than the other? And if men are great enough to fly in our time, their greatness consists in this, that they perceive more facts than Icarus? And when they grow great to soar to Uranus, and to goad gold into uranium, their greatness will consist in a perception of facts, in a growth of consciousness? And, meantime, each of the boons that rebukes the hope of human or brute, each punishment which we stumble on, or bread of rueing which we bedrench and chew, is due to a defect of perception, a lack of consciousness of facts? Let us be convinced of this. But now, tell me: the things that present themselves to Mind as facts, are they not of two kinds? True and untrue?'

'That is so,' I said.

'So that greatness of mind, which consists in perceiving facts, consists in perceiving the untruth of the untrue? and the truth of the true? Is this so?'

'That must be so,' I agreed.

'So that greatness of mind consists in these two: (1) Scepticism, and (2) Proneness to truth—on the understanding that, though we call them two, yet they are but two phases, or faces, of the same one quality of Mind, namely, the faculty of perceiving facts?—of perceiving the untruth of the untrue, which we call scepticism? and of perceiving the truth of the true, which we call proneness? Is that so? And since the negative, scepticism, and the positive, proneness, are but two phases, or faces, of the same golden louis, must not the scepticism of any mind be an *exact* measure, or mirror, of its proneness to truth, as its proneness to truth must be an *exact* measure, or mirror, of its scepticism? as we see in savages and children, who have *exactly* so little proneness as they have little scepticism? And in philosophers, who have *exactly* so much proneness as they have much scepticism? Is all this sure, Shiel?'

'All this certainly seems to be so,' I conceded.

'But as to Caesar,' said Monk. 'My business is to prove to you that there is scarce today a schoolboy in England who is not more sceptical, i.e., who has not a greater proneness to truth, and faculty of perceiving facts, i.e., who is not a greater mind, than Caesar. But have you, my friend, a 'Gallic War' at hand that you could lend me?'

'I have,' I answered, and ran and got it.

'I only hope that I shall be able quickly to find one of the passages which I have in my mind,' muttered Monk, rushing through the pages, but he quickly found something, and begged me to read it aloud, since his eyes that night were sick.

In the passage—which I translate—Caesar is describing (from hearsay) certain German things, and he says: 'In it (the Hercynian Forest) are many species of beasts which are not seen in other places, of which the most memorable are as follows:

' "There is a bull that has a stag's figure, from the middle of whose forehead, between the ears, one horn sticks up, taller and straighter than any horns known to us; and from its top, like palms, branches arch out far. The nature of the male and female is the same, the same shape and size of horn.

' "There are also some beasts called elks. These resemble he-goats in figure and colouring, and they have legs without any joints in them, so do not lie down to rest, nor, if by any chance they fall down, can they get up again. Tree-trunks serve as beds for these creatures; on tree-trunks they prop themselves, and so, only a little leaning, take their rest. And when huntsmen discover their haunts from their footprints, they cut through the trees thereabouts so much as to leave a semblance of trees still standing; then when the elks come and lean on the trees as usual, the elks' weights break the weakened trees, the elks tumble with the trees. (And, as they cannot get up again, the hunters come and take them so.)" '

'But, my friend,' said Monk, when I had read it, 'is this thing true, that there were such bulls and elks in the Hercynian Forest?'

'No,' I said.

He leant forward sharply, asking, '*How do you know?*'

'I do not trouble to ask myself how I know,' I answered, 'I only know that I know.'

'But as to a Lancing lad,' he said, 'one who has no special knowledge as to elks; if one were to tell him this thing as to elks, is it not certain what he would say? Would he not murmur, "draw it mild"?'

'Μαλιστα γε,' I replied. 'The boy would certainly employ words of such a kind.'

'And is not this a fact like Cotopaxi,' said Monk, 'that statements about the cosmos that to a Lancing lad seem comic Caesar solemnly swallowed, and did not wink? Shall we not say that God has been jogging men? and that there appears here such a growth in scepticism, in general intelligence, or proneness to truth, i.e., in greatness of mind—such a growth—for we laugh at Caesar in the same tone in which we laugh at infants and monkeys, without troubling to ask ourselves how we know the untruth of his statements—so great a growth, that Caesar and the people of his time must be defined as lower types of mind and life, we being somewhat to them as they to Bushmen, one stage above apes? and that it is beneath the dignity of modern men of your kind any longer to speak of suchlike types of life as 'great,' even though we still permit ourselves to ape their apish pages of legislation and foolish institutions? Of course, with a machine-gun under cover, one Rugby fag would easily have smashed ten thousand tenth legions, generalled by ten thousand Caesars; with one gunboat grumbling a Rugby brogue would have rolled up many Roman empires; and by the Roman world would certainly have been worshipped as that which he is, Mercury come with thunders from the pinnacles of Olympus. But that is not what I wished to show, but this, that, without the gun or the gunboat—though it is not fair, mind, to take the boat from the boy, since the boat is proper to him; he invented it, he or his uncle, or cousin; and Caesar would eagerly have invented it, if great enough; though, if he had attempted it, God would have mocked him, would not have cashed his cheque, since he would have been seeking to perceive truths of the universe proper to a higher type of life than his. Still, take the boat from the boy: then, I say that our boy, by his scepticism and proneness to truth, is of so far higher a type of mind and life than Caesar, that he would not have failed to prove himself in every respect as superhuman compared with Caesar. Or do you need me to adduce more proof of this?'

The Pale Ape and Other Pulses

'No,' I said, 'for one proof of a thing, if it be a sure proof, is enough; and no more is needed.'

'Very good,' he said, 'but if the mind of Caesar was of this kind as compared with Rugby lads, how was it as compared with Spencer's or Kelvin's?'

'It was of a very much lower evolution,' I said.

'And so, by definition, a savage?'

'Yes,' I said.

'But as to Mr Bernard Shaw,' he said: 'is he a savage?'

'Why, no,' I answered.

'But do you know whether that is true what has been told me, that this Mr Shaw has published the criticism that he is the best mind of our time?'

'I do not know if it is true,' I replied, 'but I, too, have been told by a friend that he has published this criticism.'

'And if it is true that he has done so, is it not a savage criticism?' asked Monk.

'I think it a fatuous criticism,' I answered; 'but I confess I do not see why you call it savage.'

'Let us consider it,' said Monk. 'Since the trait of mind is consciousness, or the perception of facts, then the signal of a *great* mind will be this, will it not, that it will perceive new facts—at any rate, some one fact that other minds have not contrived to perceive? Will not this be the signal of a great mind?'

'It cannot but be so,' I assented.

'But as to Mr Shaw: has he, then, perceived something new of the universe that you know of, that was not of the surface and froth of things?'

'No,' I said.

'Has Mr H.G. Wells?'

'Is it not he who has "discovered the future"?' I said.

'A new discovery?'

'No,' I said, 'since it lay subconscious in all men and conscious in some; but still something of a discovery—with an assault, a consciousness, a largeness of thought, which were novel. Let us stretch a little, and give credit to fiction-writers, for if other men have a thought, that is not surprising; but if a fiction-writer has a thought, it is surprising; since fiction-writers have been such a tiny tribe.'

'That is very much so,' said Monk. 'But do you, then, a critic of intellects, as of machines which perceive facts, place Mr Wells on a level with, or above, or below Mr Shaw?'

'Above,' I said.

'A little above? or well above?'

'Well above.'

'But are you sure, my friend, of this?'

'There is very little possibility of error,' I said, 'in the judgments of critics on suchlike things.'

'Let it be so, then,' he said. 'But as to Signor Marconi: tell me: has he perceived something new of the universe?'

'Yes,' I said, 'or wondrously nigh to new, and more things than one, be sure:'

'And do you as a critic of intellects place Mr Wells on a level with him, or above, or below?'

'Below,' I said.

'A little below? or well below?'

'Well below.'

'To me, too,' he said, 'what you say seems to be very much so: for, oh, my friend—we know his face—what a very temple and sacred place is that man's cranium wherein his Creator has elected to make his dwelling-place. How grandly it ramps and carries its ramparts, looking nearly as noble as it is—the brow of Caesar crowded with a thousand Caesar's crowns. Believe, Shiel, nearly everything that it thinks is as true and sacred as nearly everything that the skulls of other men think is untrue and profane. But since some are well above Mr Shaw, and those some well below other some, how wild appears this criticism of Mr Shaw that he is above all.'

' "Wild," if you like,' I said, 'but you said "savage".'

'But are not the criticisms of savages and children wild?' he asked, 'and this criticism in particular, is it not rich in a certain skittishness, due to an unconsciousness of facts? in a certain kicking up of the heels, for one's own part, at the vague universe? rich, too, in its childish or savage over-belief?'

'I see the skittishness,' I said, 'but not quite the over-belief.'

'Is it not over-believing,' said Monk—'that is, *super*-stitious, *aber*-glaubig—because, like the over-beliefs of savages, it is a fantasy built upon fact? built upon a consciousness in Mr Shaw of some actual intellectual energy? just as the over-belief of negroes that the corpse is hurrying home is built upon an actual quickening of the pace of the funeral? in each case a large and fantastic conclusion being elaborated on a puny basis *of* fact? And is not this savage?'

'True,' I said, 'Nevertheless, let us look at it with some sweetness and light—'

'Ah!' he cried: 'but think, Shiel, of sticking the sweetness before the light, the cheap before the topaz of Ethiopia! And they are not the very best of friends! for light has a rather unsweet way of giving darkness warning to quit.'

'Then,' said I, 'I will say with some humour. Mr Shaw is a *farceur*! and his statements do not necessarily represent his beliefs. Even when he is serious beneath his farce, all the same, unknown to him, there is a lower and lowest stratum of farce beneath his seriousness: and this is skittish, but not, so to say, if I am a critic, skittishness of *intellect*. As to "credulity," he is truly sceptical; and if he has perceived no new fact, he has perceived many facts previously perceived by others; and that with much clearness and consciousness: Besides, one lie does not make a liar, nor one savage statement a savage—unless, indeed, it be such a statement as Caesar made as to elks, proving a furiously unsceptical stage of mental evolution.'

'Let it, then, be as you say,' answered Monk. 'Besides, I am not blind to the fact that Mr Shaw is partly to be pardoned in this, because of the now chronic rawness of the estimate that the feeble folk of art-writers, and artists in general, have formed of themselves, an estimate in which they cannot help being propped by the babbling and rawness of the populace. Curious fatuity! But how well would it be for the world if it could recognise its great men, and would stop erecting monuments to its petty men, who tickle it with pleasant little pictures and plays, tales and ditties. Baron Tennyson lies smiling with himself in Westminster Abbey, but try to find in 'In Memoriam,' which moans to be thoughtful, a thought that was not some other man's thought; so that there is today many a mechanic gaining four pounds a week in motor-works and elsewhere of greater mind than the Baron, but will not be buried in the Abbey, nor, I think, will Marconi, causing all the gods and even geese to mock at our Simple-Simon simplicity. For that is rather true of art-writers, so far, what Socrates said: 'Taking up, therefore, some of their poems that appeared the most elaborately written, I asked what was their meaning, that I might learn something of them; and I am ashamed, indeed, O Athenians, to tell you the truth; for I discovered in a short time concerning the poets that they did not effect by wisdom that which they did, but by a certain enthusiastic energy, like prophets, and those that utter oracles; and at the same time I perceived that they considered themselves, on account of their poetry, to be the wisest of men in other things, in which they were not so.' So Socrates—and you yourself, I perceive, Shiel, will occasionally pen pleasant tales possessing no particular pressure of philosophy that I can see, or reason to be written, save their pleasantness, and this with wise titles and a certain bravura and burden, as though, forsooth, you were parturient with news of the universe: which is well for King's-jesters and artistes, but a little beneath the dignity, I conceive, of gifted intellects. Thus much, at any rate, as to Mr Shaw. But as to Dante—was he a savage?'

'I have such a fondness,' I began to say, 'for that *di parlar si largo fiume*—'

'I also,' said Monk; 'but my question was not as to the amiability of Dante, but as to whether Dante was a savage, i.e., whether he had far less scepticism and far less proneness to truth, than high minds. Did not Dante believe, and crib, everything that anybody ever said?'

'Why, no, he once differed from Aristotle,' I answered.

'Ah! I did not know that. But you know, do you, that the whole scheme of the Inferno is hawed on a misunderstanding by Cicero of something that Aristotle said? that, in fact, a thing had only to get itself written in a book, and Dante took it for "learning," as every child does, and accepted it as certain—as when someone writes that lightning is a swift wind that gets ignited by friction, Dante gives that as his discovery, never asking himself whence the wind comes, or how it gets ignited, or why, being ignited, it does not fire everything? but, since the brain then had not the strength, the practice, the nimbleness, to think of several explanations, and select the best, catching, as all savages do, at the first explanation of a thing, triumphing in any explanation, and resting on that as on a prop, to prop his wee weak top, as children in learning to walk catch at the first thing? Is this a truth as to every page that Dante wrote? For I know that you know Dante in rather an expert way.'

'Yes,' I said, 'all this is true as to Dante.'

'Why, then,' he asked, 'did you say at first that Dante was not a savage?'

'Because,' I answered, 'I had not then clearly before my mind what a savage is; and because Dante was, after all, such a great poet.'

'But not a great mind?'

'Well, no.'

'So, then, you can have a great poet who is not a great mind? With what, then, does he write his poetry, if not with his mind? You can have a great wrestler, a great singer. But do not these do their feats with something else than their mind? Is this the case with a poet?'

'No,' I said.

'Do you say, then, that Dante was not a great poet, since he was of weak mind?'

'Yes, I say so now,' I said; and I added, 'I should not have used the word "great," but should have said what I meant—a pleasant, a delicious, poet—pure water from the muses' well, I think.'

'There I agree with you,' Monk said, 'though he was not *often* a delicious poet, either; for a poet who begins his verses with "Oh, predestination!" is often apt to pen the opposite of poetry. Certainly, Beatrice was the dullest young woman that ever flew from star to star. With admirable artifice one is led to expect her all through the Inferno and Purgatorio, but when the girl does turn up, how great is her bathos! "I will now treat this subject," she says—*tratterò*—a stock word of the scholastics—and when she starts to treat, ah! who shall stop her? It is not merely that her treatings are empty of verity, but that they are empty of relevance, babblings whose fantasticalities lack any bearing, the most baby-like, the most brainless, on actualities; as when she explains to Dante in a prolonged "treating" that the spots on the moon are not due to "rare and dense," as people "down below" believed, but to an unequal diffusion of the Divine Virtù; for, since the moon was to Dante only a luminous mist, through which bodies could pass, the thought was far from cropping up in such a top as his that her spots might be owing to broken surfaces, though 1,700 years before it had occurred to Socrates that the moon might be a mass of earth: and I think that among the most comic things I see in the cosmos is the bringing out of new editions of such old authors "*With Notes*" and solemn comments on their pratings by modern ratepayers, the Rev. Philip Wicksteed, and other solemn scholars and unjesting gentlemen. As to his pretty trick of expression, I think with you that there are the very prettiest ripples of poetry when he stops being philosophic; but it must be said that the task that he set himself in harmony was far too hard for him, for the three rhymes in each triplet are not simple rhymes like cook, took, look, but double rhymes like summer, mummer, hummer—far too hard; so that he is hardly ever saying what he is impelled to say, but what he is compelled to say. And he is nearly always being philosophic—such philosophy! as though something could come out of nothing.'

'What precisely do you mean by this?' I asked—' "something coming out of nothing"?'

'But, my friend,' said Monk, 'can one think well under laughing-gas? or chloroform? To think at all one must be conscious?'

'Yes,' I said.

'And consciousness is a knowledge of facts?'

'Quite so,' I said.

'So, without a knowledge of facts, thought is impossible?'

'I see that,' I said.

'Do you say, then, that thought was a new thing on earth in the nineteenth century, since knowledge was a new thing? And that it was quite in vain for the ancients to sit down and think hard about things, as savages and apes do, without having any knowledge of anything?'

'Yes, if knowledge, as you say, was a new thing in the nineteenth century.'

'Practically, was it not?' said Monk. 'It is impossible to know anything, except by experiment! for if you go guessing you are perfectly certain to guess all over the place; and experiment, roughly speaking, was a nineteenth century thing? As to such a man as Dante, it may be said that he knew nothing. He knew that the sky looks blue, and he knew some Euclid, and the names of the constellations. The rest of his "learning" consisted in having at his finger-ends a string of Greek myths, which was not knowledge—not knowledge of things, BE-ing, I AM—and never could a little help him to think. We two here, do we not owe the whole tone of our souls to the recent discovery that the universe is no nook? But Dante's universe, the cosy human home! of which a human female was the queen. For although his sun was but a lamp and planet of the earth, all his stars shone by that tiny sun's shine, though, ages before, Philolaus and some Pythagorians had had the notion that our globe might be rolling round a sun which was the centre of everything. Nor was this toy-universe filled by his God! "O our Father, who stayest in Heaven", he says—"in Heaven, not because Thou art circumscribed, but because of the greater love which Thou hast for the first-created beings up there." And notice that facility—so deliciously characteristic of children—with which his intellect accepts both of two contradictory concepts. He has heard it said that "God is not circumscribed"; and he has heard it said that God is circumscribed by the greater love which He has for the first-created beings up there, compelling Him to live up there. He believes both—*easily*, and does not one bit care whether in the same phrase he says that God is not circumscribed, and that God is circumscribed. And I say, let modern men continue to revel in the pretty tricks of expression of suchlike types of life, but let no modern man—if he *is* genuinely modern—if he has diligently made himself worthy to be called by that name whereby the lords of the earth are called—let him not in reading these people read them as equals, nor any longer deign to give to them the name of "great," since that is beneath his dignity, and, indeed, ungodly. Enough, however, as to Dante. But as to Milton: Is Milton still not a savage?'

'We will now say of Milton that he was a savage,' I said.

'Yes, but have you reflected how essentially a savage, my friend?' asked Monk. 'Do you recall to yourself that Milton lived definitely in the dawn of the day of Revelation? Thirty years or so (my dates may be shaky) before his birth Copernicus had closed his eyes, holding that Holy Book that he had indited in his hand. Little Milton cared. By the date of his birth, Galileo had discovered the isochronism of the pendulum, had proved that all bodies fall with an equal velocity, had invented the water-thermometer, and with his new optic tube had noted the moons of Jupiter, the ansated form of Saturn, the spots on the sun, the phases of Venus. I think that before Milton was a lad, Kepler must have published his "Three Laws"; and when Milton, a young man, called upon Galileo, an old man, in Italy, Galileo had given out his "Dialoghi delle nuove Scienze." And let Milton's proneness to truth be estimated by the fact that in this new activity of intellect he not only had no part, but it did not a little dig the nigger to any tingling. The cosmography in "Paradise Lost" is Ptolemaic! because it was Ptolemaic in the "Divine Comedy"—as if Milton had never *heard* of Copernicus. One of the things which I can never understand is how all savages did not always *see* that our globe goes about the sun, an inability I can no more sympathise with than they grasp Grotthüs's doctrine of travelling hydrogen in electrolysis, or the flashes of light on which we fly: they are to be forgiven for this, as I am to be forgiven for not seeing myriads of things on the face of nature that men will yet see: but how great must be the negro grain of a being, who, when the thing which he cannot see for himself has been seen for him by seers, and revealed to him, receives God's holy truth with indifference or unbelief, with a top preoccupied with Greek and negro crotchets and the resurrection of the dead, clinging to night, and for some motive or other liking it more than light!'

'I see that what you say of Milton is true,' I said, 'though he is my favourite poet.'

'Mine are Job and Lucretius,' said Monk, 'and I think that Milton comes next for me. . . . I love his pretty trick of expression, and his *os magna sonans,* and I love children and negroes. But I don't love unconsciousness in grown-up Circassians. And is it not a thing very ridiculous that unsceptical critics should still in our day be teaching the people in their reading to say of suchlike types of life, not "ah, how agreeable," but "ah, how great"? But so it will continue to be, until the government begins to give to the citizen an education intimate with things, BE-ing, I AM, and not with myths. Myths and Milton were intimates! his ambition being to beat the poor Dante (who could not read Greek), in having at his finger-ends a string of Greek and Biblical things, his knowledge of which he was more eager to exhibit than to give ear to the things of God, that His elect were then investigating: so that about the time when Huygens was adapting the pendulum to the clock, when Torricelli was weighing the air, when Mariotte was discovering the law of pressure, and Römer the velocity of light, and von Guericke was making an air-pump,[1] we find the schoolman-mind of Milton proving his proneness to truth by pouring forth polemics on church-government and the resurrection of the body; yes, and just when he was whirling out a world of such words as "Hail, holy light, offspring of heaven first-born," Newton was writing this: "When I understood this I left off my aforesaid Glassworks: for I saw that telescopes were limited, not so much for want of glass, as because that *Light itself is a heterogeneous mixture o f differently refrangible rays.*" Think of the interval betwixt these intellects, in quiddity and quantity, the chasm! Think of "offspring of heaven first-born"! He saw candles: and he saw light: and he saw candles that did not give out any light, but he never saw light that was not given out by candles, or by some kind of matter: should not the littlest infant's intellect instantly pitch to the decision that light must be the child of some passion of matter? that matter must antedate light? that candlelight cannot exist without a candle? or sunlight without a sun? But he had heard that somebody had asserted that light was "first-born ('let there be light!')," and his wee weak top, that caught at all things as a prop, was so blocked up and pre-occupied with showing off his knowledge of a hotch-potch of such borrowed crotchets, as the black of Congoland cocks a battered top-hat on his head, and, naked else, rakishly promenades so arranged to parade his charm, that such a thing as thinking was as distant as Wittiput from his sinciput. Shall we say, then, that Milton was a savage, not as compared with high minds, but as compared with Newton?'

'We shall say so,' I said. 'But was not Newton, then, one of the high minds? Or are we to say that Newton, too, was something of a savage?'

'But, my friend, is that not certainly so?' asked Monk. 'Supposing that Copernicus, and Kepler, Galileo and Newton had not made their investigations, and supposing that, nevertheless, the mind of man had gone on evolving as it did—though that's

---

[1] And Papin a steam-boat!

impossible—then, is it not certain that at the birth of the nineteenth century a million minds in Europe and America would instantly have leapt to the discoveries of those splendid fellows? They are not, to tell the truth, very abstruse. And since the discoveries that appeared to them enormous appears to us small and obvious, shall we not say that they were rather savages? Let us say this, then, with respect to Newton as compared with Kelvin and Edison, though we say it with our heads bent, as to no other savage.'

'Let it be so, then,' said I: 'but as to poets, and that beauty of theirs which you admit, but despise, think how great in usefulness, Monk!'

'That *I* despise?' replied Monk: 'but, my friend, I do nothing of this kind, since I well descry the truth that that beauty of poets is more useful than wireless; nay, that it is the fruit of a true perception in poets: for, in truth, perception, if empty of emotion, of the mood of music, the flush of love, and stress of Eros, is perception pale and lame, like electricity stricken sick if empty of potential. As a matter of fact, Hertzian waves are wonderful and Divine: and to whatever extent Marconi's perception of them is empty of a Divine piety and emotion of Wonder, empty of that baby amaze of Job and cat's abstraction staring at the staring moon in a universe new-made that day, to that extent must his perception of Hertzian waves be inert and imperfect. In this respect, then, poets, painters, tale-tellers have been true perceivers, for they have perceived (*what* they have perceived—the moon moving, human moods and dooms, etc.) in an emotional or impassioned manner; and Socrates was wrong in assuming that their "enthusiasm" is not "wisdom" for it is the quiddity of wisdom, is true, and has proved most useful in seducing mankind to view the universe in this manner. So that a critic would not, in strict truth, degrade words in asserting that one poet or painter has been "*greater*" than another, since these have been true perceivers, and even new feelers; but will he not degrade words in asserting that some one of them has been "*great*" because beautiful and useful, although some of the most beautiful and useful, and newest feelers, have been known as people of feeble or sick intellects, idiots nearly, as Turner, Tasso, Scott, and a multitude more? For, at that rate, if greatness were in beauty and usefulness, the very greatest of men would be perfumers, dyers, miners: but as Plutarch observes, "we are pleased with purples and perfumes, but look upon dyers and perfumers as mean mechanics." Not therefore in beauty or usefulness is the grain of greatness, but in the depth of perception—the scepticism and proneness to truth—represented in anything. Or has this not already been proved by us?'

'Yes,' I said, 'that has been proved.'

'But as to Plato of Athens,' he said, 'is he still not a savage?'

'Truth to tell,' I said, 'I still find it difficult to think of Plato as a savage; so much so that if the definition makes him a savage, I shall be inclined to suspect the definition of error somewhere.'

'But shall we not be reasonable?' asked Monk: 'is not the definition the outcome of reasoning?'

'Yes, certainly,' I said.

'But your notion that Plato was not a savage, is it not the outcome of something else than reasoning? Has a habitual assumption, and a college prejudice, nothing to do with it?'

'That, too, is no doubt true.'

'And though reasoning is not a good guide to truth, will you not say that it is the least bad that we have when based on knowledge? and less bad than habitual assumption or prejudice?'

'I will say so, Monk,'

'So, then,' he said, 'if the definition clashes with your notion that Plato was not a savage, will you properly begin to think the definition wrong, which is the outcome of reasoning, or will you properly begin to think your notion wrong that Plato was not a savage, which is the outcome of habitual assumption? or will you incline to slight your less bad guide to follow your worse?'

'No,' I meekly said, 'I will rather choose to cling to my least bad guide than to my worst. But was Plato, then, a savage by the definition?'

'But had not Plato a skittish, credulous, over-believing mind in comparison with high minds?'

'Tell me of it!' I said.

'But was Plato not a member of a society that condemned Socrates to die because Socrates had taught the doctrine that the sun is not a god, but a stone? Is this Congoland? Or how say you? And if you reflect how very far that handful of savages are said to have surpassed us in the arts, as the Japanese also are thought to do, you will the deeper agree with the truth of my statement that greatness of mind is in no relation with the producing of pretty things, but with perception of truth, and that savages may be, and are, charming artists. Consider also how fantastic to farce, and far from the reality, are the mirages which the average don, or such fantastic doctors as Ruskin, have fashioned in their skulls of that handful of savages. Certainly, very worthy representatives of that handful of savages were Euclid and Aristotle—and Plato, too, in his way: but Newton in his youth refused to bother to con Euclid, whose truths were too obvious to him; and, of course, a modern schoolboy every night at prep spryly romps through five "riders" five times abstruser than Euclid ever brooded on—Euclid, or Archimedes, or Hiero, or Ctesebius—and darted from their baths to scream through the streets: "*eureka*!" As to Plato and his thinkings, could something come out of nothing? Can Mr Lloyd George think without statistics? without experts, and actuaries, and specialists, and a knowledge of Economy? And, if Plato chloroformed was little more unconscious than Plato unchloroformed, could Plato unchloroformed think, though he might prettily play at thinking? Did Plato believe that all knowledge is but a remembering—in which case the ancients had bad memories—and a dozen other things of this sort? did he not make an attempt to prove by dialectics the immortality of the soul of mammals, himself believing in it?'

'He did.'

'But what were the grounds of this undoubting belief of Plato's and Cato's? Were they the kind of grounds whereon high minds found their undoubting beliefs? or were they the kind of grounds whereon negro tribes weak-mindedly prop their undoubting belief in this same thesis, namely, the adumbrations and mirages of their brains, as when at a foot-funeral the pace smartens and the corpse is thought to be hurrying home? On the latter you will say? You can't imagine Signor Marconi, or even Sir Oliver Lodge, writing a book to prove by dialectics that the soul of animals is immortal?'

'No.'

'And is not this shyness of high minds about laying down the law as to the unknown the fruit of a growth of responsibility and exactitude, as when a grown-up lad casts aside his Wild-west romances? and enters seriously into business?'

'There is undoubtedly,' I said, 'that growth of responsibility and exactitude among us.'

'But in this attempt to settle once for all the immortality of the soul by logic-chopping, does there not attach to Plato and Descartes a skittishness and unconsciousness, as of a filly frisking in spring, or as of the builders of Babel saying, "come let us build to the moon, which is sometimes quite near above the tree-tops"?'

'I think I catch what you wish to point out,' I answered.

'But,' said Monk, 'if Plato was thus superstitious and skittish as compared with us, was he not a savage, what though he attained the highest moral, sociable and physical evolution of the historic ages?'

'This, too, I must admit,' I answered.

'But if Plato, the charming, and Cato, the hard-headed, and Caesar *con gli occhi grifagin,* had childish minds, shall we not say that *all* the minds of former ages were likewise savage? and that only modern minds are not savage?'

'It does seem so,' I said.

'But as to a navvy of Whitechapel who cannot read: do you still say that he is a savage?'

'Yes,' I answered, 'I still say so.'

'But suppose, Shiel,' said Monk, 'that the man leads a moderately moral life, that he sometimes washes himself and attends to his nails, that he says "tank you kindly" when anything is done for him: is such a one *far* from the average of the historic ages in the moral, sociable and physical respects?'

'No,' I said, 'but there remains the mental; he cannot read: he is far from the highest mental evolution of our age; his mind will have the notes of a child's.'

'But are you sure that this is so?' asked Monk. 'Let us look into it. We consented just now that Scepticism is the bloom of mental evolution; but of what is mental evolution itself the bloom?'

'How do you mean?' I asked.

'Tell me this,' he said: 'in what does mental evolution manifest itself?'

'In a new and higher way of thinking,' I answered.

'Just so. But did we not see that one does not think well under chloroform? That in order to think at all one must be conscious? that the more conscious one is, the better one thinks? and that consciousness is a knowledge of facts? so that the more we know of facts, the better we think, i.e., the higher our mental evolution? Did we not consent to this?'

'Yes,' I said.

'So is not mental evolution the bloom of an enlarged consciousness, the bloom of knowledge?'

'That is clearly so.'

'And "knowledge" and "science" are words of the same meaning? the one being Saxon and the other Latin?'

'Yes.'

'So mental evolution is the bloom of science? its manifestation being thinking in a certain scientific way?'

'That must be so,' I said.

'And the mental evolution of the nineteenth century, its quite new and higher way of thinking, was it not the bloom of a great growth of knowledge, or science, or consciousness?

'Undoubtedly.'

'But, come now,' he said: 'did not Lord Kelvin know more than Lord Rosebery?'

'So I suppose,' I answered.

'Yet is not Lord K.'s and Lord R.'s modern way of thinking, i.e., their mental evolution, about the same, even though mental evolution is the bloom of science, and Lord K. has the more science?'

'That is so,' I answered.

'How, then, do you account for this?' he asked.

'It can only be,' I answered, 'that all knowledge, or science, has not an equal virtue in evolving the mind and heightening its way of thinking, but that those particular facts of science which Lord K. and Lord R. have learned in common have some special virtue in this respect.'

'But, then,' he said, 'those facts can't be many, since most of the facts known by Lord K. are of a very different sort from those known by Lord R.?'

'No,' I said, 'I believe that they are even few.'

'But, surely, since they are few, and since their effect upon the mind is so mighty, must it not be that they make up in splendour and large-mindedness for what they lack in number?'

'It must be so,' I agreed.

'But, in that case, since they are few and large, you and I, as modern people, know and can repeat them off-hand: are they not these: that the nearest sun to our sun is a good many millions of millions of leagues distant? that our globe, though far, far vaster than all mortal thought—as the Isle of Wight is—is but a spattering of matter in comparison with our sun, which, nevertheless, is among the littlest of many millions of suns? that all things are changing? and changing in their sum for the better? that man is a cousin to monkeys and dogs? that living things appeared on our globe millions of eras ago? and, growing ever more knowing and august, will, without doubt, continue on it for millions of aeons to come? and some others of this vast-minded simple sort?'

'Yes,' I said, 'it can only be the consciousness of such truths as these that causes the new way of thinking of both Lord Rosebery and Lord Kelvin.'

'But, come,' said Monk: 'may not our navvy have come to know these facts in a hundred ways, even though he cannot read? May he not, besides, have pondered them in his head on his bed at night, and accepted them into his constant consciousness? And, having known the truth, shall not the truth make him free? so educating and evolving him, that he thenceforth thinks of the cosmos in a well-grown, scientific, sceptical way, and is a good deal less weak to lean upon any queer thing that he hears or fancies of the universe than Basutos are, or than Dante was? And since the further facts learned by Lord Kelvin are so like nothing in comparison with those large-minded ones, that Lord Rosebery has still somewhat the same mental evolution as Lord K., are not the further facts learned by Lord R. so like nothing, that the navvy may still have somewhat the same mental evolution as Lord R.? But he must be far from having this, in order to be a savage. Do you still say, then, that such a navvy is a savage?'

'No,' I answered, 'for I see now that he is by no means a savage.'

'But as to Cardinal Newman,' said Monk: 'do you still say that he was not a savage?'

'But was not Newman, then, a modern man?' I said: 'did he not know all those large-minded facts by the knowledge of which Lord K., Lord R., and our navvy are not savages?'

'But we did not say that by the knowledge of them they are not savages,' said Monk, 'but we said that by the knowledge of them their minds have evolved, and by the evolution of their minds they are not savages. Is that not so?'

'True,' I answered.

'Is it not a matter of common comment,' said Monk, 'that knowledge does not invariably evolve the brain, as in the case of the average graduate, and grallæ crammed for exams? In order that knowledge may effect this, must it not somehow digest itself into consciousness, since knowledge and consciousness are not exactly one thing, but consciousness is knowledge in action? Must not one, then, picture the objects of knowledge to oneself, feeding upon them in the heart, and becoming instantly conscious of them, in order that they may make us better men? And if these large-minded facts, which, once taken into the heart, infallibly save a man from kiddishness, still left the Cardinal skittish, credulous, over-believing, and stubborn, what shall be said of him? Shall we not say that through some kiddish stubbornness, or other reason, having curs, he did not hear? but skittishly kicked up his heels at the truth? and, knowing the truth, retained the unconsciousness of a savage?'

'Yes,' I consented, 'we shall say this of him, if only you are able to show that he did remain skittish, credulous, over-believing, and stubborn, in despite of light and knowledge.'

'But how shall I be able to show this, Shiel,' said Monk, 'except by appealing to your general sense of Newman's intellect? Unless, indeed, you have something written by him at hand among your books?'

'I have all his writings,' I replied, 'for I have a liking for his style.'

'I, too,' said Monk. 'But bring some book of his at haphazard, and, opening at random, read where your eye happens to light.'

On this I rose, got the Apologia, and coming again to Monk, read the following: ' "I used (when a boy) to wish the Arabian tales were true; my imagination ran on unknown influences, on magical powers and talismans; I thought life might be a dream, or I an angel, and all this world a deception, my fellow-angels by a playful device concealing themselves from me, and deceiving me with the semblance of a material world. . . . When I was fifteen (in the autumn of 1816) a great change of thought took place in me. I fell under the influence of a definite creed, and received into my intellect impressions of dogma, which, through God's mercy, have never been affected or obscured."'

'Well, that was the boy,' said Monk when I stopped; 'and how unsoiled, how blameless a boy, though spoiled, and pale! I would only remark as to the passage in general a certain grab as of the crab's claw with which early notions, through God's mercy, took hold upon his consciousness, as one sees it at its acme in Methodist and Catholic negroes: a grasp and grimness which once forced from his lips the opinion that heretics should be shown no pity.'

'No, not "heretics," ' I said, ' "heresiarchs"; I believe I can even discover the passage'—and after a hunt I discovered and read: ' "the latter (any 'heresiarch') should meet with no mercy; to spare him is a false and dangerous pity. . . . I cannot deny," he continues, "that this is a very fierce passage, but it is only fair to myself to say that neither at this nor at any other time of my life, not even when I was fiercest, could I have even cut off a Puritan's ears, and I think the sight of a Spanish *auto-da-fé* would have been the death of me. Again, when one of my friends wrote to expostulate with me on the course I was taking, I said that we would ride over him and his as Othniel prevailed over Chusan-rishathaim, King of Mesopotamia—" '

'Oh, well, let that pass,' said Monk, interrupting me, 'since no comment is necessary. With regard, by the way, to "Othniel prevailing over Chusan-rishathaim," this is a very negro thing, the referring of modern cases to Biblical ones, and finding likenesses between them. This "Othniel" is not a good instance, for it is semi-humorous, I think: but Newman was given to it. It is over-belief gone doting! as when any sudden death in Barbados will instantly bring to many a lip the words "Ananias and Sapphira". Newman, I remember, once drew an elaborate analogy between the seceding Ten Tribes and the Church of England, in order to show that, as the ten tribes were still recognised as a people "by the divine mercy," and as the Shunamite "received no command" to break off from her own people, *therefore* there is no call for an Anglican to leave his church for Rome. As to the rest of the passage which you have read, let nothing be said. The cutting off of a Puritan's ears, or a Spanish *auto-da-fé,* would have been the death of Newman, solely because of his very advanced moral evolution; as to the mentality of the whole thing, is it not a skittish and irrelevant piece of scripture to proceed from a modern pen? Fierce also and stubborn? Childish, then, and savage? You will say that this is so. But that is a mere straw, showing possibly which way the wind blows. Read something else somewhere.'

I turned some pages and met the passage: ' "It is Milner's doctrine that upon the visible Church came down from above, at certain intervals, large and temporary *effusions* of divine grace. In a note he adds that 'in the term *effusion* there is *not* here included the idea of the miraculous operations of the Spirit'; but still it was natural for me, admitting Milner's theory, not to stop short at his abrupt *ipse dixit,* but boldly to pass forward to the conclusion that, as miracles accompanied the first effusion of grace, so they might accompany the latter, and that there was no force in the popular argument that, because we did not see miracles with our own eyes, miracles were not taking place in distant places. . . .' "

'Notice,' said Monk, 'the somehow lovable skittishness—the half self-conscious skittishness—of 'distant places'; the kicking up of the heels, for one's own part, at the vague universe! Must it not have entered his head, even as he said it, that there are no more any *distant places* since the coming of steam, except in Thibet, and Caesar's "Hercynian Forest," for miracles to take place in? But little he recked! and with tight eyes frisked from behind, executing mentally that back-kick of the cake-walk. Unless, indeed, he meant "distant places," not here beneath, but on, say, the nearest star? And yet, hardly on this, I think, for the nearest star seems never to have got well into Newman's consciousness, no more than steam fully got, inasmuch as in his youth mail-coaches crawled, and his youth, as he relates, remained always with him. But this passage is so much less modern than anything in Aristotle! So read something else.'

At this I turned over, and lighted upon the following: ' "It was, I suppose, to the Alexandrian school and to the early Church that I owe what I definitely held about the angels. I viewed them as carrying on the economy of the visible world. This doctrine I have drawn out in my sermon for Michaelmas Day, written in 1831, I say of the angels, 'Every breath of air and ray of light and heat, livery beautiful prospect is, as it were, the skirts of their garments, the waving of the robes of those whose faces see God.' Again, I ask what would be the thoughts of a man who, 'when examining a flower or a pebble, suddenly discovered that he was in the presence of some powerful being who was hidden behind the visible things he was inspecting, whose robe and ornaments these objects were?' Also, besides the hosts of evil spirits, I considered there was a middle race, δαιμονια, neither in heaven nor in hell; partially fallen, capricious, wayward; noble or crafty, benevolent or malicious, as the case might be. In 1837 I made a further development of this doctrine—" '

'A *further* development?' said Monk at this point—' "in 1837"?'

'Let me finish,' I said; and I read on: ' "In 1837 I made a further development of this doctrine. I said to a dear friend, Samuel Francis Wood, in a letter: I have an idea. The mass of the Fathers hold that, though Satan fell from the beginning, the angels fell before the Deluge, falling in love with the daughters of men. Daniel speaks as if each nation had its guardian-angel. I cannot but think that there are beings with a great deal of good in them, yet with great defects, who are the animating principles of certain institutions, etc., etc. . . . Take England with many high virtues, and yet a low Catholicism: it seems to me that John Bull is a spirit neither of heaven nor hell. . . .'

'Well,' said Monk, 'all that seems to me skittish and over-believing. Does it not to you?'

'Well, yes,' I consented.

'Observe,' he said, 'that this is not mere fancy, but fancy accepted as authentic, and become *belief*. He does not say that every breath of air may be, "as it were, the skirts of the angels' garments"; but he says that every breath is, as it were, that; and he is so confirmed that it is so, that he journeys forth, urging it, in a church, upon others, laying it down as a fact that so the matter stands on that particular "Michaelmas Day".'

'The fancy, though, is pretty,' I said, 'and full of that world-wonder which you love in Job.'

'It is very prettily expressed, anyway in one sentence,' he said, 'much more prettily than in Dante and "Religio Medici," where we have the fancy in all its details; but as to your reference, my friend, to Job, really I can't help thinking dint here your criticism deeply sleeps. *Catch* Job puking such pap! Job, too, of course, is a child-mind—true: but a most robust country-child; Newman a most artificial child, a sophisticated, a sickly. Job's interest is all riveted on things BE-ing, I AM, on onyx, on coral, on spittle, on skin of teeth, on the number of the months, on Boötes, on stones, on wild asses' colts, on conies, on wild goats, on dust of gold, on fill the manners and customs of this unrolling of the Glory of the Most High God, whose gonfalons roam on their road before his eyesight: so that he lacks the time to *care* whether there are angels roguishly ogling under stones, he is so ghast with marvelling at stones themselves, at sparks that fly upward, not sideward or otherward, with marvelling that there are sparks at all, or aught at all, and "O," he calls out, "it is all as lofty as heaven, what can'st thou do? profounder down than hell, what can'st thou know?" Newman, on the other hand, in his callousness, as to the actual marvel of stones, has to manufacture a fantastic marvel of angels roguishly ogling under stones, to make stones a little interesting to him, for since a marvel to interest him has to be grotesque, in things, BE-ing, I AM, he has no gramme of interest, 'his interest is in I AM's son's mother and grandmother. Do not, then, be likening Newman with job, but with Oscar Wilde: for these two Oxford-men, so dissimilar-looking, were, in truth, beings curiously alike in fibre to the eye of criticism, Newman being a kind of white-eyed Wilde, or Wilde-in-chokey adoring *Sorrow*, Newman, too, a *roué*, luxurious, uxorious, pain his holy whore, not "pleasure," pain being his pleasure, but both men of the same mental measure, men made of mosaic, of paint and paste, infinitely artificial, fantastic, packed with padding to the pancreas, their pansies wallpaper pansies, their landscape a tapestry landscape, their sun a monstrance sun, all most aesthetically wrought!—or wrought in a way that they had heard someone say was aesthetic; and never the feet of either got down to God's grand grass and ragged ground. But as to the beauty of the fancy in question, does not a poet inform us with some plausibleness that "beauty is truth, truth beauty"? If there be no truth in the fancy, perhaps there is no true beauty. But in its possible beauty or truth we are not at present interested: for, since believed in without experiment or grounds, even if it were beautiful, and by some chance true, must it not be regarded as still negroid, over-believing, obiahish? peopling the air with demons and semi-demons, and angels? of which semi-demons Plato tells us that "through their intervention we possess every kind of divination and incantation, and the whole of magic"? investing the shapes of the fancy with a certain actualness and awe? and elaborating them with a certain precision and conviction? as some savages arranged Judgment Day on the apparition of a ship's flashlight? and as all children and savages do?'

'Yes, that certainly seems to be so,' I said. 'But read something else,' said Monk.

I turned over and read as follows: ' "First was the principle of dogma: my battle was with liberalism; by liberalism I mean the anti-dogmatic principle. This was the first point on which I was certain. Here I make a remark: persistence in a given belief is no test of its truth; but departure from it is at least a slur upon the man who has felt so certain about it. From the age of fifteen dogma has been the fundamental principle of my religion: I know no other religion; I cannot enter into the idea of any other sort of religion. . . ." '

'But is not this yet another proof of mental stubbornness?' demanded Monk.

'There is a certain stubbornness in it,' I answered.

'Notice especially,' he said, 'how remote Newman is from the modern mood where he says that departure from a given belief is "a slur" upon the man who has felt so certain of it: for even in politics a total *volte-face* is no longer reckoned much; and can anything be nimbler than the ease wherewith scientific intellects again and again give up their beliefs, standing constantly brisk and prompt to give them up the moment that their own or another's discoveries prove them in some trifle unprecise?'

'That is very much so,' I assented.

'But a Methodist negro would rather greet a martyr's death than incur "the slur" of an altering of belief? this stubbornness being owing to the fact that what the savage loves is not so much truth as his own belief and *parti pris?* and a kind of feeling that he is necessarily right? and a biped better than anybody in the binding of his fibre?'

'I suppose that this, too, is so,' I said, 'from what you have told me as to Negroes.'

'And, on the whole,' he said, 'with regard to the seeking after truth, does not the matter somehow stand somewhat in this wise: that man was made to seek after truth, but that in his childish or savage state he merely plays at seeking after it? in the childish-lovable manner of, for example, Sir Thomas Browne, or of Milton? and is skittish with respect to it, as children play at soldiers or at keeping store? but when time more matures man's mind, man enters seriously into business with respect to truth? and into real warfare because of it, in the way of a well-grown stripling? And as amid the games of children the passions gush out, with arrogances, and stubbornnesses, and personal waywardnesses, like Achilles withdrawing into his tent (though the cause of the quarrel is of no consequence), but actual business and warfare is carried on with a certain earnest and impersonal calm for their own sake, so the savage is passionate, personal and rooted in his playing at truth? and the controversies of the ages have been conducted with rages and stubbornness? like child's-play? . . . Imagine a controversy betwixt Milton and Newman! That would have been pleasant! "Fierce as ten furies, terrible as hell" . . . ha, ha. Would not Milton have new-named Newman "that pork"? and would not Newman have doomed Milton, deep, deep, even if he did not "cut off his ears"? But scientific controversies are not so conducted? but with a well-grown calm? everyone standing brisk and prompt to give up his opinion for God's sake? and not thinking this any "slur" on him? Does not the matter stand somewhat as I have stated it?'

'It seems to me to be even as you say,' I answered.

'But read further,' he said.

I turned the leaves, and read as follows: ' "As a matter, then, of conscience, I felt it to be a duty to protest against the Church of Rome: for I adopted the argument of Bernard Gilpin that Protestants were not able to give any firm and solid reason of the separation besides this, to wit, that the Pope is antichrist. . . ." '

'Well, let that, too, pass,' said Monk: 'for all that one need remark is that it seems no more sceptical to believe that the good easy Pope is antichrist than to believe that a battleship's flashlight is antichrist; moreover, Newman abandoned this belief in his latter years, proving that, if he was as over-believing as, he was at least less stubborn than, a Methodist of Barbados, who *never* abandons it: so read further.'

I again turned the leaves and read as follows: ' "Starting, then, with the being of a God I look out of myself into the world, and there I see a sight which fills me with distress. The world seems simply to give the lie to that great truth of which my whole being is so full. The sight of the world is nothing else than the prophet's scroll, "full of lamentations and mourning and woe." To consider it in its length and breadth, its various history, the tokens so faint and broken of a superintending design, the idolatries, the corruptions, the dreary hopeless irreligion, the condition of the whole race so fearfully, yet exactly, described in the Apostle's words, 'having no hope and without a God in the world'—all this is a vision to dizzy and appal; and inflicts upon the mind the sense of a mystery which is absolutely beyond human solution. . . ." '

'He prattles prettily,' said Monk at this point, 'and how prettily you read him aloud!'

'I will finish the passage,' I said; and I continued to read: ' "What will be said of this reason-bewildering fact? I can only answer that either there is no Creator, or this society of men is in a true sense discarded from His presence. And so I argue about the world—*if* there be a God, *since* there is a God, the human race is implicated in some terrible aboriginal calamity. It is out of joint with the purposes of its Creator. And now, supposing it were the loving will of the Creator to interfere in this anarchical condition of things, what are we to suppose would be the methods which might be naturally involved in His purpose of Mercy? . . . There is nothing to surprise the mind, if He should think fit to introduce a Power into the world invested with the prerogative of infallibility in religious matters; and when I find that this is the very claim of the Catholic Church, there is a fitness in it which recommends it to my mind. . . . The Church must denounce rebellion as of all possible evils the greatest; she must have no terms with it; if she would be true to her Master, she must ban and anathematise it. This is the meaning of a statement of mine which has furnished matter for one of those accusations to which I am replying: I said, 'The Catholic Church holds it better for the sun and the moon to drop from heaven, for the earth to fail, and for all the many millions on it to die of starvation in extremest agony, than that one soul should commit one single venial sin, should tell one wilful untruth.' " '

'I think that in some respects he writes well,' said Monk when I stopped, 'though wordily. But as a matter of fact, is not this passage skittish, credulous, over-believing and, above all, stubborn?'

'In what particular points do you mean?' I asked.

'Let us glance at the argument,' said Monk: 'he first of all insists upon God's existence—a singular insistence, by the way, for did any living being ever question the fact that the order of things must have a cause of some sort, a cause which we English call 'God'? But the fact of the matter is, that it is not upon the existence of the infinite God, infinitely inconceivable, that Newman is insisting, but it is upon the existence of God as conceived by the geese-heads of Greeks and negroes, viz., as a living thing, i.e., a mortal, yet immortal, an immortal mortal, a mammal or enormous tortoise inhabiting a habitat *lassù*, as Dante says, "up there." Anyway, God, he insists, exists; but the world is a denial of God's existence, "the world is out of joint with the purposes of its Creator, through some terrible aboriginal calamity," the fall of man in Eden; in which state of things, he says, it was natural that God should establish some fabric like the Catholic Church, infallible, claiming to be so, and proclaiming that "it is better for the sun and moon to drop from heaven than that one soul should tell one untruth"; as to which one can't help pausing to remark on this irreverent way of talking of the sun and moon in the same breath—and drop where to? Upon Oxford probably? Could he have had Oxford in him mind, my friend?'

'As to that, I do not know what to think,' I answered.

'But in that case,' said Monk, 'would not the splash of the sun's dropping in especial spread even to Littlemore? making some derangement even there?'

'It would without doubt,' I consented, 'spread even to Littlemore.'

'But does not the fact that he says "the sun and moon," and not "the moon and sun" seem to show that he was at least subconscious that the sun is more than the moon?'

'He seems to have been at least subconscious of it,' I answered.

'Suppose he had said "the moon and sun"! That would have been pleasant! like "sweetness and light"—the cart forty millions of millions of miles before the horse. But does not the fact that he babbles in this facile fashion in the same breath of "the sun and moon" "dropping" "from heaven" upon Oxford or elsewhere indicate that he was not instantly conscious of the truth about the sun and about the moon, or, in general, of those large-minded truths by the evolving breath of which Lord Kelvin, Lord Rosebery and our navvy of Whitechapel are no longer childish?'

'What you say does seem to have some likelihood,' I answered.

'But to go back to his argument: he bases his faith in an infallible fabric upon "the fall of man," and if his premise is good, his conclusion may be good, too. But is it not so that his clinging to that premise was skittish, credulous, and, above all, stubborn?'

'Is that a provable thing?' I asked.

'But is it not a provable thing,' Monk demanded, 'that in a former age all Britons were savages?'

'Yes,' I said.

'But we here are no longer so?'

'No.'

'So it is a provable thing that we here have evolved from lower types?'

'That is certain,' I answered.

'And is it not, moreover, a provable thing that nothing can come from nothing, and that those lower types from which we here have evolved themselves evolved from lower yet, Nature being ever like herself? And though blood-crystals and serum-precipitates had not in that day heaved the simian descent of man from a theory to a scientific thesis, as a mutter of fact was it not equally well known to thinkers at the date when Newman wrote?'

'Why, yes.'

'But Newman did not know it well? but continued to think of "a terrible aboriginal calamity," and of "a world out of joint with the purposes of its Creator"—as if such things could be!—and of the "tokens so faint and broken of design," and of our race "having no hope and being without God," though, in truth, its hope begins to grow into a vision so glorified, that "*l'occhio da presso nol sostiene*"?'

'None of all that can be denied,' I said.

'But, then, if this be so, shall we not say of Newman that his is a stubbornness become skittish, as it were of the frisking filly kicking up, for its part, its heels at the vague universe? For, if of a pair of statements, one that man rose slowly, the other that he fell suddenly, one practically proved and modern, its analogy everywhere to be noticed, the other not proved and ancient, its analogy nowhere to be noticed, and apparently foreign to Nature, Newman clung to the latter just because it was of the latter that his brain first caught an impression, "when he was fifteen," is not this a personally wayward playing at truth? and a thing rather disagreeably negroid? as the deaf adder stoppeth her ear? and will not hearken to the voice of charmers, charm they never so wisely, so Divinely?'

'Well, I consent,' I said—'on this understanding, though, that Newman would have had an answer to all this, for he would have answered that intellect is weak, and reason rickety; that only that which Holy Writ and the Church assert is certainly true; and that this you will some day discover in hell, Monk.'

'Well,' said Monk, 'at least one piece of that answer is most true, and let us say that the whole may be true—though, by the way, owing to my much greater greatness of mind, i.e., my mental evolution, i.e., my scepticism and proneness to truth, I know that it is not true in the same way that I know the untruth of the statements of negroes as regards corpses hurrying, or of Caesar as regards elks' legs, without even troubling to ask myself how I know. Still, let us say that this final reply of Newman may be true. Then, I say of it that it is precisely, to my knowledge, the final reply which a Barbados negro makes, without fail, to an opponent, my only care at present being to get you to agree that his Grace had a negroid brain.'

'Well, let it be so,' I said.

'But,' he said, 'having admitted that Newman had a mind which continued childish, you have admitted, I think, nothing which is at all likely to diminish your love of its charmingness: Here it seems, was a bud, not born to blow—because maybe the soil was thin? the air thick?—but still touched with that *mignon* endearment which the rose has outgrown: for to children and many immature things God does grant this special grace and engagingness, as Greek, gipsy, negro women exhibit a gracility which does not quite belong to the most evolved types; and the dayspring is prettier than the day.'

'Yes, I see with you,' I said, 'and this talk of ours you should let me some day publish.'

'I have no objection,' he answered—'nay, it may do good : for let the man of Balham and of Birmingham once well learn the certainty of the truths which we have been proving, and Britain may then permanently disburden herself of her most just nervousness of Germany.'

III

HE WAKES AN ECHO

'It seems incredible, but remember it was Regulus.'—PLINY.

We were down at the Abbey How, Monk's house in the Cotswolds, when Monk's weakness of the eyes—for which he wore a gold button in one ear—came upon him, and now he would cower for days over a library-grate, tamed, the green shade over his nose, his profile lighted by the fire. In fact our life was spent in the library, with every one of its procession of windows shuttered up, so that at midday we were as shut away from the sun as at midnight; and our consciousness that from outside the mansion had a look of having been deserted for ages may have confirmed our tendency to indolence, Monk giving hardly a sign of life, save an occasional shiver at the gales of autumn wawling all among the hills.

The reaction, however, in his case, was ever certain. A moment came when he stirred, and stretched; then for minutes a dead relapse; then a sitting forward with frowning thought, and now a spring up, a laugh, a mutter, 'By Jingo, I'm hungry!'

For more things than one: for cities, and the storm of things, and the thick of war. At the same time he cast the shade from his eyes, and said to me: 'Do you know what I have been thinking? That one of the big crimes would rouse and excite us.'

'No doubt of that,' I said: 'but against whom shall we commit it?'

'Oh, come, one needn't go and commit it oneself,' he said; 'what I mean is that we should first conceive the crime, construct it, then find out someone who is somewhere committing it in the world, and mix ourselves up generally in the trouble.'

'But in what possible way?' I asked, 'and—with what earthly motive?'

'Isn't crime, being a human thing, my business?' he said.

'But—really, Monk—what sort of crime?'

'Crimes—that is what I have been thinking there—are of three sorts: little—usually heard of and punished; middle-sized—heard of, but not usually punished; and big—usually never heard of.'

'But what do you call "big" crimes?'

'Those which, like Borgia's, or Gilles de Rais', are both large and dark-minded in mood; and "little", those which, like burglars' murders, are sordid in mood.'

'But suppose there are no "big crimes" going forward at present for us to "mix ourselves up in"?'

'But isn't everything going forward that ever was or will be—doomsdays, moonfalls, cries of crucified Christs, rackets of Nile-cataracts, births of whirling worlds? As for our own sun, never before, credit me, did he blaze so crazily red, or so dreadfully roar on his road—what a bustle and thrill the whole thing is! Big crimes enough, I should think.'

'Well, I am willing,' I said, 'though I like the light of day, and the pretty things that prink the sky at night, and have no wish to be shot. But how on earth—I can't even begin to conceive—'

'Wait, we shall see; first, let's dine.'

So we dined, and after dinner returned to the library where at once Monk, as he said, 'set to work,' first assuring me that there was no doubt about the result, since he had several methods in his head, and if one failed everyone would not. And now he proceeded to spend three hours in a heat of activity, pitching up ladder-steps, eagerly dashing through leaves, with now a grumble, now a shrug, a mutter, hunting the rainbow, to 'give to airy nothing a local habitation and a name.'

I saw him pry into A B C's, masses of Ordnance maps, through a shelf of old ledgers belonging to the insurance-branch of his house, piles of newspapers, books on science. At last he lit a cigar, cast himself down upon a couch, his arms behind his head, and laughed. It was then ten o'clock.

'Come,' I said, 'something has been discovered.'

'Look you,' Monk said, 'since modern men by heredity and morals are given a bent against "sin," it is ever under some compelling temptation that they commit it. Well, but in temptation there are two elements—wish, possibility; so that, if I think of a "sin" and desire to find out who is committing it, I commence by discovering those who have a roaring opportunity for doing so. Now, suppose I conceive that someone wants, for any reason, to lure a stranger or so into his clutches, what are the ideal conditions as to "opportunity" which I should seek ? Those conditions occur in the case of a man living near one of two very obscure railway-stations which have nearly the same name: so I found out the sixteen such pairs of stations which exist in Europe, and wrote them down—one such pair, I may tell you at once, being Stratton Eastern and Stratton Western in Scotland. Very good. Now, suppose on discovering this fact, I discover also this constantly repeated advertisement "Summerdale Farm. Paying guests received. Every home comfort. Climate highly recommended by the Profession. Terms moderate. Near Stratton Western, Kincardine.—Apply J.P., 'Telegraph,' Box No. 3y5." And suppose I moreover discover, firstly, that this climate, so highly recommended by the Profession, is the climate of a storm-swept coast, almost uninhabited; and secondly, that there is no record anywhere of any such farm in Kincardine as Summerdale Farm?'

'That might be ugly,' I agreed.

'You see, of course,' he went on, 'what might very well happen to a 'paying guest' who starts to get to 'Summerdale Farm.' His friends, if he has any, know that he has gone to Stratton Western; his train arrives, let us say, one evening at Stratton Western; his luggage is put upon the local cab, if there is one—upon some species of thing with wheels—and now he gives the order "Summerdale Farm." However, his driver knows no Summerdale Farm—no one knows it—it doesn't, in fact, exist. But at last the idea inevitably strikes someone that the stranger has made a mistake—that the farm must be at Stratton Eastern, not at Stratton Western; and, sure at first though our stranger is that Western it is, and not Eastern, finally, in his perplexity, and hunger, maybe, he is tempted to try Eastern, whither by the next train he goes. Here someone—maybe disguised—awaits him with a trap. "Is he not the stranger expected at Summerdale Farm?" Yes. He enters that trap; and a trap it proves. He is driven a long way, perhaps, to a place which is not Summerdale Farm, and no trace from that moment remains of that man in this world.'

'Well!' I exclaimed.

'Unless, indeed, the evil-doer has the imprudence to compromise himself by taking out a rather unusual number of policies of insurance—'

'No! *Is* there someone at Stratton Eastern who has done that?'

'Not very far from Stratton Eastern—a certain Sir Saul Ingram, as I see, residing at Feuding Manor, thereabouts. Far be it from me to assert that this good Sir Saul, who has taken out the policies, and the man who has advertised the fictitious farm are the same. Still, I have a greed on me to see this Feuding Manor, and I mean to go to it.'

'Not alone?'

'Yes, since I have a sort of guess in my head that Sir Saul Ingram may be a country squire of unquiet type, and you have said that you like the sun.'

His eye twinkled, but his tone was decided. I did not know what to say; and when I woke the next morning my Monk had already taken train northward. At nine the same evening (as it was related to me afterwards) he arrived at Stratton Eastern.

There, after making a good many inquiries, he got to hear something of the whereabouts of Feuding Manor, miles away, and set off on foot over a tract of 'links'—sand-dunes mixed with scrub—where the solitude was absolute. Great guns of wind were blowing a roar of breakers shoreward from over a dark sea chill with waters from the North Pole—a storm with something in its tone which seemed to Monk to mean that here it was no occasional comer, but the everlasting master of that coast. Warned as he had been in regard to the quicksands near the seaboard of the links, and hearing the roar of breakers grow in his ears, as he dug his way head-foremost in the teeth of the gale, he was directing his course more westward, when a great gust tugged his hat from his hands and head, and carted it into the dark. With the wind now at his right shoulder, he went on hatless for some forty minutes, till he found the ground begin to harden; and soon he was following a footpath through a wood of alders that presently thickened to a forest where he could scarcely see his hand, and then anew thinned to a wood, through which he passed downwards by a path, and now found himself in a vale, enclosed by fells and scars; and he could make out before him a lake of water.

He thought that this ought to be the place; but, as he could make out nothing with any distinctness, he stood in uncertainty a little, until up burned the brim of the moon luridly above a scar; and now he could perceive the shape of a house, darksome, low, and large, on an ait or island, lying in a lowland mere.

Not one blink of light came out from it; but, without hesitation, Monk walked down to the edge of the mere, found a causeway of stone leading to the island; went over it; passed at the end of it between two rocks like druidical 'standing-stones,' and, sending a flock of black-faced sheep bleating away through bracken, began to prowl round the grounds and house.

The ground he found very rough, without any visible road; the alders and willows huddled all one way by the continual sea-storm; and, as to the house, its structure was most intricate and quaint, the roofs of different breadths, spouts out of the straight, with an outhouse or lean-to here or there. But what struck him was the apparently hoary age of the whole, the walls being propped with beams which were themselves watery and soft with rot; and here or there a mass of masonry and beams had tumbled. Every window on both stories was boarded up; and, though Monk again and again glued his eyes to the boardings, he was able to spy no glimmer of light. All of a sudden a muffled, yet wild, howl wawled out of the house.

Plan of action Monk had as yet none: yet upon action of some sort he was resolved; and hearing, as he now stood thinking how he was to act, a horse's neigh, he followed the sound, and came to an outhouse in an alder-spinney. This proved to be a stable, and there, against the door, stood a spade, a rake, and a crowbar.

Monk took the crowbar and with it returned to the house, where, after scrambling to the roof of a low lean-to, he set to work upon a window shuttered by a sheet of iron just over the roof, the loud roar of the winds drowning the sounds of his fumbling. The roof, being mossy, was very slippery; but, lying along it, he managed presently to prise open the iron slab, which yielded with a pop, though, as it turned out, the wrench did not break the catch: this lacked a handle, and when Monk had drawn the shutter towards him against the force of the storm, and had sprung into the apartment beyond, the wind again slammed the shutter, he heard the catch click, and realised that he was a prisoner.

Light though his leap was, it shook the house, which he felt shake throughout to each gust of the gale, and here, it was clear, was the home of old decay. As he stood there in a darkness that was complete, from somewhere far away there came to his ears a cry like the wail of one rived with pain; and when upon this Monk struck a match, there, at his feet, kneeling with a face of fear, he saw a man, quite young, yet with long, white hair, clad in the rags of a dressing-gown.

Monk, having struck another match, put his left hand on the lad's head, murmuring to him: 'I am not going to hurt you; do I look, now, as if I would? Tell me who you are.' Nothing but a species of jabbering proceeded in answer out of the throat of the lad, who, opening his mouth wide, pointed inward to it. 'Ah!' said Monk, when he saw that the lad had no tongue. And he kept on striking matches, examining that prostrate shape, examining the chamber.

He saw that there were two truckle-beds, from one of which the lad had apparently just risen, the other being 'made'; and at the foot of this other—chained to it—was a cash-box, which Monk was going to investigate when the lad held him back with a grip and gaze of warning—a gaze that all at once grew aghast at a sound of footsteps coming without. Quickly now Monk struck another match, hustled the lad into a large cupboard, without shelves, in a corner, locked its door upon him, kept the key; then, flying to the lad's bed, with that lightning knack of which he, above all mortals, was a master, so arranged the bedclothes as to lend them an air of covering a slumberer. An instant later the key turned in the lock and there entered a very bulky man, bearing a candlestick with a tallow candle stuck in it. Monk, though he had purposely come to this house without a weapon, boldly faced him.

The man, dressed in a loose red shirt which bagged over his girdle, was evidently a servant, had an expression of dullness and grimness, a great fan-beard, and eyes nearly invisible, beneath their lax lids, that resembled little draperies of skin. At sight of Monk his conduct was extraordinary. He simply dropped candlestick and candle, dashed to the cash-box, and, hugging it with both arms, began to bawl 'Help!' But in one half-minute his mood of miserly affright changed into hatred; he bounded towards a stool and caught and swung it to dash out Monk's brains, but Monk made a dodge as if to seize the cash-box, and the man, seeing this in the still-burning candlelight, bounded to intercept him; upon which Monk dived and escaped out of the chamber.

Monk, after first leaving the crowbar in a corner and marking the spot in his mind, darted onward, little knowing whither, through the most curious old house which he had yet seen, where one chamber was higher or lower than the next by three or four steps, where nothing appeared quite straight, and doors hung awry, and the very floors were aslant. He went butting into triangular rooms, antic nooks, whimsical corners, till, at last, seeing a blink of light ahead, he boldly moved towards it, opened a door, and entered a room.

As he stepped in there hastened to meet him—a man; and both stood stone-still, and looked at each other.

The man—a powerful person of middle height—walked with a busy fling-out of the right leg, and with his left hand stuck in the pocket of his robe, which was tied with a cord round the waist. He wore spectacles across his broad face, and had a broad mouth and an out-sticking, stiff beard, so hairy as even to invade the fat of his cheeks.

At last he spoke, saying quite coolly—

'Well, you silly devil, what are you doing here?'

His speech was a species of rapid mutter, and even in the act of speaking, his tongue-tip was ever out, seeking for one end of his moustache to eat.

'I am here to find a brother of mine,' answered Monk.

'What name?'

'Never mind his name. The lad whose tongue you have cut out, Sir Saul Ingram.'

'Same father? Same mother?'

'Adam and Eve, you know.'

'Silly devil!' muttered the man musingly. Now, during this talk Monk had stood with his palms pressed on the round table in the middle of the room, his back towards the one door; and the baronet, who was more remote from the door, had been moving round towards it—a movement that Monk did not fail to notice, though he made no attempt to stop it. So now, with a sudden run, Ingram gained the door, closed it, locked it. He then stepped to a small chest of drawers, caught up out of one of the drawers a revolver, turned anew upon his prisoner, and now his mouth drew back in a sort of snarl that resembled a laugh.

'What you do it for?' he asked Monk, with the breadth of the table between them, and his laugh had something strained in it, cruel and hard to see, as though done by machinery which lacked oil.

'Are you going to shoot me,' asked Monk— 'an unarmed and helpless man?'

'Silly devil!' muttered Ingram, almost laughing out now, 'of course I'm going to! What you do it for?'

'I have help near; I defy you to shoot.'

'Pooh! Lie!'

'I have!'

'Lie! Look out!' He raised and aimed the weapon; his finger rested on the trigger. All the house trembled with many a weary creak to the power of the storm, while four or five seconds passed, in which the baronet appeared to be enjoying a consciousness of power before firing. The shot, however, was never fired. Instead of it there rang out a passionate shout—from outside the house, apparently—a cry in the night: 'Monk! Monk! I'll be here for you at two with the police!'

It was the baronet who seemed shot. He fell back some feet, rushed aimlessly to the door, aimlessly back again, gaping in a frank scare, realising no doubt that, if Monk's presence in the house was known outside it, then Monk's death, and the manner of it, was a matter for reflection. But in a minute he was partially reassured by Monk himself, who said to him: 'Look you, you were right; I have no help near, for that shout came from *me*, and only seemed to come from outside because I chance to be the sort of man who can do such things. But you see now, don't you, Ingram, if you are not a goose, that I wasn't altogether fashioned to be shot down by a clown like you? You couldn't, really. Try again, and I have five other ways of stopping you, some of them not so agreeable: Better keep quiet.'

Ingram eyed Monk with a grim underlook, quite undecided now, no doubt, as Monk wished him to be, which was the untruth—whether the cry had or had not come from outside. After a minute of thought, he turned away, inwardly resolving, perhaps, to wait till two, the hour mentioned by the voice that had appeared to shout from outside. After two—he would see.

It was at this point that a rap sounded on the locked door, and when Ingram opened it, there slouched in the big man in the loose red shirt whom Monk had encountered before; he bore dishes on both his palms, and was followed by a tall woman of a visage most white and gaunt, with jaundiced eye-whites, robed in a gown of rusty black, who bore on a tray a bottle, a plate, and a tablecloth. The man took not the slightest notice of Monk, but the woman eyed him curiously, with a look of rancour. No one spoke. The woman spread the table with the tablecloth, the man put on the dishes. But as she turned to go, the woman, holding up a finger, said to Ingram: 'Saul, mon, Saul, gi' heed! There be danger this nicht!'

The baronet made no answer, locked the door after them, and sat to a repast of potatoes, boiled cod, bread black as coal, whisky-and-water; and he began to eat with a greedy earnestness and to drink.

After some minutes he glanced up at Monk, who stood regarding him with folded arms, and said: 'Sit down, if you like.'

Monk sat on a chair by the table, watching for some time the guzzling of Ingram, watching the revolver at his right hand on the table, watching the great gulps of whisky which the man—who ate and drank more like a yokel than a gentleman—imbibed. At last, yielding, perhaps, to the garrulous influence of a third whisky, Ingram suddenly said: 'Silly devil! What you do it for?'

'Do what?' asked Monk.

'What you come here for?'

'I found out that you were up to some kind of mischief, and came to stop you.'

'Mischief—eh? Know what I am?'

'No. Tell me.'

'I am the only exact scientist in the world.'

'Oh, come, not the only one.'

'See those three big books there on the shelf? They are all in manuscript. I wrote them. Going to burn them before I die. Almost the whole secret of body and soul is in them—the secret of life.'

'By Jove! And by what methods?'

'There's only one way—persistent human vivisection.'

'By Jove!'

The baronet's words for a moment seemed to burn Monk's brain, which was yet no stranger to notions of horror; but here was something new to him: and he gaped with a grain of something resembling reverence at that greasy, plump face, as Ingram drained yet another glass.

'Know what I shall probably do with you?' said the baronet. 'Good thing you came. Infect you with a culture of rabid germs which I have on hand, then vivisect, perhaps, if I have time. The dumb fellow you saw—young parson from Cambridge—am driving mad for sake of living brain. Doctors say, you know, that they can't discover any morbid anatomy in mad brains. Silly devils! No morbid anatomy! Oh, good Lord! Silly devils!'

Ingram grinned sweetly to himself at this, grovelling with a full mouth over his meal.

'But how on earth do you drive people mad?' asked Monk.

'Fear, torture, horror, chiefly. Other things, too; have eighty-eight snakes, one jaguar, and a monster grouse with four legs in the house. Simple solitary confinement sometimes. Depends on diathesis of patient.'

'Well, you are candid enough,' said Monk. 'How if friends are really coming to rescue me at two? I'll naturally repeat all this.'

'No, you don't, friends or no friends. Suppose I wanted to hide you from them—alive—on the premises, think I couldn't? Why, I have seventeen people here now, undergoing various preparations, and you might search as you choose, you wouldn't find one. A man like me can devise a sure hiding-place, I suppose?'

'If you hid me, I should call out, of course.'

'Not much you wouldn't. I could strike you dumb in three minutes without leaving a sign to show how. But you won't be here to call out. Know what I mean to do with you? Did it once before eight years ago, and once again four years ago. Put your dead body in a packing-case with gun-cotton and a time-fuse, send you off in first goods train, and thirty miles from Stratton Eastern scarcely a trace left of you, or of the van that carried you.'

'I see,' said Monk. 'But, even so, you won't escape the law, for one of my friends knows of the presence here of the dumb lad, who will be looked for, and undoubtedly found, however you may conceal him.'

'Found, will he? Your statement that someone knows that he is here, whether true or false, merely decides me to examine his brain tonight, instead of next week.'

'Still, traces of the body will be found.'

'Traces, no. His body will go with yours in the packing-case to the railway.'

'I see—I see. But tell me one thing—since science is your motive for trapping strangers into this house, how comes it that your name figures in insurance policies?'

Ingram at this glanced up angrily, stung in his honour, crying—'What! You know of that? And do you suppose that the motives of a lord of thought, of a man like me, could be tainted in that sordid way? Why, I live on about sixpence a day—except the whisky; and if I didn't have the sixpence, I'd do without. Sometimes I do take out a policy on a patient, but the money doesn't come to *me*, silly devil! I've got two misers in the house, that's all—Hubert and my sister, whom you saw just now—and I get the money to give to them, in the hope that they'll tear each other to shreds over it. Beastly misers! That man Hubert—miserly beast, murderous beast! Mad as a mad dog! Silly devil, thinks I am for ever on the look-out to steal the very money I have given him! Sleeps in the same room as fellow without tongue and no human being dare approach room a single moment. Once wanted to do for me. Mad dog!'

'I see,' said Monk. 'But is it your whisky, or what, that has made you so very candid? Doesn't it really occur to you, Ingram, that with the knowledge that you have now given me of yourself I could snuff you out without fail in five or six different ways, without lifting a finger? Could make you commit suicide, for example? or make Hubert kill you? or your sister kill you? or make you all kill one another in a mix-up? And, considering how gory a thing, Ingram, you have allowed yourself to grow into, I do here and now deliberately pass sentence of death upon you. You really shan't live through this night, I vow, you wretch!'

The baronet did not even give an upward glance at this threat, believing, maybe, that here was a diseased brain come spontaneously for his scalpel. The rude repast concluded, he now picked his teeth musingly, while a clock struck midnight; and always outside wailed the storm.

'Hubert!' presently roared the baronet, at the same time clattering a huge bell.

And now anew came Hubert slouching in.

'Look,' the baronet said to, him, 'in the dissecting-room closet, and carry the top one of those three long boxes to your room. Dumb Wilson and this man have got to go into it, and you've got to take them to the station at five in the morning. Understand?'

Hubert made a sound not unlike the grunt of a pig.

'And don't go holding matches and things over the box, now, silly devil!' said Ingram, grinning one of his grim smiles: 'it's got guncotton in it.'

Hubert grunted, but did not move.

'Well, why don't you go?' asked Ingram.

'Why must the box be e'en stowed in my room?' asked Hubert.

'Oh, go away, you, and do what I tell you!' said the baronet. 'Who the deuce wants to steal your daft money? I'm not even going to enter your room!'

Hubert grunted, reassured, and went out. And now Ingram at once began to make his preparations for the investigation of the dumb lad's brain, taking two instrument-cases from a bureau, examining three scalpels, a trephine, and a saw, one by one, over the lamp, and laying them side by side on the sill of a window, each of the three scalpels being wrapped in a piece of chamois leather. The dim room was crowded all round with shelves, on which stood hundreds of chemical jars, and, like all the house, was pervaded with a breath of the laboratory, a scent of research, and also a certain taint of death. The baronet had just laid down the instruments side by side on the window-seat, when a face with jaundiced eyes peeped in, saying: 'Saul, mon, I wad ha' speech wi' ye.'

The baronet stalked to her, and, while a little outside the door they stood talking, Monk stole close and hearkened.

'Saul, mon,' the woman said, ' 'tis no ower weel this nicht, I'm doubting. I hae heard your talk wi' yon callant—'

'Well, what's the matter now, Elspeth?' asked the baronet impatiently.

'Are ye minded to mak' ony mair operations on Wilson tonicht, Saul?' she asked. 'Tak' a fule's counsel, and no do it, for 'tis e'en a long wark, and ye wad no hae the time.'

'Why can't you be quiet? What is it you want with me?' asked the baronet.

'Split Wilson's throat at once like a heather-blutter's, Saul,' she answered, 'and yon callant's, too, and pit them baith tegither into the box for the station. Tak' a fule's counsel, for I feel a sair fricht, mon, on me. Ye canna hae the time for mair long operations, for ye kenna what aid this man may e'en ha' outside; and here is Hubert threeping that one o' the dangerous snakes has escaped, and I near swafing awa' wi' fright—'

Monk, his whole plan of action now decided upon, stopped to listen to no more; but, moving from the door, flew lightly round the crowded shelves, searching till he found a bottle marked 'Phosphorus,' which contained some waxy, semi-transparent sticks in water. This he took down, and took out one of the phosphorus sticks, first throwing some of the cold water on his fingers so that their warmth should not cause the phosphorus to break into flame; and, now, running to the window-sill, he took one of the three scalpels which lay there out of its chamois leather wrapping, made the inner fold of the leather damp with some water to keep it cold for some minutes at least, and then, putting the stick of phosphorus with the scalpel, wrapped it up anew. He had barely put back the bottle in its place when the baronet came in again, stalked to the window, hurriedly put all the rolls of leather into an outer pocket of his robe, phosphorus and all, and set to calling out 'Hubert!'

'Look you,' said Monk, now frowning balefully, 'let me save you some trouble, sir. You are now calling this Hubert, I think, in order to send him for the dumb lad, whom you desire to be taken to your dissecting-room. Well, I say now to you that the lad is gone—has escaped—is at this moment free—'

Ingram turned quite white.

'What are you saying?' he asked.

'He is gone, I tell you. If you don't believe me, go and see. I set him at liberty myself.' At those words the baronet flew. To this moment the disappearance of Wilson had not been discovered, probably owing to Monk's life-like placing of the bed-clothes when he had locked away the dumb lad in the cupboard. At any rate, so intense was the baronet's care at this ugly news that he even forgot to lock Monk in—only for one instant, indeed, for he flew back, transferred the key from the inside to the outside, turned it, then in wild flight was off anew, making for Wilson's chamber—which was Hubert's, too; and he was just off when Hubert, in answer to his summons, turned the key, entered, and was looking round to see the baronet, who had called him, when Monk burst out laughing.

'Why, whom are you looking for?' asked Monk. 'Not the baronet, surely? Tut, man! Where's your head? He only called you to get you out of the way while he went into your room. He told you just now that he wasn't going there at all, didn't he? Well, but as a man of the world, you can easily guess that he's in want of a little ready cash tonight, of all nights, to buy my silence. Take my advice: lie low—say nothing.'

At these words the man's face passed through all the expressions of disbelief, belief, rage, lunacy; and suddenly, casting up his arms, he took to his heels. Monk had the hope that in the man's access of miserly fright he would omit to lock the door in his flight, and he did; but, after one moment's forgetfulness, he, too, darted back to the key, turned it, and was away again.

Monk, then, was still a prisoner; but he now no sooner found himself alone than he began to shout, in a perfect imitation of Ingram's voice: 'Hi! Elspeth! Elspeth!' and when in a minute the baronet's sister peeped in, looking keenly round for her brother, Monk, bowing, said to her: 'The baronet has just left the room, madam. I see that he is in a great hurry to make his experiment on the dumb lad, and is now gone to get all ready; but, hurry as he may, I tell you that he will hardly have time. Look you, will you make a bargain with me?'

'Weel?' asked Elspeth, with a crafty twitching of the cheeks and eyes.

'Madam,' said Monk, 'I stand this night in a huge danger; but so do you: and if I show you how to save yourself, will you save me? Is that a bargain?'

'Ye-es,' said the woman.

'Well, I'll tell you. In one half-hour my friends will be here, and as they have reason to believe that Wilson is here, the only hope for you really is to have Wilson out of the house in the box before they come; but, since the baronet is bent upon his experiment on Wilson, and won't give it up, there seems really nothing for you to do but to destroy the lad with your own hands now—this moment—as he lies a-bed, before the baronet can get him for the experiment; for the baronet will have no use for the dead body, it is the living brain that he is bent on studying. So now I have told you how to act, will you save my life in return?'

'We'll e'en see,' answered Elspeth, with twitching eyes of craft; but she saw fully the force of Monk's remarks, which accorded with her own views—saw that Wilson must, in truth, die by her hands, since by no other. And at once making up her mind, she turned to the bureau, unlocked a drawer by one of the bundle of keys at her girdle, and drew forth a horn-handled dagger, her purpose, as Monk well knew, being to spring first upon him, stab him, and then hurry to the dumb lad's bedside. But while she was still stooping over the bureau, Monk had caught up Ingram's water-jug, which was still half-full of water, and had hidden it behind his back, at the same time looking down at the floor, which he found to slant somewhat, like many of the floors of the house; and as the woman was in the act of raising herself to turn upon him, there hissed forth between Monk's teeth the two words: 'A snake!'

'A snake!'

Elspeth glared with panic where he pointed, and her glance saw in the gloom a wiry form gliding over the floor towards her—a snake created by Monk, who, having previously heard her say that one of the baronet's poison-snakes had escaped, had now, out of the water-bottle held behind his back, poured an undulating rivulet over the floor. The woman flew; and, as she flew, again glanced backward, only once more to behold the infuriated pursuit of the snake over the slanting floor; nor gave she any third glance, but—serpents being clearly her weak point—sent throughout the house a shriek, and was gone, leaving the door open, Monk after her, tracking the sound of her footfalls, himself all unmarked, through the vast intricacies of that house which held so many ghastly secrets, towards Wilson's apartment.

The situation at that moment in the room of Wilson, Monk declares that he knew with a precision almost as absolute as though he saw it. He had sent the baronet to search for Wilson, and he had sent the miser Hubert to search for the baronet. Now, Monk was certain that Ingram had a real fear of Hubert's growls and miserly furies, and he knew that no sooner would Ingram have discovered the absence of Wilson than he would hear the oncoming of the snorts and wrathful grunts of Hubert; upon which it was certain that the baronet, to avoid a scene, or something worse, would wish to secrete himself. But Monk knew that there was absolutely no hiding-place in that room, save two—the cupboard, and the rumpled bedclothes of Wilson's truckle-bed. The cupboard, containing Wilson, Monk had locked. It was natural, therefore, that Ingram, knowing that Hubert was still ignorant of the disappearance of Wilson, would scuttle well beneath Wilson's bedclothes and pretend to be Wilson asleep. And Monk had now effectually prompted Elspeth to the murder of Wilson in his bed; provided she did which quickly and quietly, it was sure as doom she would stab her brother.

Something more or less corresponding to these calculations must really have taken place. Hubert, on entering Wilson's room, must have struck a match, stared round, observed no baronet there, and now, perhaps, was about to go out again, when he must have heard footsteps—the footsteps of Elspeth coming to kill Wilson. Hubert's miserly suspicions must at once anew have burst into bloom, and he must have crouched down somewhere to watch what would take place. Elspeth then went in, Monk by that time being close behind her, though before he could reach the door, she had shut and secured it; and he stood keenly listening outside. And now the woman, moving no doubt on hands and knees, steel in hand, in the deep darkness crawled for the bed on which lay her brother, the supposed Wilson: for suddenly—short, but most raucous—Monk heard the outburst of a shout.

At this outcry of the murdered baronet, Hubert most likely leapt up: for presently Monk heard Elspeth explaining to him her motive for disposing at once of the dumb lad; and this was followed by a noise of shuffling feet when the body was being raised and placed in its packing-case, which was waiting there to receive the remains of Monk and Wilson. The garment worn by Wilson was of the same sort as that worn by Ingram, and no suspicion of the truth could have occurred to the criminals, who were sufficiently well advised to strike no matches over the gun-cotton in that box; and Monk heard the drop of the lid over the deposited body.

And now he knew that there was need for haste. In the box was gun-cotton, and in the baronet's pocket was a piece of phosphorus, for Monk, who could be ruthless, had doomed all the three. That phosphorus must quickly fire at the warmth of a still warm body packed into that confined space, the moistened chamois-leather which wrapped it round being now nearly dry. Now, therefore, to the spot where he had deposited the crowbar Monk darted, then back again to the room; outside which, at about the spot where the cupboard which contained Wilson stood, he began to dig deeply at the oak boarding with heavy heaves of the body. Within, Elspeth and Hubert must have hearkened with a paralysis of awe to those earnest strokes of the crowbar, to that breath of Monk's breast, while on he toiled in the momentary expectancy of death, till at last the oak was crackling, a plank splintered, another, and an opening was there. Monk put in his hand, felt the contact of chilly flesh, dragged the lad out, tossed the meagre form over his shoulders, and now, as though the fiend was after him, went flying, with many a blind stumble and fumble about the house. Wilson's arm clasped his neck, almost choking him, and from the dumb throat moaned a whimpering; while Monk, gasping beneath his load, roamed onward in random trepidation, till, spying a gleam like moonshine through a crack, he again and again drove his back against some boarding, tumbled outward, and, by a drop down of fifteen feet, was rolling in bracken.

Catching up Wilson afresh, Monk now made paces from the house; and had not run thirty yards, when behind him a disturbance like the bursting of some tremendous drum had the earth atremble; whereupon Monk, glancing backward, saw, like startled grouse in the midst of a spout of glare, a swarm of débris flying. Then followed three more brisk bangs; and the explosion, which was quite local to Wilson's room, was over. But some instinct of general ruin held Monk rooted where he stood during two full minutes of dreadful expectation; at the end of which, at a point not very remote from the place of the explosion, a case of masonry disengaged itself from the house, and thumped in powder to the ground; there came a greater rage of the gale; the house seemed to totter to its downfall; a larger wall of mason-work tumbled outward in a smoke of dust; from the interior there pealed forth, joined in one choir a shriek of many voices; and a moment later the whole area of the mansion nodded, roared, and hastily rushed into ruin. On Monk's breast lay the dumb lad sobbing.

A BUNDLE OF LETTERS
'Was the stranger's nose a true nose, or was it a false one?'—STERNE.

I
BLANCHE BATHURST TO EMILY HOLMES

' . . . Yes, Emily, I'm really in for it now! have promised, dear, and *been kissed*. . . . But the hornets'-nest! you can't conceive, for they all mean me, of course, to be cast a victim to that old baldhead Lord Isambard so as to connect the family with the aristocracy, and the mere suspicion of this makes them furious. Not that they know yet of my *solemn* engagement, but Edmond has suggested something to papa, and from mamma I have got *such* a piece of dignity; while my brother Claude said this morning, after breakfast, "why, we don't really know the fellow—his grandfather may have been a Moonlighter"; and a little Looloo chimed in that "it was far-fetched for a child like Blanche, hardly eighteen and a half yet, to be thinking of such things at all." Fancy that infant putting in her oar!

'How shall I describe Edmond to you? Tall, of course, and, in contrast with my own oaten loveliness, olive-dark; age about twenty-six; moustache like a negro's dream. Perfection save for one little—disfigurement?—a raspberry mark on his left middle finger! and his manner, dearie, all dignity, taciturnity, reserves of strength, so that I'm a bit nervous of the being! He looks as if he really meant people to do the thing that he likes; and as he happens to like *me*, I'm rather afraid that my lofty family will fail to stop him, in spite of forty old Lord Isambards, though it is quite true that we hardly know him exhaustively. Papa in his old judicial days was chums with his lawyer father, and Edmond himself is one of those lawyers who have never practised. . . .'

II
EMILY HOLMES TO BLANCHE BATHURST

'I was beginning to be astounded at your silence of two weeks, Blanchie, and now at last I know all the gushing reason, though, of course, I don't take your letters too seriously, since there *are*, you know, one or two matters in this scheme of things that one really should not treat freakishly, even at eighteen "and a half," as your Looloo truly remarks! . . . Singular to tell, I, too, have something big to give you in the matter of news—a business quite a month old now, and I should have overwhelmed you with the whole budget of details before but for the fact that mamma's illness kept me from settling down to the recounting of everything; and then my ingrained reticence shrank from giving you to taste of this strange fruit till it was well ripe. Frankly, then, girlie, I too—am *engaged*! Digest that, and forgive me for being over-long mum, since some natural shame at the flightiness of my age has restrained me from too soon prating. Now, however, you shall have it all launched into your ear in one heat; though, first of all, I can't help remarking upon the strangeness of the fact that your engagement and mine—if I can call yours an engagement—should be marked by circumstances so strikingly alike in point of time when, for instance—of time how long—and then the good man who has so given me his heart has not been too long known to us, nor been long here at St Arvens, just as your Mr Edmond (Mr Edmond *what*, by the way? think of not mentioning!) has not been long near you at Ash Thomas. This Ernest of mine also is Irish, and pretends to a profession—medicine—which he has never practised —both moneyed loungers, then. And now for the most marvellous part of all! for supposing that I, instead of you, had first written, then, in describing my nibbler, I might have used the very words in which you sketch yours—to the very raspberry mark! "Twin brothers," one might almost say, but, then, that can hardly be, since so far I have no notice of any brother in the case. . . .

'The resemblance is only on the outside, however, since my Ernest is hardly blessed with that so haughty "dignity," those "reserves of strength" which you laud in Mr Edmond—rather a good job, perhaps, since in this union your Emmie is certainly destined to be "the predominant partner," darling. Better so.

'I am for the moment all lovelorn for he left me without explanation about three weeks ago—indeed, he seems a great vagabond—but I expect him back daily. By the way, his last note to me was dated from Ashton, so that he was then quite close to Ash Thomas and to you.

'I'll write soon anew, and from you meantime look for a serious letter, perfect loyalty to your people, and a heart tempered by some little sort of head. . . .'

III
BLANCHE BATHURST TO EMILY HOLMES

'He wishes me to run away! The day before yesterday old Lord Isambard formally offered to me—I am in far too much agitation to tell you now of that awful scene, and of all the hullabaloo that the old brute has brewed for me in the house. I could get only one week's grace at his hands, and now Edmond is at me, saying that there is no way out save running, and that it is pressing, pressing! So, then, what is one to do? Dear, if you were only here with me! He has broken abruptly with the family now, and doesn't visit any more—oh! he is proud. They are all watching me, I know—hornets, hornets—and are in arms against you also, I am ashamed to say, for as I came in your last to the news of your engagement I kissed the letter before everybody, when Looloo called out some rudeness about "that Miss Holmes," mamma coughed, and Claude, assuming papa's "bench" manner, haw-hawed that "should the least unwholesome influence, from whatever quarter arising, appear to be brought to bear upon a young sister of his, he for one would feel no hesitation in taking the most obvious means to make it ineffectual!"—which perhaps means that he may dare to intercept your letters—I don't know; therefore I implore you to send them for the future to the Ashton post office, and Jenny, who is my only friend, will fetch them. Edmond leaves his usually at an agreed place, the beech-tree by Ritching Old Gate, and it is my good Jenny who fetches them; but having gone away a little on "highly important business," as he says, he is for the moment writing to the post office. . . .

'You say that your Mr Ernest last wrote you from Ashton near here? It is a coincidence that Edmond tore himself from me one evening to go there, and his last letter to me on the eleventh was dated from St Gompers, near you, so we seem to be going deep into coincidences . . . I have no question of yours to answer that I can remember—only this, that Edmond's name is O'Rourke. . . .'

IV

EMILY HOLMES TO BLANCHE BATHURST

'Ernest returned before I had time to write him as to his double who haunts you, and even now that he is here about me I have not yet sought to sound him. . . . You see, dear, I don't believe in coincidences; I dislike them, and this particular one I want to fathom in my own way and time.

'Meanwhile, the queerness of the thing deepens quite overmuch for my liking. That Ernest should write me from your countryside, and then Edmond you from mine—two men so apparently alike!—neither making any mention of the other, does seem to mean some species of mystery, and mystery in connection with myself is just what I won't stand.

'They are brothers, however; that is now ascertained, for both are O'Rourkes, and—here is a marvel!—that one note of difference between them that I noticed before is now, to my bewilderment, no more, for I do now see in Ernest a good deal of that "dignity" revealed in eye, pose, presence which you mentioned as a note of Edmond, and it is as if in his brief absence from here some sobering influence has turned my Ernest into a sterner man! Or is all this only my fancy? I am worried, dearie, aggrieved, and angry with myself and with everything. . . .

'Still I wait. Let *him* speak, for I really do not feel equal to the effort of forcing a revelation. His way has undergone such a change! You are to know that he hasn't once boldly kissed me in a good stark manner ever since his coming back—not once! I get formal caresses, my dear, eggs without salt—crowds of these, indeed, as if an effort were made to compensate quality with quantity! Yet the rogue was all on his knees three weeks ago.

'During the forenoon of the eleventh, the day on which you say that Edmond wrote you from St Gompers, as Ernest and I were strolling over the sands it got strongly into my head to have it out then and there with him, and the question was in my mouth; but somehow, when I looked at him, my will seemed to fail me, for the fellow's thoughts were far enough from me, *cela se voyait*, and I held my tongue. He was away on one of his long rambles all the rest of that day, going, as he told me afterwards, to—St Gompers! However, in the evening when he called at the house, and he and I were by ourselves, out it came at last, for I said then to him:

' "Do you know, I am still rather in the dark as to your relatives?"

'Ah, he shot me at once such a shrewd, quick look.

' "My relatives?" he says.

' "Have you any others," I said, "besides your mother and three sisters?"

' "Well—some," he says; "hosts of cousins."

' "In England?"

' "Yes," in a tone which meant "no more."

'And I, strange to tell, was done.

'But the next day, when we were again strolling over the harbour sands, I made another still bolder plunge, suddenly asking him if by chance he knew anybody named Edmond O'Rourke, and, frightened as I felt, I felt also "Now I have him," for he must either fib outright—and I thought that he would hardly do that—or bare his bosom. My dear, as the words passed my lips the man turned perfectly pallid.

' "Well, I do know such a person," he answers. "Do you—by chance?"

' "I know his name," I answered—a statement which seemed to scare him, he looked so queer.

' "How?" he asked, shortly, sternly.

' "I have heard it from a friend," was my answer.

' "Which friend?" he asked, looking over the sea—to hide his face, as I believe; but some instinct restrained me from mentioning your name, and I answered,

' "You wouldn't know her."

'Then there was silence for a while, till he remarks: "O'Rourke is hardly an uncommon name; there are many Edmond O'Rourkes and many Ernest O'Rourkes, so that, if you have seen such a name in the newspapers—"

' "Newspapers?" I said, stopping him too soon. "I have said that I heard it from a friend."

' "Quite so," he says, and that was all. I was as wise as ever.

'What is one to do with such a man! One would say that I am afraid of him—I! But this much is obvious—for the present we must remain where we stand, budging neither backward nor forward. You have written me another rather startling letter, darling. I quite supposed that the word "elope" had gone out with wigs and powder. I feel sure that both Lord Isambard and your father are to be reasoned with, and this Edmond of yours must be more restrained. As to resorting to any trickeries in directing my letters to you, that I won't do. Mr Claude is only a naughty boy, and I confide in your mother's common sense to check any such nonsense as he menaces. Do write soon and fully. . . .

V

BLANCHE BATHURST TO EMILY HOLMES

'Twice today has Jenny trudged to Ashton, and no line from you, dear Emmie. Oh, why don't you write? for, indeed, I am in deep, deep distress now, and most dreadfully lonely. I do not sleep—don't speak to a soul. They have some kind of scent, I know, of Edmond's secret letters, so I have been voted "rebellious". Jenny has got a month's warning, and when she goes I shall be all alone, while on the other side this Edmond is ever at me with his letters—such letters!—demanding me as his lawful own, a perfect stranger ordering me to forsake my father's home to go I don't know where with him; and I negotiate, I show slow and sluggish, but a fault in my heart can't quite say No—the dear. So what is one to do? Ah, if you were only here with me! But not even a letter from you, and in three days' time I am under orders to "make Lord Isambard happy!" Forgive if I can give no thought to aught but my poor little self. I can't ask after your Ernest—no interest for the moment; and where is the likeness you spoke of between your love and mine? Yours will be all calm to its end, like your calm self; mine all typhoon. But you will, will write instantly? If he has beaten you in my heart, he shan't teach my head to believe that you are not the best and sagest on earth. . . .'

VI
EMILY HOLMES TO BLANCHE BATHURST

'It seems to me wild beyond believing, Blanchie, that Claude or anyone at the Hall should even conceive the thought of stopping a letter of mine to you; and yet of course, poor dear, I wrote; and since this one *must* reach you—no miscarriage this time, for your life, as u far as I can read into your last, depends upon it—I send this to the Ashton office, and have just telegraphed you the words, "Do be good till you hear again," as a first hint of the disgraceful story that I have to give you. For my own part in it I don't overmuch agonise, I assure you; some little self-disgust perhaps; but, ah! for your poor little lambkin heart I do feel a qualm, and so soon as I have any chance of success I shall importune your mamma to lend you to my bosom, that I may woo and lure you back to your laughter. Meantime, you are to try to smile with that fullness of scorn which I feel, since this miserable being is certainly worth no more.

'I speak of "being," you see: singular, girlie—not dual; for indeed there is only one of them—only one, not two! Ah, no, they are not twin brothers, Blanchie, but nearer yet and dearer still, that so masterful Edmond of yours and that so fond Ernest of mine. Like two dewdrops, they have flown into one before my face. Oh, cheap that we have been to this fellow, who is now no doubt laughing his hardest at us two pigeons.

'How do I know? Mainly by second-sight, though I am not without my proofs, too. How easy with the new light to explain why "Ernest" should write me from your countryside, "Edmond" you from mine. Not two, but one! That is the phrase of shame which keeps up its ache in my brain. . . . And only listen to this. The time is evening, two days ago; the place, the drawing-room, I sitting dutifully on a stool at the feet of this gallant Gamaliel, feeling all the time that I ought to be at mamma's bedside, who is still very ill, but trying to look fond, though; far from feeling so, mainly because *he* is not so; for my lord sits chill and absent. Of stage-embraces we have had enough. I have sung myself hoarse for him (he pretends to be enormously fond of my voice). No more singing, then; but—happy thought—the album. I plant it on his knee, insisting that he interest himself in my friends. He turns a leaf, conceals a yawn, another, another; then he starts—visibly—turns gold-colour, the second time that I have seen the good man do that. But vigorous male beings don't turn gold for nothing, so one looks at the photograph on which his gaze is fixed, and notes that it is—yours!

'He speaks first: "You know Miss Blanche Bathurst, then?"

' "She is my friend, Ernest," I say.

'Ah what a wild look of scare came into that man's eyes!'

' "But do you, Ernest?" I asked.

' "Certainly—I have seen her," says he, this time with a boyish blush.

' "And she you?"

' "Why, yes, she too."

'Not another word I said; at that moment a knowledge of the whole shocking truth shot through me.

'You don't want more proof, but I have more. Listen! It was raining that night, and as he had brought a walking-stick I gave him an umbrella when he rose to go, so he left the stick behind, and the next morning, I happening to pick up this stick, my finger pressed a spring, the gold top flew open, and lo, in the hollow space lay a little photo of—*you!*

'Clearly he is attached to you. I found the next day that he carries about a handkerchief of yours like a big schoolboy, for he dropped the tiny rag, and I could catch sight of your initials. He adores you, then, as he was adoring me a month ago, as he will adore some other gosling this day month—a gallant little Gamaliel this!

'I haven't breathed a word to anyone. I have my reasons. I must hear from you; and then I shall endeavour to impress strongly upon this gallant how grave a matter it is to tamper with an English gentlewoman's love. . . .'

VII
BLANCHE BATHURST TO EMILY HOLMES

'Still no line from you, dear Emily, only the ominous wire, "Do be good till you hear again," which, by the way, was read by everybody, for I had to show it; but no other line, now when I die for your counsel. I haven't sent Jenny to Ashton to see any more, for I know that you won't send there now, and Edmond is sending his now to the Ash Thomas post office. For me no hope now, love—all, all's over; and oh! I do feel so outcast, wicked, lost, swallowed in awe, like one falling, falling for ever, down into nothingness. He ought to love me well—I part with all for him. It is for tonight, everything arranged for me by him and Jenny—Jenny jubilant. The stupid being has had much to do with my deciding so soon. She had received a month's warning, but now "feels all right," assures me that it is "the only way out in suchlike cases," and "all will end for the best." I spend tomorrow at a halfway inn; on the seventeenth to meet him at St Pancras at 11a.m.—then the Deluge. . . . By much study have got all details into my disordered head . . . I give you name of hotel in London to which if he wills, I shall go, as have been there before. His last to me again dated from St Gompers, so has been staying near you for some time . . . Love . . . Good-bye . . . in wildest haste. . . .'

VIII
EMILY HOLMES TO BLANCHE BATHURST

'Fate is all against us again, my poor wild love, for I can hardly fly to you, mamma lies so ill, and I must not leave her even for a day, if a letter will do as well, so I send this to the London hotel which you name, and since it will reach London before you, *immediately on reading it* you are to start in a cab to Waterloo Station, and bring your poor wounded bosom to me—your poor bruised, ill-used little bosom to your only refuge now!

'I wrote, you know, oh! of course I wrote—my last being directed to the Ashton office, but you were foolish before it could get to you, you see, you poor, poor goosie! Would to God that your brother, in stopping the others, had gone one step lower and *read* them, for then he would have unveiled your lover to you and saved you from yourself! But if not from yourself, from the man at any rate you shall be saved—I'll take care of that, if there be virtue in a woman's will, for he won't meet you at the station, not if I have to forge gyves of iron to peg him here—Heaven help me. Meantime, home, home to my heart (and then none need ever know at all the cause of your mutiny, for have you not eloped to me. . . . ?

IX
JENNY PRICE TO EMILY HOLMES

'Dear Miss Holmes,—I expect you'd scarce remember me, not seeing me these two years, but still, miss, no doubt Miss Blanche have written you something about me these last few weeks, saying as how I was helping her in her love-affair and that; so I take the liberty of writing to you, miss, to tell you as how everything has turned out queer with poor Miss Blanche since she's been up in town. I never was so down in the mouth, miss, nor I don't know what in the world to do for the best; for, first place, that shabby Mr O'Rourke did not turn up at the station, and the poor soul went downright out of her mind with the shame and fright, for she had had no end of a strain put on her nerves those last few days, and on the journey up went off into fits more than once; so what with not meeting Mr O'Rourke, and low her state was, and the strangeness of all away from her home, in London all alone, she all but had hysterics in the cab to the hotel, and she dropped her poor head on my shoulder and moaned so it went to anyone's soul, miss.

'So when she got to the hotel, pale as any ghost, they gave her your letter, saying as how she was to go to you now, and her lover was a faithless villain and that; and 'tisn't for the likes of me to blame you, miss, but that letter was a bit too strong like for her, seeing as she's a very high-strung young lady, is Miss Blanche, and she's been raving ever since, and the doctors they say it's brain-fever, and a bad case. If anything was to happen, what should I do? People'd be saying as it was me as was the cause of all, and I should never be able to fancy myself on this side Jawdon. I don't really know what to do now, for Mr Edmond wherever he is, don't know our address, write to her ma or pa I dursn't, and though I've pawned most of the things, what I've got won't last long the rate we're going, so do please, miss, write me what to do, as it is useless to think of moving her—the doctors wouldn't think of such a thing, but perhaps you can suggest something. . . .'

X
EDMOND O'ROURKE TO ERNEST O'ROURKE

'. . . I write you this, my dear fellow, with as much joy at your triumphant acquittal as sorrow at the series of ill-lucks to which my becoming your substitute before the good Miss Holmes has given rise. I tell you frankly, my good fellow, that "the importance of being Ernest" has appeared to me in so new and strong a light that I now regret having done the thing, for the whole ruse has gone askew through the stupid chance that Blanche and Miss Holmes are the closest of chums, and I now believe that it would have been far sounder politics on your part to have given into Miss Holmes's ear the gist of the charge brought against you, even though brought through your own imprudence, and to have trusted to her good heart to dismiss the affair beforehand. I know quite well that the evidence against you was strong, and I don't forget that your acquaintance with Miss Holmes had not been of such long standing as easily to bear the strain of such a scandal; but still, with such a girl—a girl, I give you my word, Ernest, worth her weight in gold—it would have been the safest, as, in any case, it would have been the bravest way.

'However, you chose the shyer course, dragging me in without asking my opinion, and when you had gone so far I could hardly refuse—when could I refuse you aught?—to take my part in your plan. I quite see, mind you, that there was no way of explaining your absence from Miss Holmes's side save by my taking your place, or else by a plain statement that that absence was forced upon you; but this plain statement might, I say, have been made by you, and would have saved no end of woes.

'As to Miss Holmes, she has acted beautifully. I tell you so; and if ever this girl becomes yours, Ernest, you will possess a pearl of such worth as is given to few to own.

'You will recall that when you came to Ashton that day to inform me of your scrape I mentioned to you my thought of dragging my darling from the grasp of her guardian dragons. It wasn't merely that they were on the point of casting her a victim to that old rake Lord Isambard, but I tell you, Ernie, the impertinence of those people went beyond all bounds, and in regard to *our* family, too, you know. . . . At all events, I pressed for flight, and finally, by Heaven's help, got her to venture. . . .

'Good then—each detail was arranged. I was to meet her at St Pancras Station at 11a.m. on the seventeenth, and, so as to be in London by the night of the sixteenth, I meant to leave Miss Holmes by the 5.20 of the sixteenth, though if I missed the 5.20 train there was still another at midnight. Well, I had given Miss Holmes two days' warning of my departure, little guessing the significance of her look of alarm as I informed her of my purpose of going away—such a look, though she said nothing. So on the sixteenth, sharp at 4 p.m., I went to bid her good-bye. Her way towards me that day was less strained than it had been; but she was palish, and in her good brown eyes brooded, I now remember, a look of some pretty grim significance.

' When I said: "I am come to say good-bye," her answer was:

' "How very often you run away from me!"

' "But this time," I said, "it is a matter of no little importance that takes me."

' "Ah!" she said; "and you go by the 5.20?"

' "Yes," I answered.

' "Well, but you still have over an hour," she said; "and I ought to make the most of you while I have you, so you are to take me for a last row."

'Nothing delights her more, as you know, than a bit of boating in the charming little St Arvens harbour, and in this way she and I have passed some part of most days; so out upon the water I took her, the sea looking like a round lake, and straight out we rowed, she sitting on the cushions, I plying strongly at the oars, for she likes the sensation of flight that the light gliding gives. Well, as you are aware, she is rather one of the still, staid ones, but that afternoon she talked, she sparkled, she chatted. I couldn't at all guess what was animating her, but her face glowed, and I grew so amused by her pretty prattle that I quite forgot the passage of time in the pleasure of her company. We were soon pretty far from the coast; the water had grown to a dark ground, and our petty ship began to dip and swagger like the big ocean ones, so that at last I had to stop Miss Holmes's chatter with the remark: "We should be getting back now, for we have never been half so far before."

' "What is the time?" she asked.

'I looked at my watch, and gave vent to a vexed sound.

' "What, it is later than you thought?" she asked.

' "It is five minutes past five," I said. "I've missed my train."

' "Oh!" she said ruefully.

' "I must only take the midnight train now," I said.

' "Quite so," she says—"the midnight train; meanwhile, there is no need now for us to hurry back, and the deep sea has such a fascination for me. Just let me take the paddles a little!"

'A little vexed, I got into her place and gave her mine, and I can see her again, my good fellow, as she sat there pulling, silent now, her lips rigidly fixed together, a few of her brown hairs blown about by the rising breeze, spray beating against my face, as our boat, winged like a gull by her strong strokes, flew over the ocean's floor, out and still out, till some raindrops turned my admiration of her to dismay, and looking forth, I saw storm-wrack rolling up over the horizon's edge.

'This I pointed out to her, saying, "The very best thing that we can do now is to hurry back as fast as we can."

'Something in the tone of her answer struck me cold. "Now?" she says. "What, already? Very well, then—*now*."

'In that same instant the deed was done, my dear fellow. With a little outpush on each side she cast our oars into the billows, and I, looking backward, saw them bobbing on the world of waters thirty yards astern.

'Of that night's griefs, for her and for me, I will give you each item when we meet; all I need inform you of at present is that she braved it like the great girlie that she is: rain and brawling squall and frothing breakers, and never one sigh from her!

'At first, I declare, I thought the girl stark crazy—till all the meaning of her grim act was made clear to me, this, of course, being her only possible plan to prevent the meeting between Blanchie and me at St Pancras the next morning, and the row of the winds could not drown the harsh, trenchant impeachment in which she charged me with deceiving her, with meaning to deceive her Blanche! How coldly she regimented her facts before me, proof on proof, I cowering under her lash, my face turned away from her, unable to clear myself, the secret being yours and not mine! Only once, when I wished to throw my jacket about her, and she haughtily forbade my approach, I then, for her sake, almost betrayed you; but remembering that you were still unacquitted I held my tongue.

'Several times during the night we were quite nigh to drowning, particularly when, about two hours before the dawn, a current brought us close upon the half-round of rocks that they call Hawtry Rocks. I'll describe to you when we meet the feat of luck by which we cheated death. Near three in the morning it became bitterly cold, and some swells broke over the boat that nearly swamped us. I then caught Miss Holmes's hands in order to warm them, and would you believe? even then, though only half-conscious she would have none of me. However, I had her garnered in my arms when at half-past four an outgoing smack overhauled and picked us up, all signs of life at that hour having left her. Now, however, the worst is over; and though during two days the doctors shook very grave heads, and though she remains unconscious, her condition is no longer said to be "dangerous."

'So far, then, has our affair brought us. "All's well, however, that ends well, and since a letter from Blanchie, found on Miss Holmes, had in it the address of a London hotel, I have thus been able to find the poor child, whom horror at not meeting me at the station threw into a dangerous state; but she, too, appears to be doing well; and I, meantime, am speeding daily between the two, haunting the railway, my heart drawing me to my darling in London, and all my sense of respect back to the bedside at St Arvens.

'Everything now depends upon their getting better, and upon your speedy re-appearance; and, given these, I have nothing but good outlooks for our future and theirs. . . .'

HUGUENIN'S WIFE
'Ah! bitter-sweet!'—Keats.

HUGUENIN, my friend—the man of Art and thrills and impulses—the *boulevardier,* the *persifleur—must,* I concluded with certainty, be frenzied. So, at last, I reasoned when, after years of silence, I received from him this letter:—

' "*Sdili,*" my friend; that is the name by which they now call this ancient Delos. Wherefore has it been written, "so passeth the glory of the world."

'Ah! but to me it is—as to *her* it was—still Delos, the Sacred Island, birthplace of Apollo, son of Leto! On the summit of Cynthus I look from my dwelling, and within the wild reach of the Cyclades perceive even yet the offerings of fruit arriving from Syria, from Sicily, from Egypt; to festival—I note the flutter of their holy robes—the breeze once more floats to me their "Songs of Deliverance".

'The island now belongs almost entirely to me. I am, too, almost its sole inhabitant. It is, you know, only four miles long, and half as broad, and I have bought up every available foot of its face. On the flat top of the granite Cynthus I live, and here, my friend, I shall die. Fetters more inexorable and horrible than any that the limbs of Prometheus ever felt rivet me to this crag.

'A friend! That is the thing after which my sick spirit famishes. A *living man*: of the dead I have enough; of living monsters, ah, too much! and a servant or two, who seem persistently to shun me—this is all I possess of human fellowship. Yet I dare not implore you, my old companion, to come to the comfort of a sinking man in this place of desolation. . . .'

The epistle continued in this strain of mingled rhapsody and despair, containing, moreover, a long rigmarole on the Pythagorean dogma of the metempsychosis of the soul. Three times did the words 'living monsters' occur.

From London to Delos is a journey; yet, conquered during a long vacation by an irresistible impulse, and the fond memories of other days, I actually found myself, on a starry night, disembarking on the sands that bound the once renowned harbour of the tiny island, and my arrival may be dated by the fact that it took place just two months before the extraordinary phenomena of which Delos was the scene during the night of 13th August, 1890. I first crossed the ring of flat land that almost encircles the islet, and then commenced the ascent of the central rise, the air slumbrous with the breath of rose, jasmine, almond, with the call of the cicala, the shine of the firefly. In forty minutes I had walked into a tangled garden, and placed my hand on the back of a tall man, habited in Attic garments, who was pacing there.

With a start he faced me.

'Oh,' he said, panting, and clapping his hands upon his chest, 'I was awfully startled! My heart—'

It was Huguenin, and yet not he. The beard rolling over his snowy robes of wool was still ebon as ever; but the fluff of hair that floated with every zephyr over his face and neck was a lifeless fluff of wool white. He stared at me with the lifeless and cavernous eyes of a man long dead.

When we entered the dwelling together, the mere appearance of the building was enough to convince me that in some mysterious way, to some morbid degree, the past had fettered and darkened the intellect of my friend. The mansion was of Hellenic type, but nothing less than mad in extent—a desert more than a habitation, a Greek house multiplied many times over into a congeries of Greek houses, like objects seen through angular glasses. It consisted of a single storey, though here and there on the flat roof there rose a second layer of apartments, attained by ladders. We walked through a door—opening inwards—into a passage, which took us to a courtyard, or *aule,* surrounded by Corinthian pillars, and having in the middle an altar of marble to *Zeus Herkeios.* Around this court were ranged chambers, *thalamoi,* hung with velvets; and the whole house—made up of a hundred and a hundred

Huguenin's Wife

reproductions of such courtyards with their surrounding chambers—formed a trackless Sahara of halls through whose labyrinths the most crafty could not but fail to thread his way.

'This building,' Huguenin said to me, some days after my arrival, 'this building—every stone, plank, drapery—was the creation of my wife's wild fancy.'

I stared at him.

'You doubt that I have, or had, a wife? Come with me; you shall—see her face.'

He now led the way through the windowless house, lighted throughout the day and night by the reddish ray shed from many little censer lamps of terra-cotta filled with *nardinum*, an oil pressed from the blossom of the fragrant grass *nardus* of the Arabs.

I followed Huguenin through a good number of the rooms, noticing that, as he moved slowly onward, he kept his body bent, seeming to seek for something; and this something I quickly found to be crimson thread, laid down on the floor to afford a clue for the foot through the mazes of the house. Suddenly he stopped before the door of one of the apartments called *amphithalamoi*, and, himself staying without, motioned me to enter.

Now I am hardly a man of what might be called a tremulous diathesis, yet it was not without a tremor that I looked round that room. At first I could discern nothing under the glimmer from a single *lampas* hanging in the middle, but presently a painting in oils, unframed, occupying nearly one side of the room, grew upon my sight: the painting of a woman: and my pulses underwent a strange agitation as I gazed on her face.

She stood robed in flowing ruby *peplos*, with her head thrown back, and one hand and arm pointing starkly outward and upward. The countenance was not merely Grecian—antique Grecian, as distinct from modern—but Grecian in a highly exaggerated and unlife-like degree. Was the woman, I asked myself, more lovely than ever mortal was before—or loathsome? For Lamia stood there before me—'shape of gorgeous hue, vermilion-spotted, golden, green and blue'—and a kind of surprise held me fixed as the image slowly took possession of my vision. The Gorgon's head! whose hair was snakes; and as I thought of this I thought, too, of how from the guttering gore of the Gorgon's head monsters rose; and then, with abhorrence, I remember Huguenin's ravings as to 'monsters'. I stepped nearer, in order to analyse the impression almost of dread wrought upon me, and I quickly found—or thought that I found—the key: it lay in the lady's eyes: the very eyes of the tigress: greedy glories of green glaring with radii of gold. I hurried from her.

'You have seen her?' Huguenin asked me with an eager leer of cunning.

'Yes, Huguenin,' I said, 'she is very beautiful.'

'She painted it herself,' he said in a whisper.

'Really!'

'She considered herself—she *was*—the greatest painter since Apelles.'

'But now—where is she?'

He brought his lips to my ear.

'Dead. *You*, at any rate, would say so.'

Well, to words so apparently senseless I would pay no attention then; but they recurred to me when I unearthed the circumstance that it was his way, at certain intervals, to make furtive visits to distant districts of the dwelling. Our bed-chambers being close together I could not fail, as time passed, to notice that he would rise in the dead of night, when he supposed me drowsing, and gathering together the fragments of our last repast, depart rapidly and soundlessly with them through the vastness of the house, led always in one particular direction by the thread of silk whose crimson lay over the floor.

I now set myself strenuously to the study of Huguenin. The name and nature of his physical sickness, at least, was clear—the affection to which physicians have given the name Cheyne Stoke's Respiration, compelling him to lie back at times in an agony of inhalation, and groan for air. The bones of his cheeks seemed to be near appearing through their sere trumpery of mummy-skin; the *alæ* of his nose got no repose from their extravagance of expansion and retraction. But even this wreck of a body might, I believe, be rescued, were it not that to assuage the rage and feverishness of such a *mind* the spheres contained no thyme. For one thing, a most queer belief in some unnamed fate hanging over the little land he lived on haunted him. Again and again he recalled to me all that in the far past had been written in regard to Delos: the strange notion contained both in the Homeric and the Alexandrian hymns to the

Delian Apollo that Delos was *floating;* or that it was only held by chains; or that it had only been thrown up from the ocean as a temporary resting-place for Ortygia in her birth-giving; or that it might *sink* again before the spurning foot of the newborn god. He was never weary, through hours, of pursuing, as if in soliloquy, a species of sleepy exegesis of such scriptures as we read together. 'Do you know,' he said to me, 'that the Greeks really believed the streams of Delos to rise and fall with the rise and fall of the Nile? Could anything point more strongly to the extraordinary character of this land, its far-extending volcanic constructions, occult geologic eccentricities?' Then he might recite the punning line of the very old Sibylline prophecy—

Ἔσται καὶ Σάμος ἄμμος ἐοεῖται Δῆλος ἄδηλος; *

often, also, having recited it, he would strike from the repining chords of a lyre the theme of a threnody which, as he told me, his wife had composed to suit the line; and when to the funeral ruth of this tune—so wild with woe and whining, that I could never listen to it without a thrill—Huguenin added the sadness of his now so hollow voice, the intensity of effect upon me got to the intolerable degree, and I was glad of that pallid gloaming of the mansion, which partially hid my emotion.

'Remark, however,' he said one day, 'the meaning of the "far-seen" as regards Delos: it means "glorious" "illustrious"—far-seen to the spiritual rather than to the physical eye, for the island is not very elevated. The words "sink from sight" must, therefore, be supposed to have the corresponding significance of an extinction of this glory. And now think whether or not this prophecy has not been already fulfilled, when I tell you that this sacrosanct land, which no dog's foot was once permitted to touch, on which no man was permitted to be born or be buried, bears at this moment on its bosom a monster more loathsome than even a demon's brain, I believe, ever conceived. A literal and physical fulfilment of the prophecy cannot, I consider, be always distant.'

But all this esotericism was not native to Huguenin: his mind, I was convinced, had been ploughed into by some very potent energy, before ever this growth had choked it. I enticed him, little by little, to speak of his wife.

---

* "And Samos shall be sand, and Delos (the far-seen) sink from sight."

The Pale Ape and Other Pulses

She was, he told me, of a very antique Athenian family, which by constant effort had preserved its purity of blood; and it was while moving through Greece in a world-weary mood that, on reaching one night the village of Castri, there, on the site of the ancient Delphi, in the centre of an angry throng of Greeks and Turks, who threatened to rend her to fragments, he first saw Andromeda his wife. 'This incredible courage,' he said, 'this vast originality was hers, to take upon herself the part of a modern Hypatia—to venture upon the task of the bringing back of the gods, in the midst of fanatics, at the latter end of a century like the present. The crowd from which I rescued her was howling round her in the vestibule of a just completed temple to Apollo, whose cult she was then and there attempting to set up.'

The love of the woman fastened upon her preserver with passionate fervour, and Huguenin, constrained by the vigour of a will not to be resisted, came at her bidding to live in the grey building of her creation at Delos: in which solitude, under which shadow, the man and the woman faced each other. Ere many weeks it was revealed to the husband that he had married a seer of visions and a dreamer of dreams. And visions of what tinge! and dreams of what madness! He confessed to me that he was awed by her, and with his awe was blended a feeling which, if it was not fear, was akin to fear. That he loved her not at all he now knew, while the extravagance of her passion for him he grew to regard as gruesome. Yet his mind took on the hue of hers; he drank in her doctrines, followed her as a satellite. When for days she hid herself from him, he would wander desolate and full of search over his pathless home. Finding that she habitually yielded her body to the delights of certain seeds that grew on Delos, he found the courage to frown, but ended by himself becoming a bond-slave to the drowsy *ganja* of Hindustan. So, too, with the most strange fascination which she exercised over the animal world: he disliked it—dreaded it; regarded it as excessive and unnatural; but looked on only with the furtive eye of suspicion, and said nothing. When she walked she was accompanied by a magnetised *queue* of living things, felines in particular, and birds of large size; while dogs, on the contrary, shunned her, bristling. She had brought with her from the continent a throng of these followers, of which Huguenin had never beheld the half, since they were imprisoned in unknown

Huguenin's Wife

nooks of the building; and anon she would vanish, to reappear with new companions. Her kindness to these creatures should, no doubt, have been sufficient to account for her power over them; but Huguenin's mind, already grown morbid, probed darkly after other explanation. The primary *motif* of this unquietness doubtless lay in his wife's fanaticism on the matter of the Pythagorean dogma of the transmigration of souls. On this theme Andromeda, it was clear, was outrageously deranged. She would stand, he declared, with her arm outstretched, her eyes wild-staring, her body rigid, and in a rapid recitative—like the rapt Pythoness—prophesy of the mutations prepared for the spirit of man, dwelling, above all, with contempt, on the paucity of animal forms in the world, and insisting that the spirit of an original man, disembodied, *should and must* re-embody itself in a correspondingly original form. 'And,' she would often add, 'such forms exist, but the God, willing to save the race from frenzy, hides them from the eyes of common men.'

It was long, however, before I could get Huguenin to describe the final catastrophe of his wedded life. He related it in these words:—

'You now know that Andromeda was among the great painters—you have gloated upon her portrait of herself. Well, one day, after dilating, as was her wont, on the paucity of forms, she said, 'But you, too, shall be of the initiated: come, you shall see *something*.' She then went swiftly, beckoning, looking back often to smile on me a fond patronage, and I followed, till she stopped before a lately finished painting, pointing. I will not attempt—the attempt would be folly—to tell you what thing I saw before me on the canvas; nor can I explain in words the tempest of anger, of loathing and disgust, that stirred within me at the sight; but at that blasphemy of her fancy, I raised my hand to strike her head; and to this moment I know not if I struck her. My hand, it is true, felt the sensation of contact with something soft; but the blow, if blow there was, was hardly hard enough to harm a creature far feebler than man. Yet she fell; the film of death spread over her upbraiding eye; one last thing only she spoke, pointing to the uncleanness: 'You may yet see it in the flesh'; and so, still pointing, sped away.

'I bore her body, embalmed in the Greek manner by an artist of Corinth, to one of the smaller apartments on the roof, and saw, as I moved to leave her in her gloom, the mortal smile on her lips within the open coffin. Two weeks later I went again to visit her. My friend, she had vanished—but for the bones; and from the coffin, above that skull, two eyes—living—the very eyes of Andromeda, but full of a newborn brightness—the eyes, too, of the horror she had painted, whose form I now made out in the darkness—looked out upon me. After I had slammed the door, I fainted on the stair.'

'The suggestion,' I said to him, 'which you seem to wish to convey is that of a transition of forms, from man to animal; but, surely, the explanation that the monster, brought by your wife into the house, or born in it, imprisoned unawares by you with the dead, and maddened by famine, fed on the body, is, if not less horrible, yet less improbable.'

He looked doubtingly at me a moment, and then coldly said: 'There was no monster imprisoned with the dead.'

But at least, I pleaded, he would see the necessity of flying from that place. He replied with the avowal that it was no longer doubtful to him, from the effect which any neglect to minister to the monster's wants had upon his own health, that his life was bound up with the life of the being he stayed to maintain; that with the *second* murder which he should perpetrate—nay, with the attempt to perpetrate it, as by flight from the island—his life would be forfeited.

I accordingly formed the idea to effect the deliverance of my friend in spite of himself. Two months had now passed; the end of my visit was drawing near; yet his maladies of brain and body were not relieved: and it pained me to think of leaving him once more alone, a prey to his manias.

That very day, then, while he slept his damp trances, I started the tramp on the track of the scarlet thread. So far it hauled out its length, and the halls through which it passed were of such uniformity, and its path so wound about, that I could not doubt but that the clue once snapped at any point, the voyage along its route could be accomplished only by the most improbable chance. I followed the thread to its end, where it stopped at the foot of a ladder-stair. This I ascended to a door at its top, a door with a hole in it close to the bottom, big enough to admit a plate; but, as I placed my foot on the uppermost step, a whine, complaining low, with a wild likeness to a woman's wail, sent me skipping, sick, whence I came.

But, some little distance from the steps, I broke the thread, and, gathering it up in my hand as I ran, again broke it near the region of the mansion which we occupied.

'In this way,' I said, as I held the mass of thread to the flame of a lamp, 'shall a man be saved.'

I watched him afterwards through my half-shut eyes, as he departed, haggard and shuddering, hugging himself, on his nightly errand; and my heart galloped in an agony of disquiet while I awaited his coming again.

He was long. But when he came, he came swiftly, softly into my chamber and shook me by the shoulder. On his face was a look of unusual coolness, of dignity, of mystery.

'Wake up,' he said: 'I wish you to leave me tonight.'

'But tell me—'

'I will take no refusal. Trust me this once, and go. There is a danger here. Two of the fisher-folk of the harbour will convey you over to Rhenea before the morning.'

'But danger!' I said—'from what?'

'I cannot tell you: from the destiny, whatever it be, which awaits me. The thread on which my life depends is *snapped.*'

'But suppose I tell you—'

'Ah! . . . you hear that?'

He held up his hand and hearkened: it was a sound of howling round the house.

'It is the wind rising,' I muttered, starting up.

'But that—which followed: didn't you *feel* it?'

I made him no answer.

He now clasped with his arms a marble column upon which he rested his forehead, while with one foot he kept on patting the floor; in which posture, quite demoralised and craven, he remained for some time, while the wind continued to rise; and suddenly he span toward me with a scream in a rapture of fear.

'Now at least—*you feel it!*'

I could not deny: it was as if the island had rocked a little to and fro on a pivot.

Now thoroughly demoralised myself, I now caught Huguenin's arm, and sought to draw him from the column which, muttering low, he was again hugging. But he would not stir; and I, determined in any event to stay by him, stood hearing the earthquake's increase while he seemed to take no further note of anything, motionless but for the motion of his foot. In this way an hour went by: at the end of which interval the rocking had become strong, rapid and continuous.

There came a second, when captured by a new panic, I sprang to shake him, understanding that some lamp had been dashed down in that passion of the mansion's agitation.

'Why, man!' I cried, 'have you parted with every sense? Can't you feel that the house is in flames?'

On this his eyes, which had become dazed and dull, blazed up with a new lunacy.

'Then,' he suddenly shouted in a passion of loudness, 'I say she *shall* be saved!' The feathered cheetah!'

Before I could lay hold of the now foaming maniac, he had dashed past me into a passage. I followed in hot pursuit through rooms and corridors that seemed to reel in a furious dream of heat and reek, hoping that he, weak of lung, would fall choked and exhausted. But some energy seemed to lend him strength—he rushed onward like the hurricane; some mysterious feeling seemed to lead him—never once did he hesitate.

And after all the long chase, which ever swayed at the rocking of the land, but never stopped, I saw that the intuitions of insanity had not failed the madman—he got to the goal he gasped after. I saw him fly up the ladder, whose foot was in a pool of fire, saw him fly to the door of the tomb of Andromeda, already flagrant, and drag it open. But as he dragged it, there broke out of the room—above the roaring of the conflagration, and of the gale, and of that thousandfold growling of the ground—a shriek, shrill yet ugly with gutturalness, which congealed me in that heat; and immediately I saw proceeding from the interior a creature whose obscenity and vileness language has no vocabulary to describe. For if I say that it was a cat—of great size—its eyes glaring like a conflagration—its fat frame wrapped in a mass of feathers, grey, vermilion-tipped—with a similitude of miniature wings on it—with a width of tail vast, down-turned, like the tails of birds-of-paradise-how by such words can I express half of all the retching of my nausea, the shame, the hate . . . The fire had ere this reached the thing, and on fire I could spy it fly rather than spring at Huguenin's heart; then its fangs like grapnels buried in his breast, the gluttony of its gums that met on his gullet, I saw through a fog of feathers raining, he tottering, tearing at the feathery horror, as backward he toppled from the landing over the spot where a moment before the ladder had stood.

By blessed luck, as I rapidly ran thence, I stumbled upon some exit, to find outside the night quite cloudless, star-lit, though a whirl of all the winds of the world were whistling within the vault of sky that night. In descending, too, to the level, I remarked a rather scorched aspect of some of the leafage, and at one spot saw a series of conical openings in the ground with greenish scoriae round their edges. Lower still, I stood on a bluff, and looking over the sea, witnessed a sight sublime to wildness: for the sea, too hurried to show billow, to show ripple, and lit up deep within its depth with a sheen of phosphorescence, was speeding as if after the steeds of Diomedes with the fleetest meaning towards Delos. Delos, indeed, seemed to 'float,' to be swimming like a little doomed fowl counter to the swoop of the boundless. With the morning's light I passed away from this mysterious shrine of Grecian piety, the final sight that greeted my gaze being the still rising reek of Huguenin's grave.

MANY A TEAR

'God counts a woman's tears.'—THE TALMUD

I FIRST heard the name of Margaret Higgs one gloomy afternoon, when passing over the Chase by Tydenham, with Severn (they don't say '*the*' Severn there) trailing itself away through a vale of haze far down on my right. The aged clergyman I was making the journey with showed me the mass of rags and grey locks, where the woman sat alone on a rock on the Chase, saying to me—

'Mark that woman, a remarkable being I assure you, a woman who during sixteen years has plumbed even the deeps of human woe; for I say that if ever the arm of the Almighty bared itself to be known openly in the affairs of men, it was in that life. There, like a pine blighted by the lightning's wrath, sits Margaret now, a living pledge of that Power which governs the world.'

He spoke with no little solemnity, though I must say that when he went on to tell me the facts, he left me utterly unconvinced of this 'arm of the Almighty'; and I hope that by this time he, too, has nobler thoughts with regard to Margaret Higgs.

'I remember her when she had no resemblance to the object you see there,' he told me, 'a shapely wench with a tripping run on her toes, soft-spoken and most soft-eyed, dark blue eyes and black hair, a gay gossip—"news-hunter" they say here—with a prayer-book in her hand in the lanes on Sunday, and a name for "knocking around" with the young men; one of those earth-born souls of this part, unconscious of a world beyond Severn—save of Gloucester, because the magistrates say to the naughty ones: "Go to Gloucester for a month."

'She came of good farmer-folk in a small way, who died almost together, upon which Margaret chose to marry beneath her, a quarry-man from the Wyebanks near, a thickset, rather taciturn and nervous person, named Higgs, a widower some fifteen years Margaret's senior. He had a son of twelve or so called Fred Higgs;

and I think I have heard it said that as a girl Margaret had had the nursing of this boy, and that it was her fondness for the boy which caused the heiress to make choice of the father.

'Well, Margaret and Higgs got on very well for several years. I have observed them driving toward St Bride's of a weekend to market, frequently have called in to visit them, and they appeared happy. However, one summer there came to lodge with them a stranger—a sailor they say he was, though, as the house stands well out of the way in a bower, and as the stranger never at all showed his nose abroad, not much is known of him; one or two, however, of the Woolaston villagers lower down the mountain—a group of people known as the most "news-hunting" in the country—gave it out that the stranger was a good-looking chap, and that Margaret had lost her heart to him; a tale which was confirmed when he was one afternoon loudly ordered out of the house by Higgs, and was observed to pass out of the house and away over the mountains.

'Well, some time after nine that night, when the boy Fred Higgs went to bed, Margaret, from motives of revenge, probably, destroyed her husband; for from that night Higgs has never been seen, and a daft fellow called Felix, who would frequently roam the countryside all night, reported that near three that morning he had seen Mrs Higgs struggling in a storm across the fields towards Severn beneath the burden of a body.

'This was all the evidence to begin with, except the queer fact that Margaret breathed not a syllable to anyone with regard to her husband's disappearance; but other signs and evidences soon followed, as I have told you, from—Heaven itself.

'Owing, maybe, to the fact that this witness, Felix, was not a man able to appreciate the nature of an oath, the police took no open action in the matter; and at this apparent sluggishness of the law, you never saw such a gush of fury, every boatman for miles up the two rivers becoming an eye to scan the waters for a body; and both where the banks are all mud, and where there are reaches of beach, parties of diggers, organised by the villagers, were ferreting for a buried body.

'Well, no body was ever discovered; but by society, I can tell you, a way was discovered to avenge itself, and the woman was punished. The baker's cart ceased to wait at Woodside farm, the butcher declined to deal; even so far off as St Bride's and the

Forest of Dean Margaret Higgs could neither sell her starved calf nor get meal for her pig, nor find a forgiving smile.

' "Her's done away wi'n right enough," was the word everywhere: "hanging be too good for she, and shame ought to cover the face of the police."

'Passing by the farm one morning, I walked up the garden-path, and saw Margaret. The round of industry there was suspended now, her stepson appeared to be aiming shots at imaginary rabbits, and the young woman, swinging her knee between her hands, was seated on the door-sill of her snowy low home. She sprang up to offer me a chair, and I said then sorrowfully to her: "Well, Mrs Higgs, things are not so well with you as they have been," at which she at once became visibly inflamed, and cried out, "the gossiping, news-hunting lot, ignorant as wagon-horses! I do have nothing off they, Mr Somerset! They don't keep me! Why should I trouble about what they have to say?"

' "But how, Mrs Higgs, do you propose to live, to manage the farm?" I asked.

' "I did live and find bread for the boy before, and I'll do it again, sir," she answered.

' "But for one to defy many is up-hill work, and you without a protector now," I said . . . "Tell me the truth, Margaret," I added, "is Higgs dead?"

'She stood against the wall, eyeing the ground, and after a silence said with a shrug of her shoulders: "Er *be* dead, I suppose—God knows; I don't."

'Well, I was angry at this callous shrugging, and left her at once.

'The next Sunday she dared to come to church, and as I surmised that this would be resented, especially as she walked up the aisle with so haughty a toss of the head, I uttered in my sermon a few words as to the beauty of Christian forbearance. But it had no effect, and all up the back lane that leads steeply to Woodside, though it was a stormy afternoon, Margaret was followed by the congregation—most of them her cousins, and cousins of one another. They did not at first molest her, but uttered coughs, whistles, catcalls; all which she endured without looking round, till by becks and signs they managed to induce her boy to leave her side and join the enemy, and thenceforth the walk became a crossfire of abuse yelled from side to side, the woman hastening on in front afraid, with a grey face, but defiant eyes on fire, the people eagerly speeding upon her heels with no peaceable meaning.

' "Go on!" she shouted to them, laughing with a rather ghastly grin of the mouth—"you gossiping, news-hunting lot! Shame ought to cover your face!"

' "Where's Higgs?" they all roared at her.

' "Go on, you! ignorant as wagon-horses, with your silly, foolhardy questions!"

'And so till they came to her house, where the crowd surrounded her; and now, finding herself at bay, her defiance suddenly failing, the woman broke into tears, and falling to her knees, called out upon the Almighty in passionate tones of reproach, saying "What have I done, my good God? If I have done any wrong, send that my house may be burnt to the ground, may every evil befall me, may I be struck paralysed from my crown to my foot—" a vow so apparently hearty, and so awful to the villagers that they went away and left her.

'But that night her house was burned to the ground.

'When the crowd had left her, she had flung herself upon a couch in the house, where she had remained in the grip of an ague till nine in the night; and getting up then to go to bed her still trembling hand had dropped the lamp . . .

'The news of that thing flew that night like loosened effluvia, and in a few minutes Woolaston was at Woodside. They found the boy, Fred Higgs, confined in the house by the fire, for in the first panic Margaret had run out, calling out to him, but he had been asleep, and now was screaming at his window, which was too little for him to squeeze through to leap to the ground. Seeing this, some of the crowd darted off to look for the orchard-ladder, when Margaret herself, to the awe of all, dived back into the fire, and presently appeared tearing at the framework of the boy's window, half of which was a fixture, and half a sideward slide. Well, as she was ever a person of great strength, the woodwork gave way to her tuggings, leaving space for the leap to the ground, and they came down safely.

'Fred Higgs was taken home by Price, the grocer; and Margaret, now all bald and baked on one side of the face, found a shelter in her stable with the body of her starved horse, which had died that day.

'But the woman's spirit was not yet broken. When, the next morning, Morgan, the policeman, called to invite her, things being as they were, to make a clean breast of what had happened to Higgs, she still sat dumb, rocking her body to and fro. She seems to have entertained still the crazy hope of carrying on the farm on which she was born, but that same day Mr Millings, Loreburn's land-steward, called to tell her that, of course, she must go now, offering, however, to give her a price for her implements, etc., which no one else would buy of her. These terms she had to accept; but she showed then as ever a fierce determination not to leave the place of her birth, and like a spider whose web has been torn, at once the woman set mutely to work to build up her life anew.

'On the third day after the fire she came with her face in bandages to my daughter, Nina, who owned a cottage high up there near the Chase; and though I felt bound to warn my daughter of the danger of letting, she chose to do so. On this the woman went away to Newport, bought there some new things, took her sow and fowls to her new abode, and was about once more to commence housekeeping. But it was not to be: for when all was ready, and she went down to Price, the grocer, who had taken in her boy, the boy roundly refused to go with her, saying to her: "No mother, I don't want to see thee face never again."

'These words seemed to strike the woman quite silly; and turning toward the crowd for pity, with a wry mouth that tried to smile, she let slip the words: "Why, it was for him chiefly I did it!"

' "Did it! You hear her? Did what?" cried some, while the rest of the boors booed and hissed her.

' "Come with your mother, hearty," wooed the woman to the boy, "don't be hard."

' "Thee go away," said the boy, emboldened by the mob, "thee bisn't my own mother, nor I never did despise anybody so much as I do despise thee, never in all my life, and shame ought to cover thee face."

'Margaret looked awe-struck at this last disaster. She said nothing more, but throwing her arm languidly at him was gone with lagging steps, as if broken down now, given over, cowed, and done for; nor from that day, I think, did she ever show any resistance to whatever was done to her, except once, when she threw a stone at a throng of boys who were pursuing her.

'Morgan, the policeman, however, and I also, thought that with regard to the boy, to whom from his youth the woman had ever been a good mother, a hardship had been done her; especially as without his help her new nook of land would be of little use to her. So after three weeks of talk the grocer formally agreed to give up the boy; and the same morning Morgan, happening to be passing up there, called to Margaret across her gate that her boy would be coming back to her at once. Upon this she seems to have run to stand under an ash tree at the end of the lane to see him coming up the hill; several persons, hurrying past in the rain, saw her standing there that day with her dress thrown over her head; and though the boy did not come for some hours, there she stood patiently on the look out, until the afternoon had become late and dark with storm. At last the boy came. But it was to find her lying helpless on her right side, apparently struck by lightning—the ash, at any rate, had been shivered, and she was found paralysed right down one side. Babbling with her blighted tongue, she begged the boy to give her a hand to try to get her home without uttering a word to anyone, but he, as if out of his wits, flew down the hill, howling out the news to the four winds.

'Well, however deep the woman's sin, what followed for her that evening is really shocking to recount, for a legion of fiends seem to have taken possession of the people to make a scene out of pandemonium on the mountain that evening. The words arose, "drum her out"—for, of course, whatever doubt may have lingered in any mind with regard to Margaret's guilt was gone now, since all that her vow had called down upon herself was now fallen upon her; nor did the rain and darkness make any difference; with one accord the crowd started up the mountain. Happily, she guessed their approach, and in her terror, gathering whatever forces remained to her, she fled before them, managing to drag her frame into some bush before they reached the tree; while they, going on to her cottage to find her, and not finding her, threw all her new goods into a hurly-burly, and by accident or design burned to the ground my daughter's house. It was not till the next morning that Margaret was discovered lying in the field called the Morplepiece, and was then carried away by the police, to be put into the St Bride's infirmary.

'There pressure was afresh brought to bear upon the woman to make some sort of confession, but she remained as dumb as ever; and after some months was sent out with that maimed drag in her gait and speech, which even now marks her. She dared again, though now penniless and hopeless of gaining a living here, to face the load of pain that awaited her in her native place; and hereabouts, Heaven knows how, has continued to exist. My daughter Nina, whose heart has always deeply grieved for her, sometimes of an angry night will say to me: "That poor Margaret Higgs, papa; perhaps out on the Chase in it all." Aye, and I have known her go out with a groom and a lantern to look for the woman, and on discovering her under one of those two-arched kilns which are common in this part, has wooed the poor soul to come home with her. Margaret when dragged has come, but always before morning was gone again. Indeed, she had soon become much of a wild woman, imbued with the mood of stormwinds and dark nights, as shy and gloomy-eyed as those shaggy nags on the Chase, her only mates, whose manes and great tails the gales up there ever fret; so that belated yokels on their way home have often paused to hearken to some moan or laugh of hers in the dark. Once she was sent to prison, when, ever unlucky, on happening to throw a stone at a throng of boys, the stone cut one of them, and the magistrates gave her their "go to Gloucester for a month." One of these magistrates, by the way, was none other than her stepson, Fred Higgs, who had been taken up by some mysterious business man—in Glasgow they say it was—had graduated at Oxford, and is now, you may say, one of our magnates. The man has simply ignored his stepmother's existence.

'However, the new proprietor of Glanna has given orders that the woman be housed, and provided with the means of a livelihood—has let it be understood, too, that whoever injures her will incur his displeasure. In fact, during the few weeks that this Mr Ogden has been in residence his goodness to the poor has become the talk, though he seems something of a queer sort, and almost a hermit. At any rate, through him, the condition of Margaret may shortly be expected to undergo a change, though it is not easy to rescue her—she resists, appears to be suspicious, can't now believe perhaps that anyone really wishes her well—and whether she is capable of being reclaimed from her half-savage state it is hard to say: for the years alter us all, sir, the years leave the marks of their passing upon us.'

So much Mr Somerset, the aged clergyman, was able to give me of the story of Margaret Higgs, and that morose star of hers; and two days later I learned in further detail that every effort was being made to tame and help her.

But the bad destiny that seemed to have the woman in hand was not even yet done with her. Her new abode was actually ready for her, and she had agreed to go into it, glad, I suppose, poor soul, of a bed at last, when some men, digging for a foundation down by Severn, found the remains of a man.

It was near the spot where the daft Felix over fifteen years before had seen Margaret Higgs with a body on her back one dark morning, and the cry arose, 'the body of Higgs at last.'

Again, then, was Margaret taken to prison; and I, hearing of all the to-do, took train to St Bride's to witness her trial in the petty sessions there.

Of the two justices one was her own stepson, Fred Higgs, a good-looking man of not much more than thirty, and the other, the new lord of the Manor of Glanna.

As to the woman herself, she sat through it all—she was too woefully weak to stand—in a spiritless attitude, as unmoving as a statue. It was understood that, on being pressed in prison, she had admitted that the body discovered was that of her husband, buried by her; to which admission one Inspector Jonas deposed, and spoke as to the enforcing of the Coroner's warrant, and the whole story of the horror.

But what struck me from the first was the nervousness of one of the justices, the lord of Glanna—a short-built and broad-faced man, with cropped hair, and squat fingers, with which he kept tapping on his chin, tapping on his chair, tapping ever on everything near him.

And presently his keenness to procure the release of the accused became quite clear, till it was painful. One never saw a judge so jumpy in his chair, so agitated, so impatient of opposition. When his brother justice once leaned toward him, perhaps to whisper some remonstrance, Mr Ogden cried out loudly: "You be sure to shut your mouth!" and I then noticed that the very slight rocking of Margaret Higgs's body, which was going on as regularly as a pendulum's swing, suddenly ceased, and the woman seemed to start and hearken.

Evidence, however, is evidence, and no magistrate could have saved the woman from the County assizes, had it not been that at the last, when the prosecution was summing-up, saying, "there can be no doubt therefore that the remains now found are actually those of Barnaby Higgs—" Mr Ogden at those words leaped from his chair, calling out: "But how can all that be so certain to you, sir, when here's Barnaby Higgs himself, a living man, talking to ye?"

The hands which the old man spread before us shivered with strong emotion, while tears blinded his eyes. I heard Mr Somerset, seated near me on the bench, twice breathe to himself: *'My God!'* The mass of rags in the dock sprang straight with a crazy stare. Throughout the crowded room hardly a sound was heard till Mr Higgs, stepping to the rail, spoke—with a most painful agitation at the beginning, but presently more calmly and then again with wrathful agitation when, turning upon Fred Higgs, he scourged his son with invective. And ever afresh at the object of sorrow and rags arraigned before him he stretched his forefinger, with red-veined eyes, and a moan of love in his choked throat, calling her blessed, calling her saint.

It was the same Barnaby Higgs, he told the court—was rather surprised that some of them hadn't recognised him—only sixteen years older now, and a big-wig, in a frock-coat, and without a beard, but the same.

One summer there had come to the farm a man named John Cheyne—a sailorman he was—a cousin, who had got into trouble for abducting a girl, and Higgs had hidden him.

But the chap had not been three days on the place when Higgs began to be jealous.

'Though she told me that there was nothing in it, I didn't believe her, nor I don't now believe her, for I distinctly saw John Cheyne kissing, or trying to kiss, her behind the sty; and that same day, between three-thirty and four by the clock, I turned the fellow off the place.'

The sailor took his departure, but by ten in the night was back at the farm, craving to be again taken in; this Higgs refused. Cheyne pushed himself in, hot words arose, then fisticuffs, during which Cheyne, who must have had heart-disease, 'dropped down dead before a right-handed cross-counter in the left ribs, after a lead-off with the left by himself.' Some moments afterwards, Margaret, who had been out 'at fair,' walked in and saw what that was which Higgs was crouched down over on the floor.

Higgs, in the crowd of his terrors, knowing that his row with the sailor was known, could foresee nothing but the gallows; but Margaret, after sitting like a stone a long time, proposed flight, she to bury the body down by Severn, and in three nights' time to meet Higgs secretly on the Chase, to let him know whether he might safely return home.

This was agreed. Higgs ran, Margaret buried the sailor—no one suspected that he was dead, but as to the rendezvous on the Chase on the third day Higgs, ever nervous, had shirked it. Terrified by the tidings heard in his hiding that Margaret had been seen carrying a body on her back, he had not dared to return into the region of danger, but, having reached Liverpool, took ship.

'Yes,' he said from the bench, 'I abandoned her, little thinking that she'd be seriously charged with killing *me,* who knew myself to be alive and hearty, and all the time I was in South Africa I was that shy and sick of my cowardice I couldn't write to her; I preferred she should think me dead and gone. But I didn't know, I made sure she'd be going on all right in the old style. . . . Hadn't I left one to protect her, friends? Didn't I get a business friend in Glasgow to adopt him? He did nothing for her. My own son—this man—he did nothing for her. Ah! the squalls that caught her and the frosts that froze her bones were never a bit so hard on her as this bitter heart. It was for him she did it, friends, just think! She said to me that night, for she was cross wi' me, "it's not to screen *thee,* I do it," she said, "so I tell thee straight; but what kind of a life will it be for Fred with everybody having it to say he be a murderer's son?" And she kept the truth dark from him and from all—how long? For two months? For ten? While he was a dutiful boy to her? No, sixteen solid years down to this hour, though he was a beast to her. Why, sirs, talking of Christianity, there stands a Christian for you, I think? And you—you, couldn't you do some little something for her who did so much for you? Were you really bound to send her to Gloucester? And when you saw that her own husband had coward-like abandoned her, and all the crowd of them was hounding her, and the Almighty God on high Himself that ought to have been her Father was all dead agen her, and she stood dumb and astonished, was that the moment for you, too, Fred, hard heart . . . ? For if only from this confession she has made that she did kill me, I can pretty well judge what she's been through; she has confessed because, when she'd once tasted her prison cell that's proved a palace of rest to her after her kilns, and her brackens, and her barns, and her storms, she was afraid of being set free, maybe, if she didn't confess; or maybe she was too aweary to trouble to say no to aught they asked her. Oh, well, poor wounded woman, you've had it to do, haven't you, poor mute ewe, with all your wounds and bruises on you; but a bosom is here at last to guard you, Margaret Higgs, like the morning to a murky night, and the turning to a long lane, aye, a bosom is here to guard you . . . The prisoner is discharged! Officer, I give myself in charge for the manslaughter of one John Cheyne.'

It was now that the woman, babbling something, put out both her hands one moment toward her husband, but in the very act failed and fell. She was raised and taken out, and I, rushing out with the rest just behind her husband, witnessed everything that was done in vain to revive her, and the raver's frenzied vain prayers to his dead.

THE HOUSE OF SOUNDS

'E caddi come l'uom cui sonno piglia.'—Dante.

A good many years ago, when a young man, a student in Paris, I knew the great Carot, and witnessed by his side many of those cases of mind-malady, in the analysis of which he was such a master. I remember one little maid of the Marais who, until the age of nine, did not differ from her playmates; but one night, lying abed she whispered into her mother's ear: 'Mama, can you not hear *the sound of the world?*' It appears that her geography had just taught her that our globe reels with an enormous velocity on an orbit about the sun; and this *sound of the world* of hers was merely a murmur in the ear, heard in the silence of night. Within six months she was as mad as a March-hare.

I mentioned the case to my friend, Haco Harfager, then occupying with me an old mansion in St Germain, shut in by a wall and jungle of shrubbery. He listened with singular interest, and during a good while sat wrapped in gloom.

Another case which I gave made a great impression upon my friend: A young man, a toy-maker of St Antoine, suffering from consumption—but sober, industrious—returning one gloaming to his garret, happened to purchase one of those factious journals which circulate by lamplight over the Boulevards. This simple act was the beginning of his doom. He had never been a reader: knew little of the reel and turmoil of the world. But the next night he purchased another journal. Soon he acquired a knowledge of politics, the huge movements, the tumult of life. And this interest grew absorbing. Till late into the night, every night, he lay poring over the roar of action, the printed passion. He would awake sick, but brisk in spirit—and bought a morning paper. And the more his teeth gnashed, the less they ate. He grew negligent, irregular at work, turning on his bed through the day. Rags overtook him. As the grand interest grew upon his frail soul so every lesser interest failed in him. There came a day when he no more cared for his own life; and another day when he tore the hairs from his head.

As to this man the great Carot said to me: 'Really, one does not know whether to chuckle or to weep over such a business. Observe, for one thing, how diversely men are made! There are minds precisely so sensitive as a thread of melted lead: *every* breath will fret and trouble them: and how about the hurricane? For such this scheme of things is clearly no fit habitation, but a Machine of Death, a baleful Immense. *Too* cruel to some is the rushing shriek of Being—they *cannot* stand the world. Let each look well to his own little shred of existence, I say, and leave the monstrous Automaton alone! Here in this poor toy-maker you have a case of the ear: it is only the neurosis, Oxyecoia. Grand was that Greek myth of "the Harpies"—by *them* was this creature snatched away-or say, caught by a limb in the wheels of the universe, and so perished. It is quite a ravishing exit—translation in a chariot of flame! Only remember that the member first seized was *the pinna*—he bent *ear* to the howl of the world, and ended by himself howling. Between chaos and our shoes swings, I assure you, the thinnest film! I knew a man who had this aural peculiarity: that every sound brought him some knowledge of the matter causing the sound: a rod for instance, of mixed copper and tin striking upon a rod of mixed iron and lead, conveyed to him not merely the proportion of each metal in each rod, but some knowledge of the essential meaning and spirit, as it were, of copper, of tin, of iron and of lead. Him also did the Harpies snatch aloft!'

I have mentioned that I related some of these cases to my friend, Harfager: and I was astonished at the obvious pains which he gave himself to hide his interest, his gaping nostrils. . . .

From first days when we happened to attend the same seminary in Stockholm an intimacy had sprung up between us. But it was not an intimacy accompanied by the ordinary signs of friendship. Harfager was the shyest, most isolated, of beings. Though our joint housekeeping (brought about by a chance meeting at a midnight *séance*) had now lasted some months, I knew nothing of his plans. Through the day we read together, he rapt back into the past, I engrossed with the present; late at night we reclined on sofas within the vast cave of a hearth-place *Louis Onze,* and smoked over the dying fire in silence. Occasionally a

The House of Sounds

soirée or lecture might draw me from the house; except once, I never understood that Harfager left it. On that occasion I was hurrying through the Rue St Honore, where a rush of traffic rattles over the old pavers retained there, when I came upon him. In this tumult he stood in a listening attitude; and for a moment did not know me.

Even as a boy I had seen in my friend the genuine patrician— not that his personality gave any impression of loftiness or opulence: on the contrary. He did, however, suggest an incalculable *ancientness;* and I have known no nobleman who so bore in his expression the assurance of the essential Prince, whose pale blossom is of yesterday, and will perish tomorrow, but whose root shoots through the ages. This much I knew of Harfager; also that on one or other of his islands north of Zetland lived his mother and an aunt; that he was somewhat deaf; but liable to a thousand torments or delights at certain sounds, the whine of a door, the note of a bird. . . .

He was somewhat under the middle height; and inclined to portliness. His nose rose highly aquiline from that sort of brow called 'the musical'—that is, with temples which incline *outward* to the cheek-bones, making breadth for the base of the brain; while the direction of the heavy-lidded eyes and of the eyebrows was a downward *droop* from the nose of their outer ends. He wore a thin chin-beard. But the feature of his face were the ears, which were nearly circular, very small and flat, without that outer curve called 'the helix.' I came to understand that this had long been a trait of his race. Over the whole wan face of my friend was engraved an air of woeful inability, utter gravity of sorrow: one said 'Sardanapalus,' frail last of the race of Nimrod.

After a year I found it necessary to mention to Harfager my intention of leaving Paris, as we reclined one night in our nooks within the fireplace. He replied to my tidings with a polite 'Indeed!' and continued to gloat over the grate: but after an hour turned to me and observed: 'Well, it seems to be a hard world.'

Truisms uttered in just such a tone of discovery I occasionally heard from him; but his earnest gaze, his despondency now, astonished me.

'Apropos of what?' I asked.

'My friend, do not leave me!' He spread his arms.

The Pale Ape and Other Pulses

I learned that he was the object of a devilish malice; that he was the prey of a horrible temptation. That a lure, a becking hand, a lurking lust, which it was the effort of his life to escape (and to which he was especially liable in solitude) perpetually enticed him; and that so it had been almost from the day when, at the age of five, he had been sent by his father from his desolate home in the ocean.

And whose was this malice?

He told me his mother's and aunt's.

And what was this temptation?

He said it was the temptation to go back—to hurry with the very frenzy of hunger—back to that home.

I demanded with what motives, and in what way, the malice of his mother and aunt manifested itself. He answered that there was, he fancied, no definite motive, but only a fated malevolence; and that the respect in which it manifested itself was the prayers and commands with which they plagued him to go again to the hold of his ancestors.

All this I could not understand, and said so. In what consisted this magnetism, and this peril, of his home? To this Harfager did not reply, but rising from his seat, disappeared behind the hearth-curtains, and left the apartment. When he returned, it was with a quarto tome bound in hide, which proved to be Hugh Gascoigne's *Chronicle of Norse Families* in English black-letter. The passage to which he pointed I read as follows:

'Now of these two brothers the older, Harold, being of seemly personage and prowess, did go a pilgrimage into Danemark, wherefrom he repaired again home to Hjaltland (Zetland), and with him fetched the amiable Thronda for his wife, who was a daughter of the sank (blood) royal of Danemark. And his younger brother, Sweyn, that was sad and debonair, but far surpassed the other in cunning, received him with all good cheer.

'But eftsoons (soon after) fell Sweyn sick for all his love that he had of Thronda, his brother's wife. And while the worthy Harold ministered about the bed where Sweyn lay sick, lo, Sweyn fastened on him a violent stroke with a sword, and with no longer tarrying enclosed his hands in bonds, and cast him in the bottom of a deep hold. And because Harold would not deprive himself of the governance of Thronda his wife, Sweyn cut off both his ear[s], and put out one of his eyes, and after divers such torments was ready to slay him. But on a day the valiant Harold, breaking his bonds, and embracing his adversary, did by the sleight of wrestling overthrow him, and escaped. Notwithstanding, he faltered when he came to the Somburg Head, not far from the Castle, and, albeit that he was swift-foot, could no farther run, by reason that he was faint with the long plagues of his brother. And whilst he there lay in a swoon, did Sweyn come upon him, and when he had stricken him with a dart, cast him from Somburg Head into the sea.

'Not long hereafterward did the lady Thronda (though she knew not the manner of her lord's death, nor, verily, if he was dead or alive) receive Sweyn into favour, and with great gaudying and blowing of beamous (trumpets) did become his wife. And right soon they two went thence to sojourn in far parts.

'Now, it befell that Sweyn was minded by a dream to have built a great mansion in Hjaltland for the home-coming of the lady Thronda;, wherefore he called to him a cunning Master-workman, and sent him to England to gather men for the building of this lusty House, while he himself remained with his lady at Rome. Then came this Architect to London, but passing thence to Hjaltland was drowned, he and his feers (mates), all and some.

'And after two years, which was the time assigned, Sweyn Harfager sent a letter to Hjaltland to understand how his great House did: for he knew not of the drowning of the Architect: and soon after he received answer that the House *did well*, and was building on the Isle of Rayba. But that was not the Isle where Sweyn had appointed the building to be: and he was afeard, and near fell down dead for dread, because, in the letter, he saw before him the manner of writing of his brother Harold. And he said in this form: "Surely Harold is alive, else be this letter writ with ghostly hand." And he was wo many days, seeing that this was a deadly stroke.

'Thereafter he took himself back to Hjaltland to know how the matter was, and there the old Castle on Somburg Head was break down to the earth. Then Sweyn was wodewroth, and cried: "Jhesu mercy, where is all the great house of my fathers gone? alas! this wicked day of destiny!" And one of the people told him that a host of workmen from far parts had break it down. And he said:

"Who hath bid them?" but that could none answer. Then he said again: "nis (is not) my brother Harold alive? for I have behold his writing": and that, too, could none answer. So he went to Rayba, and saw there a great House stand, and when he looked on it, he said: "This, sooth, was y-built by my brother Harold, be he dead or be he on-live." And there he dwelt, and his lady, and his sons' sons until now: for that the House is ruthless and without pity; wherefore 'tis said that upon all who dwell there falleth a wicked madness and a lecherous anguish; and that by way of the ears do they drinck the cup of the furie of the earless Harold, till the time of the House be ended.'

After I had read the narrative half-aloud, I smiled, saying: 'This, Harfager, is very tolerable romance on the part of the good Gascoigne, but has the look of indifferent history.'

'It is, nevertheless, *history*,' he replied.

'You believe that?'

'The house stands solidly on Rayba.'

'But you believe that medieval ghosts superintended the building of their family mansions?'

'Gascoigne nowhere says that,' he answered: 'for to be "stricken with a darte," is not necessarily to die; nor, if he did say it, have I any knowledge on the subject.'

'And what, Harfager, is the nature of that "wicked madness," that "lecherous anguish," of which Gascoigne speaks?'

'Do you ask me?'—he spread his arms—'what do I know? I know nothing! I was banished from the place at the age of five. Yet the cry of it still rings in my mind. And have I not told you of anguishes—even in myself—of inherited longing and loathing. . . .'

Anyway, I *had* to go to Heidelberg just then: so I said I would compromise by making my absence short, and rejoin him in a few weeks. I took his moody silence to mean assent; and soon afterwards left him.

But I was detained: and when I got back to our old house found it empty. Harfager was gone.

It was only after twelve years that a letter was forwarded me—a rather wild letter, an awfully long one—in the writing of my friend. It was dated at Rayba. From the writing I understood that it had been dashed off *with furious haste,* so that I was the more astonished at the very trivial nature of the contents. On the first half page he spoke of our old friendship, and asked if I would see his mother, who was dying; the rest of the epistle consisted of an analysis of his mother's family-tree, the apparent aim being to show that she was a genuine Harfager, and a distant cousin of his father. He then went on to comment on the great prolificness of his race, stating that since the fourteenth century over *four millions* of its members had lived; three only of them, he believed, being now left. This settled, the letter ended.

Influenced by this, I travelled northward; reached Caithness; passed the stormy Orkneys; reached Lerwick; and from Unst, the most bleak and northerly of the Zetlands, contrived, by dint of bribes, to pit the weather-worthiness of a lug-sailed 'sixern' (identical with the 'langschips' of the Vikings) against a flowing sea and an ugly sky. The trip, I was told, was at such a season of some risk. It was the sombre December of those seas; and the weather, they said, although never cold, is seldom other than tempestuous. A mist now lay over the billows, enclosing our boat in a dome of doleful gloaming; and there was a ghostly something in the look of the silent sea and brooding sky which produced upon my nerves the mood of a journey out of nature, a cruise beyond the world. Occasionally, however, we ran past one of those 'skerries,' or sea-stacks, whose craggy sea-walls, disintegrated by the struggles of the Gulf Stream with the North Sea, had a look of awful ruin and havoc. But I only noticed three of these: for before the dun day had well run half its course, sudden darkness was upon us; and with it one of those storms of which the winter of this semi-Arctic sea is one succession. During the haggard glimpses of the following day the rain did not stop; but before darkness had quite fallen, my skipper (who talked continuously to a mate of seal-maidens, and water-horses, and *grülies*), paused to point me out a mound of gloomier grey on the weather-bow, which, he said, should be Rayba.

Rayba, he said, was the centre of quite a nest of those *rösts* (eddies) and cross-currents which the tidal wave hurls with complicated swirlings among all the islands: but at Rayba they ran with more than usual angriness, owing to the row of sea-crags which garrisoned the land around; approach was therefore at all times difficult, and at night foolhardy. With a running sea, however, we came sufficiently close to see the mane of foam which railed round the coastwall. Its shock, according to the captain, had often more than all the efficiency of artillery, tossing tons of rock to heights of six hundred feet upon the island.

When the sun next pried above the horizon, we had closely approached the coast; and it was then that for the first time the impression of some *spinning* motion of the island (due probably to the swirling movements of the water) was produced upon me. We affected a landing at a *voe*, or sea-arm, on the west coast—the east, though the point of my aim, was out of the question on account of the swell. Here I found in two *skeoes* (or sheds), thatched with feal, five or six seamen, who gained a livelihood by trading for the groceries of the great house on the east: and, taking one of them for a guide, I began the climb of the island.

Now, during the night in the boat, I had been aware of a booming in the ears for which even the roar of the sea round the coast seemed insufficient to account; and this now, as we went on, became immensely augmented—and with it, once more, that conviction within me of *spinning* motions. Rayba I found to be a land of precipices of granite and flaggy gneiss; at about the centre, however, we came upon a tableland, sloping from west to east, and covered by a lot of lochs, which sullenly flowed into one another. I could see no shore eastward to this chain of waters, and by dint of shouting to my leader, and bending ear to his shoutings, I came to know that there was no such shore—I say shout, for nothing less could have sounded through the steady bellowing as of ten thousand bisons that now resounded on every side. A certain trembling, too, of the earth became distinct. In vain, meantime, did the eye in its dreary survey seek a tree or shrub—for no kind of vegetation, save peat, could brave for a day the perennial tempest of this benighted island. Darkness, half an hour after noon, commenced to fall upon us: and it was soon afterwards that my guide, pointing down a defile near the east coast, hurriedly started back upon the way he had come. I bawled a question after him, as he went: but at this point the voice of mortals had ceased to be in the least audible.

Down this defile, with a sinking of the heart, and a singular sickness of giddiness, I passed; and, on reaching its end, emerged upon a ledge of rock which shuddered to the immediate onsets of

The House of Sounds

the sea—though all this part of the island was, besides, in the grip of an ague not due to the great guns of the sea. Hugging a crag of cliff for steadiness from the gusts, I gazed forth upon a scene not less eerily dismal than some drear district of the dreams of Dante. Three "skerries," flanked by stacks as fantastic and twisted as a witch's finger, and giving a home to hosts of osprey and scart, seal and walrus, lay at some fathoms distance; and from its rush among them, the sea in blanched, tumultuous, but inaudible wrath, like an army with banners, ranted toward the land. Letting go my crag, I staggered some distance to the left: and now all at once an amphitheatre opened before me, and there broke upon my view a panorama of such appalling majesty as had never entered my heart to fancy.

'An amphitheatre,' I said: but it was rather the form of a Norman door that I saw. Fancy such a door, half a mile wide, flat on the ground, the rounded part farthest from the sea; and all round it let a wall of rock tower perpendicular forty yards: and now down this rounded door-shape, and *over its whole extent,* let a roaring ocean roll its tonnage in hoary fury—and the stupor with which I looked, and then the shrinking, and then the instinct of flight, will find comprehension.

This was the disemboguement of the lochs of Rayba.

And within the curve of this Norman cataract, robed in the world of its smokes and far-excursive surfs, stood a fabric of brass.

The last beam of the day had now nearly passed; but I could still see through the mist which bleakly nimbused it as in tears, that the building was low in proportion to the hugeness of its circumference; that it was roofed with a dome; and that round it ran two rows of Norman windows, the upper smaller than the lower. Certain indications led me to infer that the house had been founded upon a bed of rock which lay, circular and detached, within the curve of the cataract; but this nowhere emerged above the flood: for the whole floor which I had before me dashed one reeking deep river to the beachless sea—passage to the mansion being made possible by a massive causeway-bridge, with arches, all bearded with sea-weed.

Descending from my ledge, I passed along it, now drenched in spray; and, as I came nearer, could see that the house, too, was to half its height more thickly bearded than an old hull with barnacles and every variety of bright seaweed; also—what was very surprising—that from many spots near the top of the brazen wall ponderous chains, dropping beards, reached out in rays: so that the fabric had the aspect of a many-anchored ark. But without pausing to look closely, I pushed forward, and rushing through the smooth waterfall which poured all round from the roof, by one of its many porches I entered the dwelling.

Darkness now was around me—and sound. I seemed to stand in the centre of some yelling planet, the row resembling the resounding of many thousands of cannon, punctuated by strange crashing and breaking uproars. And a sadness descended on me; I was near to tears. 'Here,' I said, 'is the place of weeping; not elsewhere is the vale of sighing.' However, I passed forward through a succession of halls, and was wondering where to go next, when a hideous figure, with a lamp in his hand, stamped towards me. I shrank from him! It seemed the skeleton of a lank man wrapped in a winding-sheet, till the light of one tiny eye, and a film of skin over a portion of the face reassured one. Of ears he showed no sign. His name, I afterwards learned, was Aith; and his appearance was explained by his pretence (true or false), that he had once suffered *burning*, almost to the cinder-stage, but had somehow recovered. With an expression of malice, and agitated gestures, he led the way to a chamber on the upper stage, where, having struck light to a taper, he made signs toward a spread table, and left me.

For a long time I sat in solitude, conscious of the shaking of the mansion, though every sense was swallowed up and confounded in the one impression of sound. Water, water, was the world—a nightmare on my breast, a desire to gasp for breath, a tingling on my nerves, a sense of being infinitely drowned and buried in boundless deluges; and when the feeling of giddiness, too, increased, I sprang up and paced—but suddenly stopped, angry, I scarce knew why, with myself. I had, in fact, caught myself walking with a certain *hurry*, not usual with me, not natural to me. So I forced myself to stand and take note of the hall. It was large, and damp with mists, so that its tattered, but rich, furniture looked lost in it, its centre occupied by a tomb bearing the name of a Harfager of the fourteenth century, and its walls old panels of oak. Having drearily seen these things, I waited on with an intolerable consciousness of solitude; but a little after midnight the tapestry parted, and Harfager with a rapid stalk walked in.

In twelve years my friend had grown old. He showed, it is true, a tendency to portliness: yet, to a knowing eye he was in reality tabid, ill-nourished. And his neck stuck forward from his chest; and the lower part of his back had quite a forward bend of age; and his hair floated about his face and shoulders in a wildness of awful whiteness, while a white chin-beard hung to his chest. His dress was a robe of bauge, which, as he went, waved aflaunt from his bare and hairy shins; and he was shod in those soft slippers called *rivlins*.

To my astonishment, he spoke. When I passionately shouted that I could gather no fragment of sound from his moving mouth, he clapped both his palms to his ears, and then anew besieged mine: but again without result: and now, with an angry throw of the hand, he caught up his taper, and walked from the apartment.

There was something strikingly unnatural in his manner—something which reminded me of the skeleton, Aith: an excess of zeal, a fever, a rage, *a loudness,* an eagerness of gait, a great extravagance of gesture. His hand constantly dashed wiffs of hair from a face which, though of the saffron of death, had red eyes—thick-lidded eyes, fixed in a downward and sideward gaze. When he came back to me, it was with a leaf of ivory, and a piece of graphite, hanging from the cord tied round his garment; and he rapidly wrote a petition that, if not too tired, I would take part with him in the funeral of his mother.

I shouted assent.

Once more he clapped his palms to his ears; then wrote: 'Do not shout: no whisper in any part of the building is inaudible to me.'

I remembered that in early life he had been slightly *deaf*.

We passed together through many apartments, he shading the taper with his hand—a necessary action, for, as I quickly discovered, in no nook of the quivering building was the air in a state of rest, but was for ever commoved by a curious agitation, a faint windiness, like an echo of tempests, which communicated a universal nervousness to the curtains. Everywhere I met the same past grandeur, present raggedness and decay. In many of the rooms were tombs; one was a museum thronged with bronzes, but broken, grown with fungoids, dripping with moisture—it was as if the mansion, in ardour of travail, sweated; and a miasma of decomposition tainted all the air.

I followed Harfager through the maze of his way with some difficulty, for he went headlong—only once stopping, when with a face ungainly wild over the glare of the light, he tossed up his fingers, and gave out a single word: from the form of his lips I guessed the word '*Hark!*'

Presently we entered a very long chamber, in which, on chairs beside a bed, lay a coffin flanked by a file of candles. The coffin was very deep, and had this singularity—that the foot-piece was absent, so that the soles of the corpse could be seen as we approached. I saw, too, three upright rods secured to a side of the coffin, each rod fitted at its top with a little silver bell of the sort called *morrice,* pendent from a flexible spring. And at the head of the bed, Aith, with an air of irascibility, was stamping to and fro within a narrow area.

Harfager deposited the taper upon a stone table, and stood poring with a crazy intentness over the body. I, too, stood and looked at death so grim and rigorous as I think I never saw. The coffin looked angrily full of tangled grey locks, the lady being of great age, bony and hook-nosed; and her face shook with solemn constancy to the quivering of the building. I noticed that over the body had been fixed three bridges, like the bridge of a violin, their sides fitting into grooves in the coffin's sides, and their tops of a shape to fit the slope of the two coffin-lids when closed. One of these bridges passed over the knees of the dead lady; another bridged her stomach; the third her neck. In each of them was a hole, and across each of the three holes passed a string from the morrice-bell above it—the three holes being thus divided by the three tight strings into six semi-circles. Before I could guess the significance of all this, Harfager closed the folding coffin-lids, which had little holes for the passage of the three strings. He then turned the key in the lock, and uttered a word which I took to be 'come.'

Aith now took hold of the handle at the coffin's head; and out of the dark parts of the hall a lady in black walked forward. She was tall, pallid, of imposing aspect; and from the curvature of her

The House of Sounds

nose, and her circular ears, I guessed her the lady Swertha, aunt of Harfager. Her eyes were quite red—if with crying I could not tell.

Harfager and I taking each a handle near the coffin-foot, and the lady bearing before us one of the black candlesticks, the obsequies began. When I got to the doorway, I noticed in a corner there two more coffins, engraved with the names of Harfager and his aunt. Thence we wound our way down a wide stairway winding to a lower floor; and descending thence still lower by narrow brass steps, came to a portal of metal, where the lady, depositing the candlestick, left us.

The chamber of death into which we now bore the body had for its outer wall the brazen outer wall of the whole house at a spot where this closely approached the cataract, and was no doubt profoundly drowned in the world of surge without: so that the earthquake there was urgent. On every side the place was piled with coffins, ranged high and wide upon shelves; and the huge rush and scampering which ensued on our entrance proved it the paradise of troops of rats. As it was inconceivable that these could have eaten a way through sixteen brazen feet—for even the floor here was brazen—I assumed that some fruitful pair must have found in the house, on its building, an ark from the waters. Even this guess, though, seemed wild; and Harfager afterwards confided to me his suspicion that they had for some reason been *placed* there by the original builder.

We deposited our load upon a stone bench in the centre; whereupon Aith made haste to be away. Harfager then repeatedly walked from end to end of the place, scrutinising with many a stoop and peer and upward stretch, the shelves and their props. Could he, I was led to wonder, have any doubts as to their soundness? Damp, in fact, and decay pervaded everything. A bit of timber which I touched crumbled to dust under my thumb.

He presently beckoned to me, and, with yet one halt and 'Hark!' from him, we passed through the house to my chamber; where, left alone, I paced about, agitated with a vague anger; then tumbled to an agony of slumber.

In the far interior of the mansion even the bleared day of this land of bleakness never rose upon our gloom; but I was able to regulate my gettings-up by a clock which stood in my chamber; or I was called by Harfager, with whom in a short time I renewed more than all our former friendship. That I should say *more* is curious: but so it *was:* and this was proved by the fact that we grew to take, and to excuse, freedoms of speech and of manner which, as two persons of more than usual reserve, we had once never dreamed of permitting to ourselves in respect of each other. Once, for example, in our pacings of aimless haste down passages that vanished in shadow and length of perspective remoteness, he wrote that my step was very slow. I replied that it was just such a step as suited my then mood. He wrote: 'You have developed a tendency to *fret.*' I was very offended, and said: 'Certainly, there are more fingers than one in the world which *that* ring will fit!'

Another day he was no less than rude to me for seeking to reveal to him the secret of the unhuman keenness of his hearing—and of mine! For I, too, to my dismay, began, as time passed, to catch hints of shouted sounds. The cause might be found, I asserted, in a fervour of the auditory nerve, which, if the cataract were absent, the roar of the ocean, and the row of the perpetual tempest round us, might by themselves be sufficient to bring about; his own ear-interior, I said, must be inflamed to an exquisite pitch of fever; and I named the disease to him as the 'Paracusis Wilisii'. When he frowned dissent, I, quite undeterred, proceeded to relate the case (that had occurred within my own experience) of a very deaf lady who could hear the drop of a pin in a railway-train*; and now he made me the reply: 'Of ignorant people I am accustomed to consider the mere scientist the most ignorant!'

But I, for my part, regarded it as merely far-fetched that he should pretend to be in the dark as to the morbid state of his hearing! He himself, indeed, confessed to me his own, Aith's, and the lady Swertha's proneness to paroxysms of *vertigo.* I was startled! for I had myself shortly previously been roused out of sleep by feelings of reeling and nausea, and an assurance that the room furiously flew round with me. The impression passed away, and I attributed it, perhaps hastily, to some disturbance in the nerve-endings of 'the labyrinth,' or inner ear. In Harfager,

---

* Such cases are known to many medical men. The concussion on the deaf nerve is the cause of the acquired sensitiveness; nor is there any limit to that sensitiveness when the tumult is immensely augmented.

The House of Sounds

however, the conviction of whirling motions in the house, in the world, got to so horrible a degree of certainty, that its effects sometimes resembled those of lunacy or energumenal possession. Never, he said, was the sensation of giddiness altogether dead in him; seldom the sensation that he gazed with stretched-out arms over the brink of abysms which wooed his half-consenting foot. Once, as we walked, he was hurled as by unearthly powers to the ground, and there for an hour sprawled, bathed in sweat, with distraught bedazzlement and amaze in his stare, which watched the racing walls. He was constantly racked, moreover, with the consciousness of sounds so peculiar in their character, that I could account for them on no other supposition than that of a *tinnitùs* infinitely sick. Through the roar there sometimes visited him, he told me, the lullaby of some bird, from the burden of whose song he had the consciousness that she derived from a very remote country, was of the whiteness of foam, and crested with a comb of mauve. Or else he knew of accumulated human tones, distant, yet articulate, busily contending in volubility, and in the end melting into a medley of musical movements. Or, anon, he was shocked by an infinite and imminent crashing, like the monstrous racket of the crackling of a cosmos of crockery round his ears. He told me, moreover, that he could frequently see, rather than hear, the particoloured wheels of a mazy sphere-music deep, deep within the black dark of the cataract's roar. These impressions, which I protested *must* be merely entotic had sometimes a pleasing effect upon him, and he would stand long to listen with a lifted hand to their seduction: others again inflamed him to a mad anger. I guessed that they were the cause of those '*Harks!*' that at intervals of about an hour did not fail to break from him. But in this I was wrong: and it was with a thrill of dismay that I soon came to know the truth.

For, as we were once passing by an iron door on the lower floor, he stopped, and for some minutes stood listening with a leer most keen and cunning. Presently the cry '*Hark!*' escaped him; and he then turned to me and wrote on the tablet: 'Did you not hear?' I had heard nothing but the roar; and he howled into my ear in sounds now audible to me as an echo caught far off in dreams: 'You shall see.'

He took up the candlestick; produced from the pocket of his robe a key; unlocked the iron door; and we passed into a room very loftily domed in proportion to its area, and empty, save that a pair of steps lay against its wall, and that in the centre of its marble floor was a pool, like a Roman 'impluvium,' only round like the room—a pool evidently profound in depth, full of a thick and inky fluid. I was very perturbed by its present aspect, for as the candle burned upon its surface, I observed that this had been quite recently *disturbed,* in a style for which the shivering of the house could not account, since *ripples* of slime were now rounding out from its middle to its brink. When I glanced at Harfager for explanation, he gave me a signal to wait; and now for about an hour, with his hands behind his back, paced the chamber; but then paused, and we two stood together by the pool's margin, gazing into the water. Suddenly his clutch tightened on my arm, and I saw, with a touch of horror, a tiny ball, probably of lead, but daubed blood-red by some chemical, fall from the roof, and sink into the middle of the pool. It hissed on contact with the water a whiff of mist.

'In the name of all that is sinister,' I whispered, 'what thing is this?'

Again he made me a busy and confident signal to wait, moved the ladder-steps toward the pool, handed me the taper. When I had mounted, holding high the light, I saw hanging out of the fogs in the dome a globe of old copper, lengthened into balloon-shape by a neck, at the end of which I could spy a tiny hole. Painted over the globe was barely visible in red print-letters:

'HARFAGER-HOUS: 1389-188.'

I was down quicker than I went up!

'But the meaning?' I panted.

'Did you see the writing?'

'Yes. The meaning?'

He wrote: 'By comparing Gascoigne with Thrunster, I find that the house was *built* about 1389.'

'But the last figures?'

'After the last 8,' he replied, 'there is another figure not quite obliterated by a tarnish-spot.'

'What figure?' I asked.

The House of Sounds

'It cannot be read, but may be surmised. As the year 1888 is now all but passed, it can only be the figure 9.'

'Oh, you are depraved in mind!' I cried, very irritated: 'you assume—you *state*—in a manner which no mind trained to base its conclusions on facts can bear with patience.'

'And you are irrational,' he wrote. 'You know, I suppose, the formula of Archimedes by which, the diameter of a globe being known, its volume also is known? Now, the diameter of that globe in the dome I know to be four and a half feet; and the diameter of the leaden balls about the third of an inch. Supposing, then, that 1389 was the year in which the globe was full of balls, you may readily calculate that not many fellows of the four million and odd which have since dropped at the rate of one an hour are now left within. The fall of the balls *cannot* persist another year. The figure 9 is therefore forced upon us.'

'But you assume, Harfager!' I cried: 'Oh, believe me, my friend, this is the very wantonness of wickedness! By what algebra of despair do you know that each ball represents one of the scions of your house, or that the last date was intended to correspond with the stoppage of the horologe. And, even if so, what is the significance of it? It can have *no significance*!'

'Do you want to madden me?' he shouted. Then furiously writing; 'I swear that I know nothing of its significance! But it is not evident to you that the thing is a big hour-glass, intended to count the hours, not of a day, but of a cycle; and of a cycle of five hundred years?'

'But the whole contrivance,' I passionately cried,' is a baleful phantasm of our brains! How is the fall of the balls regulated? Ah, my friend, you wander—your mind is debauched in this brawl of waters.'

'I have not ascertained,' he replied, 'by what internal works, or clammy medium, or spiral coil, dependent probably for its action upon the vibration of the mansion, the balls are retarded in their fall: that was a matter well within the skill of the medieval mechanic, the inventor of the clock; but this at least is clear, that one element of their retardation is the smallness of the aperture through which they have to pass; that this element, by known laws of statics, will cease to operate when no more than three balls remain; and that, consequently, the last three will fall at almost the same instant.'

'In Heaven's name!' I exclaimed, careless now what folly I poured out, 'but your mother is dead, Harfager! Do you deny that there remain but you and the Lady Swertha?'

A glance of disdain was all the answer he then gave me as to this.

But he confessed to me a day later that the leaden drops were a constant sorrow to his ears; that from hour to hour his life was a keen waiting for their fall; that even from his brief sleeps he infallibly started awake at each descent; that in whatever region of the mansion he chanced to be, they found him out with a crashing *loudness;* and that each crash tweaked him with a twinge of anguish within the ear. I was therefore shocked at his declaration that these droppings had now become as the life of life to him; had acquired an entwining so close with the tone of his mind, that their ceasing might even mean for him the reeling of Reason: at which confession he sobbed, with his face buried, as he leant upon a column. When this paroxysm was past, I asked him if it was out of the question that he should once for all cast off the fascination of the horologe, and escape with me from the place. He wrote in mysterious reply: 'A *three-fold* cord is not easily broken.' I started, asking—'How threefold?' He wrote with a bitter smile: 'To be in love with pain—to pine after aching—is not that a wicked madness?' I stood astonished that he had unconsciously quoted Gascoigne! 'a wicked madness!' 'a lecherous anguish!' 'You have seen my aunt's face,' he proceeded; 'your eyes were dim if you did not see in it an impious calm, the glee of a blasphemous patience, a grin behind her daring smile.' He then spoke of a prospect at the terror of which his whole soul trembled, yet which sometimes laughed in his heart in the form of a *hope.* It was the prospect of any considerable increase in the volume of sound about his ears. At that, he said, the brain must totter. On the night of my arrival the noise of my boots, and, since then, my voice occasionally raised, had produced acute pain in him. To such an ear, I understood him to say, the luxury of torture involved in a large sound-increase around was an allurement from which no human virtue could turn: and when I said that I could not even conceive such an increase, much less the means by which it could be effected, he brought out

The House of Sounds

from the archives of the mansion some annals kept by the heads of his family. From these it appeared that the tempests that ever lacerated the latitude of Rayba did not fail to give place, at intervals of some years, to one mammoth madness, one Samson among the merry men, and Sirius among the suns. At such periods the rains descended—and the floods came—even as in the first world-deluge; those *rösts,* or eddies, which ever encircled Rayba, spurning then the bands of lateral space, burst aloft into a whirl of water-spouts, to dance about the little land, upon which, converging, some of them discharged their waters: and the locks which flowed to the cataract thus redoubled their volume, and crashed with redoubled roar. Harfager said it was miraculous that for eighteen years no such grand event had transacted itself at Rayba.

'And what,' I asked 'in addition to the dropping balls, and the prospect of an increase of sound, is the third strand of that *"threefold cord"* of which you have spoken.'

For answer he led me to a circular hall which, he said, he had ascertained to be the centre of the circular mansion. It was a very large hall—so large as I think I never saw—so large that the amount of wall lighted at one time by the candle seemed nearly flat: and nearly the whole of its area, from floor to roof, was occupied by a column of brass, the space between the wall and column being only such as to admit of a stretched-out arm.

'This column,' Harfager wrote, 'goes up to the dome and passes beyond it; it goes down to the lower floor, and passes through that; it goes down thence to the brazen flooring of the vaults and *passes through that* into the bedrock. Under each floor it spreads out, helping to support the floor. What is the precise quality of the impression which I have made upon your mind by this description?'

'I do not know,' I answered, turning from him: 'ask me none of your enigmas, Harfager: I feel a giddiness. . . .'

'But answer me,' he said: 'consider *the strangeness* of that brazen lowest floor, which I have discovered to be some six feet thick, and whose under-surface, I have reason to think, is somewhat *above* the bed-rock; remember that the fabric is at no point *fastened* to the column; think of the *chains* which ray out from the outer wall, apparently *anchoring* the house to the ground. Tell me, what impression have I *now* made?'

The Pale Ape and Other Pulses

'And is it for *this* you wait?' I cried. 'Yet there may have been no malevolent intention! You jump at conclusions! Any fixed building in such a land and spot as this would at any time be liable to be broken up by some sovereign tempest! What if it was the intention of the builder that in such a case the chains should break, and the building, by yielding, be saved?'

'You have no lack of charity at least,' he replied; and we then went back to the book we were reading together.

He had not wholly lost the old habit of study, although he could no longer get himself to *sit* to read; so with a volume (often tossed down) he would stamp about within the region of the lamplight; or I, unconscious of my voice, might read to him. By a whim of his mood the few books which now lay within the limits of his patience had all for their motive something of the *picaresque*, or the foppishly speculative: Quevedo's 'Tacaño'; or the system of Tycho Brahe; above all, George Hakewill's 'Power and Providence of God.' One day, however, as I read, he interrupted me with the sentence, *à propos* of nothing: 'What I cannot understand is that you, a scientist, should believe that life ceases with the ceasing of breathing'—and from that moment the tone of our reading changed. For he led me to the crypts of the library in the lowest part of the building, and hour after hour, with a *furore* of triumph overwhelmed me with books proving the length of life after 'death.' What, he asked, was my opinion of Baron Verulam's account of the dead man who was heard to utter words of prayer? or of the bounding bowels of the dead convict? On my expressing unbelief, he seemed surprised, and reminded me of the writhings of dead cobras, of the long beating of a frog's heart after 'death.' 'She is not dead,' he quoted, 'but *sleepeth*'. The idea of Bacon and Paracelsus that the principle of life resides in a spirit or fluid was proof to him that such fluid could not, from its very nature, undergo any *sudden* annihilation, while the organs which it pervades remain. When I asked what limit he, then, set to the persistence of 'life' in the 'dead,' he answered that when decay had so far advanced that the nerves could no longer be called nerves, or when the brain had been disconnected at the neck from the body, as by rats gnawing, then the king of terrors was king verily. With an indiscretion strange to me before my residence at Rayba, I now blurted out the question whether in all this he could be referring to

The House of Sounds

his mother? For a while he stood thoughtful, then wrote: 'Even if I had not had reason to believe that my own and Swertha's life in some way hung upon the final cessations of hers, I should still have taken precautions to ascertain the march of the destroyer on her frame: as it is, I shall not lack even the exactest information.' He then explained that the rats which ran riot in the place of death would in time do their full work upon her; but would be unable to reach to the region of the throat without first gnawing their way through the three strings stretched across the holes of the bridges within the coffin, and thus, one by one, liberating the three morrisco-bells to tinklings.

The winter solstice had gone, another year began. I was sleeping a deep sleep by night when Harfager came into my chamber, and shook me. His face was ghastly in the taper's glare. A change within a short time had taken place upon him. He was hardly the same. He was like some poor wight into whose surprised eyes in the night have pried the eyes of Affright.

He said that he was aware of strainings and creakings, which gave him the feeling of being suspended in airy spaces by a thread which must break to his weight; and he begged me, for God's sake, to accompany him to the coffins. We passed together through the house, he craven, haggard, his gait now laggard, into the chamber of the dead, where he stole to and fro examining the shelves. Out of the footless coffin of the dowager trembling on its bench I saw a water-rat crawl; and as Harfager passed beneath one of the shortest of the shelves which bore one coffin, it suddenly dropped from a height to dust at his feet. He screamed the cry of a frightened creature; tottered to my support; and I bore him back to the upper parts of the palace.

He sat, with his face buried, in a corner of a small chamber, doddering, overtaken, as it were, with the extremity of age, no longer marking with his *'Hark!'* the fall of the leaden drops. To my remonstrances he responded only with the moan, 'so soon!' Whenever I looked for him, I found him there, his manhood now collapsed in an ague. I do not think that during this time he slept.

On the second night, as I was approaching him, he sprang suddenly upright with the outcry: 'The first bell is tinkling!'

And he had scarcely screamed it when, from some long way off, a faint wail, which at its origin must have been a fierce shriek, reached my now feverish ears. Harfager, for his part, clapped his palms to his ears, and dashed from his place, I following in hot chase through the black breadth of the mansion: till we came to a chamber containing a candelabrum, and arrased in faded red. On the floor in swoon lay the lady Swertha, her dark-grey hair in disarray wrapping her like an angry sea; tufts of it scattered, torn from the roots; and on her throat prints of strangling fingers. We bore her to her bed in an alcove; and, having discovered some tincture in a cabinet, I administered it between her fixed teeth. In her rapt countenance I saw that death was not; and, as I found something appalling in her aspect, shortly afterwards left her to Harfager.

When I next saw him his manner had undergone a kind of change which I can only describe as gruesome. It resembled the officious self-importance seen in a person of weak intellect who spurs himself with the thought, 'to business! the time is short!' while his walk sickened me with a hint of *ataxie locomotrice.* When I asked him as to his aunt, as to the meaning of the marks of violence on her body, bending ear to his deep and unctuous tones, I could hear: 'An attempt has been made upon her life by the skeleton, Aith.'

He seemed not to share my astonishment at this thing! nor could give me any clear answer as to his reason for retaining such a servant, or as to the origin of Aith's service: Aith, he told me, had been admitted into the palace during the period of his own absence in youth, and he knew little of him beyond the fact that he was extraordinarily strong. *Whence* he had come, or how, no person except the lady Swertha was aware: and she, it seems, feared, or at least persistently flinched from admitting him into the mystery. He added that, as a matter of fact, the lady, from the day of his coming back to Rayba, had with some object imposed upon herself a dumbness on all subjects, which he had never once known her to break through, except by an occasional note.

With an ataxic strenuousness, with the airs of a drunken man constraining himself to ordered action, Harfager now set himself to the doing of a host of trivial things: he collected chronicles and arranged them in order of date; he docketed or ticketed packets of documents; he insisted upon my assistance in turning the faces of paintings to the wall. He was, however, now constantly stopped by bursts of vertigo, six times in a single hour being hurled to the ground, while blood frequently guttered from his ears. He complained to me in a tone of piteous wail of the wooing of a silver *piccolo* that continually seduced him. As he bent, sweating, over his momentous nothings, his hands fluttered like aspen. I noted the movements of his whimpering lips, the rheum of his sunken eyes: sudden doting had come upon his youth.

On a day he threw it utterly off, and was young anew. He entered my room; roused me from dreams; I observed the lunacy of bliss in his eyes, heard his hiss in my ear:

'Up! *The storm!*'

Ah! I had known it—in the nightmare of the night. I felt it in the air of the room. It had come. I saw it lurid by the lamplight on the hell of Harfager's face.

A glee burst at once into birth within me, as I sprang from my couch, glancing at the clock: it was eight in the morning. Harfager, with the naked stalk of some maniac prophet, had already taken himself away; and I started out after him. A deepening was clearly felt in the quivering of the edifice; anon for a second it stopped still, as if, breathlessly, to listen; its air was troubled with a vague gustiness. Occasionally there came to me as it were the noising of some far-off lamentation and voice in Ramah, but whether this was in my ear or the screaming of the gale I could not tell; or again I could hear one clear chord of an organ's vaunt. About noon I spied Harfager, lamp in hand, running along a corridor, with naked soles. As we met he looked at me, but hardly with recognition, and passed by; stopped, however, and ran back to howl into my ear the question: 'Would you *see?*' He then beckoned before me, and I followed to a very small opening in the outer wall, closed with a slab of brass. As he lifted the latch, the slab dashed inward with instant impetuosity and tossed him a long way, while the breath of the tempest, braying through the brazen tube with a brutal bravura, caught and pinned me upon a corner of a wall, and all down the corridor a long crashing racket of crowds of pictures and couches followed. I nevertheless managed to push my way on the belly to the opening. Hence the sea should have been visible; but my senses were met by nothing but a vision of tumbled tenebrousness, and a general impression of the letter O. The sun of Rayba had gone out.

In a moment of opportunity our two forces got the shutter shut again:

'Come!'—he had obtained a fresh glimmer, and beckoned before me—'let's go see how the dead fare in the great desolation:' and we ran, but had hardly got to the middle of the stairway, when I was thrilled by the consciousness of some great shock, the bass of a dull thud, which nothing save the thumping to the floor of the whole lump of the coffins could have caused. I looked for Harfager, and for a moment only saw his heels skedaddling, panic-hounded, his ears stopped, his mouth round! Then, indeed, fear reached me—a tremor in the audacity of my heart, a thought that now at any rate I must desert him in his extremity, and work out my own salvation. Yet it was with hesitancy that I turned to search for him for the last farewell—a hesitancy which I felt to be not unselfish, but selfish, and unhealthy. I rambled through the night, seeking light, and having happened upon a lamp, proceeded to seek for Harfager. Several hours went by in this way, during which I could not doubt from the state of the air in the house that the violence about me was being wildly heightened. Sounds as of screams—unreal, like the shriekings of demons—now reached my ears. As the time of night came on, I began to detect in the greatly augmented baritone of the cataract a fresh character—a shrillness—the whistle of a rapture—a malice—the menace of a rabies blind and deaf. It must have been at about the hour of six that I found Harfager. He sat in an obscure room, with his brow bowed down, his hands on his knees, his face covered with hair, and with blood from the ears. The right sleeve of his robe had been rent away in some renewed attempt, I imagined, to manage a window; and the rather crushed arm hung lank from the shoulder. For some time I stood and eyed him mouthing his mumblings; but now that I had found him uttered nothing as to my departure. Presently he looked sharply up with the call '*Hark!*'—then with impatience, 'Hark! Hark!'—then with a shout, 'The second bell!' And *again*, in immediate sequence upon his shout, there sounded a wail, vague yet real, through the house. Harfager at the instant dropped reeling with giddiness; but I, snatching up a lamp, dashed out, shivering but eager. For some while the wild wailing went on (either actually, or by reflex action of my ear); and as I ran for the lady's apartment, I saw opposite to it the open door of an

The House of Sounds

armoury, into which I passed, caught up a battle-axe, and was now about to dart in to her aid, when Aith, with a blazing eye, shied out of her chamber. I cast up my axe, and, shouting, dashed forward to down him: but by some chance the lamp fell from me, and before I knew anything more, the axe sprang from my grasp, and I was cast far backward by some most grim vigour. There was, however, enough light shining out of the chamber to show that the skeleton had darted into a door of the armoury, so I instantly slammed and locked the door near me by which I had procured the axe, and hurrying to the other, secured it, too. Aith was thus a prisoner. I then entered the lady's chamber. She lay over the bed in the alcove, and to my bent ear grossly croaked the ruckle of death. A glance at her mangled throat convincing me that her last moments were come, I settled her on the bed, curtained her within the loosened festoons of the hangings of black, and turned from the cursedness of her aspect. On an *escritoire* near I noticed a note, intended apparently for Harfager: 'I mean to defy, and fly; not from fear, but for the delight of the defiance itself. *Can* you come?' Taking a flame from the candelabrum, I left her to her loneliness, and throes of her death.

I had passed some way backward when I was startled by a queer sound—a crash—resembling the crash of a tamboureen; and as I could hear it pretty clearly, and from a distance, this meant some prodigious energy. In two minutes it again broke out; and thenceforth at regular intervals—with an effect of pain upon me; and the conviction grew gradually within me that Aith had unhung two of the old brass shields from their pegs, and holding them by their handles, and dashing them viciously together, thus expressed the frenzy that had now overtaken him. When I found my way back to Harfager, very anguish was now stamping in him about the chamber; he shook his head like a tormented horse, brushing and barring from his hearing each crash of the brass shields. 'Ah, when—when—' he hoarsely groaned into my ear, 'will that ruckle cease in her throat? I will myself, I tell you—*with my own hand*—oh God . . .' Since the morning his auditory fever (as indeed my own also) appeared to have increased in steady proportion with the roaring and screeching chaos round; and the death-struggle in the lady's throat bitterly filled for him the intervals of the grisly cymbaling of Aith. He presently sent twinkling fingers into the air, and, with his arms cast out, darted into the darkness.

And again I sought him, and long again in vain. As the hours passed, and the day deepened toward its baleful midnight, the cry of the now redoubled cataract, mixed with the mass and majesty of the now climatic tempest, took on too intentional a *shriek* to be longer tolerable to any reason. My own mind escaped my sway, and went its way: for here in the hot-bed of fever I was fevered. I wandered from chamber to chamber, precipitate, dizzy on the upbuoyance of a joy. 'As a man upon whom sleep seizes,' so I had fallen. Even yet, as I passed near the region of the armoury, the rapturous shields of Aith did not fail to smash faintly upon my ear. Harfager I did not see, for he, too, was doubtless roaming a hurtling Ahasuerus round the world of the house. However, at about midnight, observing light shining from a door on the lower stage, I entered and saw him there—the chamber of the dropping horologe. He sat hugging himself on the ladder-steps, gazing at the gloomy pool. The final lights of the riot of the day seemed dying in his eyes; and he gave me no glance as I ran in. His hands, his bare arm, were all washed with new-shed blood; but of this, too, he looked unconscious; his mouth was hanging open to his pantings. As I eyed him, he suddenly leapt high, smiting his hands with the yell, 'The last bell tinkling!' and ran out raving. He therefore did not see (though he may have understood by hearing) the thing which, with cowering awe, I now saw: for a ball slipped from the horologe with a hiss and mist of smoke into the pool; and while the clock once ticked another: and while the clock yet ticked, another! and the smoke of the first had not perfectly thinned, when the smoke of the third, mixing with it, floated toward the dome. Understanding that the sands of the mansion were run, I, too, throwing up my arm, rushed from the spot; but was suddenly stopped in my flight by the sense of some stupendous destiny emptying its vials upon the edifice; and was made aware by a crackling racket, like musketry, above, and the downpour of a world of waters, that some waterspout, in the waltz and whirl, had hurled its broken summit upon us, and burst through the dome. At that moment I beheld Harfager running toward me, his hands buried in his hair; and, as he raced past, I caught him, crying: 'Harfager, save yourself! the very fountains, Harfager—by the

The House of Sounds

grand God, man'—I hissed it into his inmost ear—'*the very fountains of the Great Deep* . . . !' He glared at me, and went on his way, while I, whisking myself into a room, closed the door. Here for some time with weak knees I waited; but the eagerness of my frenzy pressed me, and I again stepped out, to find the corridors everywhere thigh-deep with water; while rags of the storm, bragging through the hole in the dome, were now blustering about the house. My light was at once puffed out; but I was surprised by the presence of *another* light—most ghostly, gloomy, bluish—mild, yet wild—which now gloated everywhere through the house. I was standing in wonder at this when a gust of auguster passion galloped up the mansion; and, with it, I was made aware of the *snap* of something somewhere. There was a minute's infinite waiting—and then—quick—ever quicker—came the throb, snap, pop, in spacious succession, of the anchoring chains of the mansion before the hurried shoulder of the hurricane. And *again* a second of breathless stillness—and then—deliberately—its hour came—the house moved. My flesh worked like the flesh of worms which squirm. Slowly moved, and stopped—then there was a sweep—and a swirl—and a pause! then a swirl—and a sweep—and a pause! then steady labour on the brazen axis as the labourer tramps by the harrow; then a heightening of zest—then intensity—then the final light liveliness of flight. And now once again, as, staggering and plunging, I spun, the notion of escape for a moment came to me, but this time I shook an impious fist. 'No, but, God, no, no,' I gasped, 'I will no more go from here: here let me waltzing pass in this carnival of the vortices, anarchy of the thunders!'—and I ran staggering. But memory gropes in a greyer gloaming as to all that followed. I struggled up the stairway, now flowing a river, and for a good while ran staggering and plunging, full of wild rantings, about, amid the downfall of roofs, and the ruins of walls. The air was thick with splashes, the whole roof now, save three rafters, having been snatched by the wind away; and in the blush of that bluish moonshine the tapestries were flapping and trailing wildly out after the flying place, like the streaming hair of some ranting fakir stung reeling by the tarantulas of distraction. At one point, where the largest of the porticoes protruded, the mansion began at every revolution to bump with grum shudderings against some obstruction: it bumped, and while the lips said one-two-three it three times bumped again. It was the mænadism of mass! Swift—still swifter—in an ague of flurry it raced, every portico a sail to the gale, racking its great frame to fragments. I, running by the door of a room littered with the ruins of a wall, saw through that livid moonlight Harfager sitting on a tomb—a drum by him, upon which, with a club in his bloody fist, he feebly, but persistingly, beat. The speed of the leaning house had now attained the *sleeping* stage, that last pitch of the spinning-top; and now all at once Harfager dashed away the mat of hair which wrapped his face, sprang, stretched his arms, and began to spin—giddily—in the same direction as the mansion—nor less sleep-embathed, with lifted hair, with quivering cheeks. . . . From such a sight I shied with retching; and staggering, plunging, presently found myself on the lower floor opposite a porch, where an outer door chancing to crash before me, the breath of the tempest smote freshly upon me. On this an impulse, partly of madness, more of sanity, spurred in my soul; and I spurted out of the doorway, to be whirled far out into the limbo without.

The river at once rushed me deep-drenched toward the sea—though even there, in that depth of whirlpool, a shrill din, like the splitting of a world, reached my ears. It had hardly passed when my body butted in its course upon one of the arches, cushioned with seaweed, of the not all demolished cause-way. Nor had I utterly lost consciousness. A clutch freed my head from the drench; and in the end I heaved myself to the level of the summit. Hence to the ledge of rock by which I had come, the bridge being intact, I rowed myself on my face under the thumps of the wind, and under a rushing of rain, like a shimmering of silk through the air. Noticing the same wild shining about me which had blushed through the broken dome into the mansion, I glanced backward—and saw that the dwelling of the Harfagers was a memory of the past; then upward—and the whole north heaven, to the zenith, shone one ocean of variegated glories—the *aurora borealis,* which was being fairly brushed and flustered by the gale. At the augustness of which sight, I was touched to a gush of tears. And with them the dream broke! the infatuation passed! a palm seemed to skin back from my brain the films and media of delusion; and on my knees I threw my hands to heaven in thankfulness for the marvel of my rescue from all the temptation, the tribulation, and the breakage, of Rayba.

THE SPECTRE-SHIP

'Groans, and convulsions, and a discoloured face, and blacks, and obsequies.'—Bacon

I

'Odin sends out his Valkyrs to choose the slain,' said the Viking Sigurd to his nephew, Gurth; 'I go, and may not return: you know my will—see, Gurth, that you do it.'

His hands were on the heads of two children of nine, he kissed them, and leapt to his *yolle,* in which two champions rowed him to his dragon-ship lying near. As the lug-sail bulged hugely to the breeze, and the long galley stepped, gay with gilt spar and purple flag, down the *fjord,* Sigurd, on the poop, turned from his steering-oar and waved a hand. The setting sun glittered on his rich war-gear, he looming big, a towering bulk, with the long tile-beard of Assyrian kings, a white wire showing here and there in the russet. He waved his hand—his eighty rovers roared the refrain of a sea-song—and a bend hid them from the bay.

The bay was at the inner end of the winding *fjord,* a greensward sloping gently up from the beach, crowned at the top with an edge of forest; and midway stood the low 'burg', or manor-house, of the Viking's domain. To this turned Gurth, holding a hand of each of the children. So fast he walked that he dragged them; his grasp hurt them; exultation dancing in his heart and gloomy eye. He was master at last—perhaps for good—for 'Odin sends out his Valkyrs', and Sigurd the Viking was but mortal man.

Gurth, at a time when most men were warriors, was not a warrior; one saw that in his face—a puffy face, dark as a Norman's, seamed with deep lines, and hairless, with shifty eyes, and a broken nose. His back stooped deeply, and, standing by Sigurd, his head just reached the Viking's shoulder.

The Pale Ape and Other Pulses

He sat late that night in the wide hall, while around, on benches, lolled the residue of Sigurd's retainers, drinking mead from horns, and from the long hearths by the table sprang the fire-smoke to the open louvres in the roof. Gurth, brooding, sat at the table-head, fingering his embossed cup. Presently he sprang up, somewhat fuddled, and there was silence. 'Men,' he said, 'I am your over-man now; if there be thrall, or churl, or champion here disputes that, let him say it. But by the belt of Thor—!' he peered cunningly round, but no one stirred. 'Sigurd,' he continued, 'is gone a-Viking in Britland. *When* he may return, who knows? Meanwhile, we here have scarcity of much—of corn, fabrics, gold. Sigurd was a free-hand, a feaster, winking at sloth, so it were brave and bloody. I am for gathering together and husbanding. No idleness on the lands while I lord it here! Let every thrall do his sweating: everyone bring his share from land or sea. He who fails will know me better. I call a cheer!'

Malignity and a painful anxiousness wrinkled the face of Gurth: but, slowly, the men stood up and drank.

When a snore or two began to sound, he rose and glided across the courtyard. Frigga's lamp now westering low in the heavens. After passing three corridors, he tapped at a door, and was admitted into a chamber by old Gunhild, the *vala* of the burg. He sat near her, peering into her face.

'Well, now,' he said, 'have you wrought the spell for me?'

The old dame, robed in white, nodded meaningly far within her wimple.

'And is the good hap of Frey, *vala*, or the mischief of Loki to rule this life of mine?'

Gurth's soft hands were writhing clammily together, an agony of interest gazing from his eyes upon the grave old face.

'Loki or Frey?' she said, looking away at the setting moon: 'both, if you must know.'

'Ah . . . ! tell me.'

'You will conquer the living.'

His eyes closed.

'But beware of the dead.'

'How! the *dead*!'

The *vala* pointed a bent finger to a corner, where, on two beds, lay the children, the hair of the girl, Gerda, spreading over

The Spectre-Ship

the coverlet like a mat of gold, the arm of Hrolf, the son of Sigurd, lay under his head, the fist clenched.

'If harm come to *them*,' said Gunhild, 'All-father will see to it, I tell you.'

Little Gerda was an orphan, the daughter of a neighbouring Jarl, a close comrade of Sigurd, who, dying, had committed her to Sigurd, together with his lands and burg; and the last injunction of the Viking to Gurth had had reference to the marriage of the children, as soon as they should attain something like maturity. It was a project dear to his soul, and a foreboding that this his expedition might be one of those unending sails that brave men take at the behest of Heaven, had lent stern emphasis to his command.

'If harm come to *them* . . .' said Gunhild.

'But, look here, *vala*,' coaxed Gurth, spreading his hands, 'I *mean* no harm to them! Harm, do you think? As for the boy, if his father comes not back, in a few Yules we send him Viking, where let him bide the chances of the sea-fight; and fine, we all say, is death in the fight. As for the girl, seven, eight, passing summers will find her fit and marriageable. And why should not I, myself—?'

'What?'

'Well—*vala*—marry her.'

Gunhild looked calmly sidelong at his oily face.

'And so make quite sure of the Jarl's lands, Gurth?'

He chuckled. 'A wish to get, and increase in store, is but natural to us all.'

'Yet do *you*, Gurth,' she answered, shaking her finger at him, 'curb well your lust for wealth! for if I read right the signs—but fie! Gerda is for none of your marrying: there is grey already in your hair.'

'When—when will Sigurd return?'

'You mean to ask,' she said bitingly, 'whether he will return at all.'

'Well, put it so.'

'But I cannot tell. Only I know this, that he is of those high and great warriors who *do* return, though the world oppose them. And I say to you, Gurth, do your will and prosper; but beware of wrong to *those*.'

Gurth rose, bent his knee, and walked away, a greyness of morning now mingling with the dark.

II

In nine years no one any longer expected Sigurd: for the cruises of the Vikings were annual; and the bones of a hero absent nine years were well known to whiten on some shore, or roll with the tides of the ocean-flood.

Gurth, meanwhile, had 'conquered the living'. The rovers disliked him, but the trophies of their excursions they laid at his feet, that slight, dark man acquired an iron power over them. Ditlew, the Berserk, the jötun-furious, and least erect of all the spirits of the burg-guard, on returning from a voyage on the Throndheim coast, deeming himself ill-rewarded with booty, had deserted at dead of night, and sped fugitive, his horse burdened with stolen things; and Ditlew, a huge body ending in a broad-bearded coffee-pot, had reached a point where fear of pursuit no longer troubled him, when, springing from the dark of the forest, stood before him—Gurth. Ditlew did not suspect that Gurth was trembling with even chillier fears than he himself, although six thralls lurked near to protect him; and the sword-arm of the Berserk hung inert in the presence of this alert eye and all-divining brain. He returned submissively with Gurth, and from that night was like a cur, waiting upon the glance of his master. So, one by one, by force, by fraud, Gurth 'conquered' them.

One, however, no device could tame: when young Hrolf, at seventeen, had been ordered to sail a-Viking, and dying to go, had refused Ditlew, at a glance from Gurth, dragged him to the bay: and not till the Norway coast was low on the horizon did they release him. At once Hrolf sprang from the poop. His return he announced by firing a shed on the crag which was the watch-tower for the signalmen posted to flash the approach of enemies by means of beacons, Gurth believing himself invaded, while Hrolf dried his scarlet and yellow Viking-clothes at the burning shed.

At eighteen no love of opposition could longer keep him from the sea-joy. Gerda, sprung gracile now like the trepid gazelle on the crag-top, did the clasp of his ring-mail coat, and with a mock

The Spectre-Ship

curtsey put 'Tyrfing,' his grandfather's falchion, into his hand, while Hrolf stooped, and brushed with his lips the pink bloom of her cheek. She hardly noticed the caress then; but four days later, folding his clothes, he being then in mid-ocean, remembered, and blushed.

So Hrolf had drunk delight of battle, and come back brown; and the brine had thrashed him out a reddish beardlet. Gerda at the signal of his coming went fluttering down the *fjord*; and he, seeing her white dress, put off from his 'schip,' and met her without the usual kiss; and they walked to the burg together, while Gurth, seeing them come, said: 'Not too hasty, my young birds! Your wings grow fast, but I have a grave thought to clip them.'

Half a mile off, in the forest's depth, was a lakelet, and there through many an autumn afternoon Gerda had drifted in her skiff among the sedge of the shallows, hearing the chatter of the kittiwakes, or of tern, gull, osprey. It was there that from behind a tree, two days after his coming back, Hrolf stood watching the lake flooded with the after-glow of the set sun, and, floating in the midst of it, Gerda, all glorified, transfigured, her head sunk, her chest heaving in the sort of gentle trouble with which the ducks heaved on the lake's swell. Presently, by a glance almost intuitive, she saw Hrolf's red sleeve peep, and went pale—starting so, that the paddle slapped into the water. Hrolf, as if something momentous had happened, breathed to his tree: 'Odin! she's dropped her oar!'

He ran out then, shouting, to the shore.
'Wait, I am coming.'
'No!' she cried from far.
'What do you say?'
'Do not trouble.'
'But what will you do?'
'It is all right.'
'What is?'
'You will wet yourself.'
'I? Not a bit.'
'You will.'
'I am coming.'

He plunged down the rushy scaur, routing scaup and whimbrel, swam to the oar, and, like a water-dog, towed it to the boat. With commotion, apprehension, she beheld him come, and half stood, red and blanched.

'There, I said you would!'
'Would what?'
'Wet yourself.'
'Well, of course—'
'You said you wouldn't.'
'Ha! ha! But I am quite used to all that now.'
'You are such a very old—Viking.'
'I have killed my man.'
'And you have a beard.'
'And *you* are not the same, either.'
'I? Why not?'
'You seem so different since I have come back.'
'I am sorry for that, Hrolf, we were always such friends. Why different?'
'You look to me taller, and your eyes—how wonderfully blue your eyes are, Gerda!'

She bent them down, muttering something, looking upon the ebb and flow of her own bosom, in which the keenest pang shrieked for passion.

'And, look here'—he was close to her, his hand on the gunwale—'you did not—kiss me—when I came back.'
'Who didn't?'
'You didn't.'
'Why, Hrolf, are you sure?'
'Don't you suppose I'd remember?'
'You never asked, Hrolf.'
'Well—but can I come in?'
'No—don't! Hrolf, you will upset—'
'Let me!'
'But you couldn't!'
'If you sit heavily over yonder, perhaps I could.'

She went, and he made an effort, but at his long-legged mass the skiff cranked deeply. He gave it up.

'Stupid shell!' he said.

Gerda leant more heavily over the other side.

'Now, once more—try—' she said.

The Spectre-Ship

He tried again, and the next moment Gerda was in his arm in the water, his other hand clinging to the skiff's keel.

'Well, now—!' he gasped.

Her hair, wrapped about her head under a gold band, was hardly wet, and she could swim like a fish; but her eyes were closed, the woman in her being, or pretending to be, faint.

'Darling! Gerda!'—he was kissing her lifted lips—'You will be ill—'

Her arm tightened about him; her eyes opened and laughed, and closed anew at the renewed fury of his lips.

But Gurth, at the burg-door, seeing them approach bedraggled, strolled to meet them, and noticed their faces, the new meaning in their looks, the complicity, and bliss.

'How now?' he cried.

'Oh, nothing—go away,' said Hrolf: 'fell into the water.'

Gurth said to himself: 'Tonight.'

Then, close by Gerda, he whispered:—'Tonight I want to speak to you privately. You must come to the water-butt outside the burg, about nine—you hear?'

The world swam in a dream to her, so that she hardly heard, but answered: 'Yes.'

At the burg she snatched her hand free, and ran to change; then, in haste, rushed into the sanctum of Gunhild, to fall at the *vala's* knees, burying away her face, trembling: and Gunhild, gifted in heart-sight, understood, and stroked the gold, and bent her cheek to the ruby ear, crooning the rune:—

> 'Now may All-father,
> Odin, the work-skilled,
> Tunefullest song-smith,
> Gallant sea-rover,
> Faultless true-guesser,
> Guileful entangler,
> Odin wind-whispering,
> Grant that it end well!'

III

'*Marry* me?' said Gerda.

'Ay, that,' said Gurth.

It was nine near the water-butt.

She meant to laugh, but a sob burst from her lips.

Gurth held her wrist, his dark eyes alight.

'No tremblings! no faintings and flutterings! You are mine. I have nurtured you for this. Not a word! If you rebel—if you tremble—I cut off your hair, I pinch and nip your pretty graces, and grind you to my will like corn beneath the quern—you hear?'

'But who are you that you dare—'

'Silence! and him, too, remember—your young strutting cockerel—'

'*Him*! why, he can protect himself and me from a thousand such as you, Gurth Hermodsson!'

'Go!'—he flung her from him; 'say a month from now to prepare yourself within! And, meanwhile, you will be watched, be sure. Now run and tell your *vala* that it is I who swear it by the Thor's thunder!'

And to the *vala* Gerda did run, to sob the tale into the sibyl's ears. At midnight Gunhild stood alone, mumbling spells over a fire in a platter, and before morning had matured a plan in her world-wise brain.

She had Hrolf into her room, to tell the news: whereat 'Tyrfing' leapt, and Hrolf was all for war. But the *vala*, threatening and entreating, won him to a calmer mood.

'The will of Loki is set strongly against your ever having Gerda at all,' she said; 'everything is against you. Unless you have the manhood to curb that hot blood, you may give up hope and be done.'

He sat and listened. Her plan was flight, which seemed to her the only way of averting tragedy from the house of the Sigurdssons. The craft of Gurth she knew, his luck and knack of gaining an end; and she roused all her old acuteness to a combat of wits with him, she very feeble now, and this her final fight.

So Hrolf and Gerda should be seen no more together; on the third day Hrolf should pretend a journey to a neighbouring burg; and in the night the two should wait at appointed spots on the

The Spectre-Ship

crags, Hrolf having secretly returned. She knew that Gurth's spies watched them; but that night she would summon Gurth, and while they talked, Frid, one of her women, would bolt the door outside, so that Gurth would be her prisoner. Frid would then run and light a peat fire at the back of the burg-wall, a signal for the children to meet and ride away; for his spies, not finding Gurth, would not dare or care to follow. Without danger the two could then fare away to Jarl Svegdir's burg on the Ivan *fjord*, who would not be slow to grant them asylum; and, once wedded, their battle was more than half won.

On that third night, then—a gale blustering through the drizzly gloom—Gerda stood muffled, wet, on the crags north of the *fjord*, while Hrolf watched from the southern cliffs. The hour appointed for their meeting was about nine. But at ten no signal-fire had shot up.

Gurth was then walking up and down the hall, his hands behind his back, and every time he came to the door, he opened it slightly and looked out into the night. Men lolled silent about the room; the log-fires burned bright; and the eye of Ditlew, the Berserk, with the sleepy fidelity of a watch-dog, followed every step of Gurth in his ceaseless, feline pacing.

Toward eleven Hrolf said to himself: 'Beard of Thor! but will it never come?' and Gerda, trembling, haggard with terror, groaned aloud: 'Oh, some dreadful chance must have happened!'

At this hour Gurth, stopping before Ditlew, said: 'You are sure young Hrolf is back?'

'Yes,' Ditlew answered, 'I saw him.'

'And the girl?'

'Haeng, the house-churl, has had an eye upon her today.'

'And where is Haeng?'

'I thought the lout was here.'

'No, you see: he is not,' Gurth said, with a sly smile. 'Get up now, and have the six horses I spoke of this morning ready at the door. And just take red brand from the fire, and kindle me a flame at the back of the burg-wall yonder.'

Ditlew stared.

'Do it,' said Gurth, and continued his walk.

By that time Hrolf was saying to himself: 'Has Gunhild, then, played us false?' when he saw the flare at the appointed spot, and crying, 'good!—at last,' galloped through the forest to the other side of the *fjord*, near the cliff-edge of which he leapt off, and found Gerda.

'Quick now,' he panted, 'the way through the forest—'

'Hrolf,' she whispered, 'I have such a fear—Why was the signal so late?'

As she began to weep, he took her in his arms to the horse, lifted her to the pillion, sprang, and cantered.

A man, meanwhile, had crept from a cleft behind them, and run to the burg—the house-churl Haeng; and he rushed in to whisper to Gurth: 'They are off—through the forest!'

'To horse! to horse, you six!' Gurth cried, stamping, his eye flashing—'young Hrolf and my ward, Gerda—the way through the forest!'

Six fellows ran to the waiting horses, two snatching flambeaux from the sconces. These, as they entered the forest, heard the tramp of Hrolf's horse before them. But it was doubly weighted, and not the best of the burg: nor was the chase long. Presently Hrolf was lying on his back, bound, though 'Tyrfing' had passed through Haeng, the house-churl, and had chasmed the shoulder of Ditlew, the Berserk.

Meantime, Gurth as soon as his six had galloped from the door, sped across the courtyard, but his for a moment stopped, hesitating, full of doubts, then ran, and stopped, and ran again. At last, when near the *vala's* chamber, he drew off his *rivlins* from his feet, and crept, on tip-toe, to her door, which was fastened on the outside; and with an utter stealthiness Gurth undid the bolts. Fright and the triumph of his cunning fought for mastery in his face, but fright was uppermost: for the *vala* had thought to imprison him, and he had imprisoned her, the holy of the gods. Having noiselessly undone the bolt, he crept backward, took his slippers, and pelted back across the courtyard.

Listening at the door three days before he had heard the *vala* detail her scheme to Hrolf, and several plans had then passed through his brain: he might arrest the children at once; he might have men posted at the appointed spots to seize them separately. But he had decided that the lad must be caught in the act of snatching his ward from his control, in order that the subsequent cruelties which he intended might find justification in the eyes of the burg-men. His delay of hours in kindling the fire for their meeting had been prompted by the mere wantonness of the terrier playing with its prey.

In the morning a woman, entering the *vala's* chamber, found her sitting with both hands stiffly clenched, a stare of surprise and pride in her eyes. She, the long-honoured, in her old age, had been slain by an indignity, and Gurth had walked on tip-toe lest ears already dead should mark him—as the wicked flee when no man pursues.

IV

Success made of Gurth Hermodsson something of a devil—success and the death of the *vala* Gunhild. He had never dreamed of such a thing! and the incident upset and perverted him, he believing himself under the curse of heaven. For three weeks Gerda and Hrolf, each wondering where the other was, were prisoners near each other in rooms of the burg. Gerda, dishevelled, woebegone, refusing food. Twice, since the *vala's* burial, Gurth had visited her, and she had sprung to a corner, like a cat at bay, hopeless, but ready to tear, if touched. To his talk of marriage, threats of force, the slight downward curve of her lip gave answer.

'If the boy were dead!' thought Gurth, but he did not see his way, as yet, to murder, the burg-men, though subdued, being yet men, brave, and some of them might find murder intolerable. But the thought put into his head a triumphant idea, and the next day Ditlew, by instruction, slipped into Gerda's room.

He spoke kindly; told of Hrolf; that he was close to her, confined like her.

'But I come as a friend to warn you,' said Ditlew: 'I come secretly—no one knows. There's near danger hanging over the youth's head.'

'Danger!'

'Well, you know Gurth Hermodsson: he is a man must have his way. He does not *say* anything, but I know well enough what he will do, if you hold out against him.'

'To Hrolf?'

The Pale Ape and Other Pulses

'Aye. If the lad's in the way, he will be removed, I tell you. Perhaps this very night—in his sleep—'

She leapt then to him, caught him by his two sleeves, on her knees 'Ditlew! have you a cat's heart, good Ditlew? Have I ever done you harm?

'Ah, now you rave,' he said, 'what can *I* do?'

He undid her grasp and went away, leaving her on the floor.

In an hour she sent a message to Gurth, saying that she was prepared to marry him on the morrow.

༄

And on the morrow an altar on the greensward ran gory with bullock's blood, and the new *vala* chanted before it, and Gurth at last was master, beyond the tricks of chance, of the old Jarl's lands.

As if half-ashamed of the mummery, he had performed his part stammeringly, shyly awkward; but afterwards walked blithely to the burg, shrilling high a summoning horn. For Gerda he had taken a silken robe from the store-house, which she wore, to everything she acquiescing with spiritless abandonment, stipulating only that Hrolf should not be released that day, and on the next that she should be conveyed away to her father's burg, and he set free.

And beside Gurth, at the table-head, she sat through the afternoon, while freer and freer flowed the mead, and higher swelled the tumult of good cheer and forgetfulness of sorrow, till Gurth, mollified by his cup, turned for the first time to his marble bride, and said: 'Take heart, fair face! No mischief is meant you! There breathes no more harmless a rascal than thy old Gurth to them who let him go his way in quietness.'

And, as if in answer, a cheer came wafted from the bay. In a lull of the festal uproar it came, and everyone seemed to hear it. A silence fell. Gurth looked, questioning, round.

The next moment a churl came running to him to murmur:— 'Sigurd Sigurdsson *is come* back, and half his champions with him.'

The drinking-horn dropped, and the rascal toppled, collapsed, head-prone upon the table, shot in the breast. It might be said that he swooned—the world whirled from under his foot. But only for a minute.

The Spectre-Ship

He sprang, straight, sober. He beckoned to Ditlew. He whispered to Gerda, his eyes rolling round the room: 'Go now with Ditlew; later I will come to you.' He whispered to Ditlew: 'Lock her fast in the same place, and look well to the lad, too, and keep the keys. Sigurd is come. Later, keep close to me. I may want you.' Then, the Berserk and his charge having passed out, he lifted his voice: 'Men! good news for you. Sigurd Sigurdsson is *here*. Let us bid him hearty welcome, I say. But as to this marriage of mine, I would myself first tell of it to Sigurd. See, then, that *ye* say nothing. Remember! '

He turned, followed by the men, and half-way on the sward he met Sigurd.

The Viking in ten years had grown old: his beard was white, his hair was white. But that heroic frame stood still erect. His heart was calm, and the majesty of the world-warrior victorious over chance, and destiny, and death, crowned the man, ennobling the glance of his brow to something like god-likeness.

'Ah, Gurth Hermodsson!' he said, blithely calm: 'good sight to see.'

His hand fell upon Gurth's shoulder.

'And good sight, you, to see,' said Gurth—'and—strange.'

'Well, Gurth, the world is the field of battle for us poor godsons, and a man must even fight his best in it, and die. I have been away in Britland, joined to a host of Saxon-men, fighting with Scot, fighting with Pict, fighting here, fighting there. I saw the work was worth doing, and in God's name I went and did it. . . But, man, the children!'

'The children?' said Gurth.

'Aye, man.'

For thirty eternal seconds Gurth hesitated. When his lips next moved, he was a lost soul.

'The children are but lately married; are gone away together to the old Jarl's burg.'

He knew that in a day, at most, that lie must be detected—if Sigurd lived a day.

'Well said!' cried Sigurd, and patted the shoulder beneath his hand. They entered the burg, the other men, interchanging greetings, trooped in. Sigurd and Gurth sat apart in colloquy.

'But this is a merry day with you,' Sigurd said, nodding at the table.

'A holiday for the cullions here. But as to treasure, now: come back full?'

'Full, Gurth, and over-full; and a cargo, over and above, is in keeping for me at Lerwick in Hjaltland, where I last year left it.'

Gurth's eyes kindled.

'Who keeps it?'

'Old Ragnar, who jarls it now at Lerwick.'

'But it should be sent for.'

'Let it lie, man. I am weary, Gurth, of spoil and treasure, of sea-flash and sword-flash. Let it lie.'

'I will go and get it.'

'As you will.'

'This very day.'

'As you will, man.'

Sigurd's eyes were looking far away, as men, after a long night of storm, watch for morning. The goad which was urging Gurth was the necessity to be far—at once—far from the burg! and to be known by all men to be far.

Before nightfall he had forty of the men on board the *Skidblednir,* a swift dragon, and below decks, alone with Ditlew, smuggled a phial containing a green liquid into the Berserk's hand.

'There is enough for two,' he said ; 'if you fail, you had better drink the rest.'

Ditlew and others rowed to shore, and the *Skidblednir* moved down the *fjord.*

Sigurd, at supper that night, felt a stomach-gripe, and broke into the sweat of death. He was supported to his old chamber, and there for hours, from those lips which never uttered groan, burst groan on groan. Towards morning a shriek went piercing through the place, like the strong hinny of a horse in pain. But the dawn brought balm.

Men knew not what to think: it was so sudden. None dreamed of foul play, for Gurth, who might have had motive, was away. His chosen rovers hung round his couch, full of low-spoken stories of his reign and age, his heroic rage, and social soul. He was the greatest of the Vikings, they said; the type of a good man.

The Spectre-Ship

On the third morning, Hrolf and Gerda stood with the rest over him, for the new-returned rovers had insisted upon their release. And now on a bier they bore him, and laid him out on a pyre of wood raised high on the poop of his long old dragon-ship, placing beside him his gold casque, his target and sword: and his great bulk, thus raised up, lay far conspicuous in its tunic of ruby silk. The morning stormily dribbled a cold sleet that trickled tearfully from the closed lids to the beard, and guttered in streams over the great lug-sail. Down the length of the *fjord* they towed her, and moored her to a stake on the shore of an open roadstead, where, all day long, shallow rows of rollers trooped in to the funeral, crooning their coronachs; and with every heave of her beak to meet their frothy swarming, the dragon with her poop-end struck the sand, and gently shook her dead. Toward nightfall the shore was alive with rovers; and just as the sun's sinking brim broke in glory through the grey day and set the sea-breath ablaze, some of the braves held flames to the under-curve of the stern; some loosed the moorings; others, pushing, launched her forth, her scarlet sail paunching to the squall, as she walked flaming down the flame that the sunset made. From the shore, with spiritless hand-waves they called him, in chorus, a last farewell.

Such, as we know, was the form in which the Norsemen were accustomed to commit to the sea the corpses of its kings.

But, in the flurry of the moment, the dragon had somehow been pushed off before the hold of the flames was well established: and she had hardly dashed into the region of rough green swell, when the wash of the waves began to tell upon her flame. It burned low, and further out she butted into a surge, to come out of it scorched, but seaworthy, and without a spark, the corpse still unsinged. The rovers, hardly now observing, could not discern from afar that the sunset flames which wrapped her were not the flames which ravage.

The old Gunhild, by some lucky stroke of divination, had said to Gurth: ' You will conquer the living—but *beware of the dead.*'

From that part of the Norway coast to the Hjaltland Isles, there and back, was a run of six or seven days; so on the morning of the fifth day out, Gurth was returning loaded, the centre of a horizon of sea: The morning came darkly, convulsed with squalls, the wind blowing somewhat from the West of South, and the *Skidblednir*, close-hauled was steering East, labouring heavily, when at seven a man rushed below, and woke Gurth with the news that a ship, larger than the *Skidblednir*, perhaps some hostile pirate-keel, bearing upon them straight before the wind, had been sighted. Gurth, a poltroon, had his ship been empty, would still have shunned any possibility in the nature of blows; loaded as she was, he sprang from his couch, apprehension widening his eyes, crying: 'Tell them to put out every oar and run before the wind.'

In three minutes the *Skidblednir* was flying north-east from the foam of her own wide wake; in an hour the other ship, from which no oars had been put out, had disappeared; and Gurth then agreeing to resume his course, they breathed from the oars, and drew her again to the wind. But now they had somewhat lost count of their position.

At noon, through the dimness of the sunless day, they sighted that ship again bearing down upon them.

Away, then, northward: once more let the oars march regimental over the sea-room, and the gust load the loosened lug! With every swoop of the thirty blades, Gurth stooped his body forward, to help her haste, his heart whispering to the knave strange awes, his hands as chill as the hands of Sigurd.

At three they breathed afresh. But a great gale was then raging, and no soul on the *Skidblednir* had any longer any notion where they were, whither they went. A half-darkness, gloomy as doom, immured them. But at about the hour that the sun, had it been visible, would have been seen to sink, the bleakness lifted a little just south of them, and beneath that lifted curtain they dimly observed—the ship.

Away, then! . . . They needed no longer the urgings of Gurth to fly for life, for in every breast trembled a terror never felt before, nameless, vague. And now down rushed suddenly upon them the raven draperies of night—the last sight that met their eyes having been the spectre-ship.

The Spectre-Ship

They were near the Norway sea-board, did not know it, and drove straight upon one of the whirlpools that swirl in frothy fury along that coast. A roar grew gross upon them, and before long the *Skidblednir* bolted suddenly from the control of her oars, and spurted like a bird into a wide circular flight. Some were at once tossed away like feathers into the waters; the others, felled to the deck, clung to whatever they could; and, racing two cable-lengths behind them, came the ship which had chased them to this, invisible in the blackness—till a lamp, shattered in the forehold of the *Skidblednir* by her flight, belched forth an opal of smoke and fire. This light revealed, high above them, a writhing and reeling horizon; below, a well, toward which, in lessening whirls they were flying round and round an incline of churning surge. And now streaks of flying fire, streaming aft from the *Skidblednir,* having fastened upon the other ship, she, too, bloomed up into tulip bloom: and to Gurth Hermodsson, glancing abroad from his tafferel, was manifested the grim form of Sigurd lying grand and arrogant on his pyre. At this sight, Hermodsson sent to the skies a cry high above that agony-cry of the gulf, and dropped. When the *Skidblednir* bounded bow downward into the abyss he was already dead.

'But,' said Hrolf, a year afterwards, 'what if Gurth Hermodsson some day turn up? He may be alive all the time: then I should no longer be your husband.'

'That is true,' answered Gerda gravely, 'we must talk the matter over—when he comes.'

THE GREAT KING
'Belphegor was no ordinary devil:'—MACHIAVELLI

'You never,' said my Uncle Quintus, 'heard the story of the Great King? Well, that, perhaps, goes without saying, for you are unable to read cuneiform writing, and I only, and one other learned man, have as yet deciphered the history.'

My Uncle Quintus—the indefatigable man—had but lately returned from digging and delving among the ruin-heaps of Nimroud and Khosabad, and where the village of Hillah stands today, where Babylon was. It was a wild night, rags of gusts tormented the tapestries, the flicker only of the fire lighted us. We made it the centre of a mumping semicircle while my Uncle Quintus puffed from a petty pipette the smoke of some preparation of *cannabis,* which had followed him from the East.

'What you have already heard about the King,' he said, 'is that he went mad with pride; but even then you have no notion of the man's intensities—Nero, Sardanapalus, were innocents. And with all this he was a coward, too.'

The queen was Nicotris from Ionia, her Western name Moira, she having the straight nose, the bulging chin, of the daughters of the Greeks. Intercourse between East and West was not yet very close, and it is not known by what providence she was drawn to Babylon, but the King saw, and in his greed for the novel, loved her. And now was seen a spectacle: the Ionic woman was observed to acquire an altogether singular power over the mind of Nebuchadnezzar—a Chaldean king—the embodied majesty—the splendour of the heavens revealed in garments of flesh. And when Nicotris, from being loved, grew to be *feared,* all marvelled. Yet she was the mildest of women: the mighty men called her 'the suave' Queen Nicotris.

A wasting malady fell upon this lady. She lay as dead—cold in the black-stone coffin—and her maidens, with dole and plaint, annointed her lips with oil, and through the nights wailed round her their wild *nenia* for the soul flown from life, thrumming the dulcimer and ten-stringed psaltery to chaunts starry, strange, lamenting in melody many days. But when the wardens of the necropolis, followed in procession by the horned archpriests of Astarté, came to bear her from the palace to the tomb, Nicotris, starting from catalepsy, opened her blue eyes, and awoke once more to life. The like was not known before, this dual habiting of earth and the land of shadows. From that day the King ceased to love his queen.

The great stature of Nicotris, her emaciation, the pallor of her face, wrought strongly on the fancy of the King. She would pass lightly as a shadow, the diadem on her head, through the banqueting-chamber, where the King, bright with wine, sat at midnight with his ministers; and as she so passed, she would hold up, mildly smiling, a thin, forewarning finger. Then the silence of a minute, and a frown on the King's brow.

The mystery of her 'awaking from the dead' freed her from all compulsion. None could tell what dark secrets she hid within her brain, brought back from those deep, pale kingdoms into which her venturesome spirit had strayed, on what sights of terror her wide eyes had rested in all the trance of that far travel! Was she, indeed, a woman amongst women, or a true visitant from the grave? The King no longer companied with her: nard and cassia and musk could not overcome that odour of the tomb which, in his fantasy, she bore about with her; he shunned the calm of her smile; he fled the embrace of her fleshless breast; first awe, then hate, filled the heart of the King for the suave Queen Nicotris.

Yet Nicotris loved the King, though, knowing all his weaknesses, his pride, she constantly sought to curb him. Often she would draw him, in spite of himself from the revelry of wine to the moon-lit garden-paradise of the palace, they forming then a great contrast, she tall a head above him, the King obese, swart, with thick lips, and flowing beard. Often, too, she would constrain him to follow her to the top of that tremendous temple of Bel— pyramidal, seven-terraced, to symbolise the planets—where stood the observatory of the astrologers. And here, on this height, when in the dark morning Pleiades sloped steeply in the skies, the Queen would wax ecstatic, and with her scarlet-robed arm, would sweep

The Great King

from azimuth to azimuth the starry deeps, prophesying with authority of one Highest of All—asking who caused the horned horse of Astarté to haunt the earth, and whose hand hurled 'the crooked serpent' across the vault. From all this the King would turn with loathing.

But her will was law in the Court. When, for instance, the remnants of Nineveh rebelled, and it was decided that they should all be slain, the Queen walked calmly into the council-hall, and with warning, with persuasiveness, prayed for their preservation; whereupon the King dashed his sceptre down, and stalked from the hall; the Ministers passed out in silence after him: while Nicotris, left alone, bending to the big black baboon from the crags of Ararat, which ever accompanied her steps, said with her placid smile: 'You see, Pul, my friend, how these men receive the admonitions of wisdom!' Yet that day the irresistibleness of her will prevailed, and the conquered were spared.

The King was returning from hunting the lion on the plain of Dura, and passing slowly in his chariot through the labyrinth of Babylon when suddenly at a corner he saw a maiden whose beauty overcame his soul. She was daintily shod in badger's skin, and shimmered like a daughter of shahs in fine linen, and silk, and broidered work—blue and purple and vermilion—an emerald raying merrily from her forehead. Her veil being lifted, for a moment the King saw fully the vision, and then the damsel span and vanished down a shadowy alley. The King ordered two of his lords to follow, who thought they saw her enter a house, and into this they ran—the dwellings being all constructed pyramid-wise, with a terrace on the flat roof of each story, on which grew the palms, and cedars, and vines of the famed pleasure-gardens. In a nook, perhaps, of one of these the maiden hid; the people of the house did not know her; the officers tremulously sought her everywhere; but she had vanished. They questioned themselves: was this, then, a creature of air sent by destiny to trouble the brain of the King—a warning from the gods? The nervosity of Nebuchadnezzar, his terror of death, of the sight of death, of the world of spirits, had infected all his Court.

When the King reached the steps of the palace, 'Where is Nicotris, the Queen?' he asked of the cup-bearer, who presented to him, while yet in the street, a goblet of spiced wine.

'She lies ill in the forecourt of the women's quarter,' answered Vajezatha.

Many times that day did the King inquire of the state of Nicotris. An impatience possessed him as to whether she would fall again into the unnatural death-life—the hateful death without its decay, the unholy life without its pulse—perhaps to wake again? The thing, he thought, must end—he would end it. And he remembered the vision of brightness and grace in the street of the city.

He visited her in person at dawn, a fiendish intent born in his brain, the harem being a series of chambers grouped round one of the courts of the palace, and the palace itself a low structure, placed on the top of an immense platform of glazed bricks. The King passed through the gloom of a vault, guarded on each hand by winged cherubim, which formed the entrance to the harem and found Nicotris reclining on an ivory couch in one of the 'galleries,' her only guard the old ape, the faithful Pul, garrulous by her side. The King gazed long at her, a paleness on his face; he had sworn to end it—with his own secret hand. But though Nicotris could not speak, as if she divined the evil of his thoughts, as if she had heard of the meeting in the street, she lifted up a thin finger. Nebuchadnezzar turned away.

Late that same day a message came to the King declaring that Queen Nicotris had, to all appearance, entered the state of death.

She was carried by her damsels in an uncovered coffin of black marble to a corner of the paradise, if haply the breezes from the plain might again revive her, the paradise occupying a court at a corner of the platform on which the palace stood, abutting the city walls, and enclosed on two sides by the alabaster parapet of the platform, and on the other two by columns connected by curtains of silk. Here many a fountain plashed on crocus and daphne and ixia; gourd, melon, and fig; the love-apple and the henna-tree; and at one end stood a pigmy ebon temple to the God Nisroch, guarded by winged bulls. Before the steps of this the Queen was laid:

The King stepped from the banquet at midnight and walked in the garden, his brain brave with the bright wine of Iran, exultation filling him that he was free at last—for ever—from the awesome Nicotris. She should be promptly entombed, he said; no re-awaking this time! He did not dream how near the queen's body lay.

All suddenly—before the temple steps—he saw. Marble she slumbered below the moon. The King sprang backwards, groaning in pain. Panic seized him, then tumultuous rage. How came she here? It was a fate's mockery, and with the eyeballs of the striped hyena of Shinar shining in his head, like the ounce before it springs he crouched, and just so sinuously crept toward the coffin, drawing with horrid furtiveness a pigmy scimitar from his girdle. He struck. Only *once* has the hand of a man committed an infamy so mephitic. The gash slashed the integuments which ligament the hinges of the jaw together—the mouth howled agape. The King saw the redness—and saw no more.

As he ran, a sob in his throat, two eyes, questioning, upbraiding, from behind a pillar, met his own. He knew the eyes of Pul, the ape, and dashed forward to fell the beast with a stroke, but Pul vanished.

The manner of the Assyrians was to sepulchre in caves without a city, cut out of the rock, or built of painted bricks, each coffin being placed within a rock-chamber of its own, the coffin itself of stone, and the lid of a vitreous material, similar to the modern glass. In such fashion, followed by the mourning Pul, was the good Queen Nicotris, on being found mysteriously disfigured—and *now* at least supposed to be really dead—borne to her rest on the following day, the seventh of the month Adar.

Thus had the King cast off from him the coils of Nicotris. But as he passed at night-fall of that day to the halls of the harem through the now vacant bedchamber of the Queen, a new wretchedness befell him. It was dark; the curtains of the galleries were drawn; he was alone. In the obscurity—a sighing. Peering, he was aware of a something—an outline. The King turned and fled.

The distemper of the restless mind possessed the King in those days. He would leap from sleep with distraught eye and drenched hair, like a man haunted. A night-sound, the human shape of a drapery, had power to dismay him. He hated solitude. No longer did the banquet of wine work its magic of forgetfulness.

He sent in secret for the chief of the soothsayer-priestesses, who served day and night in the temple of Astarté, and she, coming in the darkest hour before the day, had conference with the King in an inner gallery of the palace, the King sitting on the edge of his couch in disarray, she doddering before him, bent with age, dry of face, with tiny bright eyes full of knowing.

'Two things,' he said, 'you shall do, or die: you shall lay the spirit that infests me; and you shall tell me the name and abode of a maiden whom, on the first of Adar, I saw in the streets of Babylon.'

'I can do even more—I can *show* the King the maiden,' answered the hag.

'How?'

'In vision first. If the King will come to an appointed spot tomorrow at midnight, alone—I will show the King this thing.'

'I will come.'

When the sibyl descended the stairway in the wall, the King rose and walked to and fro in the gallery. He looked over the endlessness of Babylon, on which the moon shone, on the pyramids, temples, the three days' journey of the city walls. From that station he could see on the plain the colossal golden image which he himself had set up. And he stamped with his foot; he brandished his arm, challenging. The thought swelled within him: 'Is not this great Babylon . . . ?'

And while the King was so thinking, arms from behind involved him, and the touch of a hand lay on his throat. He fell faint . . .

All the next day he wandered from court to court, unkinglike, with ragged head, with foam-flecked beard, and the flight of a dagger from his hand ended in the breast of a cup-bearer who approached with wine.

As night fell his brow grew gloomier, he sitting on the throne of the audience-hall, his head drooping to his knees, the majesty all gone. At midnight he dismissed all; and, looking this way and that, crouched secretly down the great stairway to the south-west gate over against the palace.

Here Zeresh, the sorceress, awaited him. They passed together over the plain, the wind soughing across the desert; and there was a threatening of thunder. But the moon shone bright.

The King stalked, Zeresh struggling to keep by him. Presently he stopped.

'Whither would you lead me?'

The Great King

'To the city of tombs, O King.'

'The *what*?'

'It is there only that I have power to show the King the vision.'

The King moved onward more slowly.

'I will tell you something,' he said, abruptly, 'and let your science unravel it. The Queen Nicotris is dead: yet, as I passed through her apartment by night, a form seemed to stand before me.'

Zeresh smiled.

'I know not,' she answered, 'but if the form was of nothing human, might it not have been that of the favoured Pul, which doubtless still haunts his mistress's chambers?'

'Yet I had ordered that the ape should be hunted from the palace. But what say you to hands, cold like the hands of Nicotris; laid on my flesh in the morning watch?'

Zeresh showed a tooth.

'Without doubt the hands of the playful Pul, oh, King, returned from banishment by climbing the palace platform.'

They had come to the ruins of Hur, where the brool of the lion, the whine of the wild cat, stalking amid the fallen walls, caught the ear. On the right the Euphrates; piled round, 'whatsoe'er of strange sculptured on alabaster obelisk, or jasper tomb, or mutilated sphinx,' outlived the wreck of the erections of the world's first cities. The desolation here was complete.

'Tell me,' the King said, 'what is the nature of the vision which waits for me.'

'The King will first enter the anti-chamber of a tomb.'

Nebuchadnezzar shuddered.

'Here heaven will descend to wanton with the nostrils of my lord.'

The sibyl had, in fact, commanded two damsels to be in waiting in the darkness, with censers exhaling vapours.

'The King,' she continued, 'will now advance, draw aside a tapestry, descend three steps, and enter the second hall of the dead; immediately a swarm of spheres will wawl sweetness to his ear.'

She had similarly secreted to this room cunning lutists with flute and dulcimer.

'Once more the King will advance, draw aside a curtain and now, before him, he shall see—'

'*Her?*'

'In a nimbus.'

'She had stationed in this third hall the most lovely of her acolytes, robed in cloth of silver; directly in front of whom a cauldron over a fire, containing a combination of natron, bitumen and sulphur, was to send up a smoke, through the obscure of which the vision should loom: and the King's' eye having rested upon her, the young priestess was to vanish into one of the side-chambers.

The wind had risen, and splashes of rain began to fall accompanied by thunderclaps.

An eagle flew low athwart their way.

'That,' Zeresh said, in the strain of the animistic anthropomorphism of the East,[*] 'is the Eagle. He gazes into the sun's heart. How strong his wing! See him preen for flight! He is the emblem of pride.'

The King glanced distrustfully at her.

They came to a tarn, by which, on one leg, stood a bittern, in the hurricane which now swept the plain.

'See,' said Zeresh, 'the bittern: he broods by the lonesome pool; gloomy he is: the emblem of the sullen mood, ever ungrateful, never content.'

The King frowned at this.

They had nearly reached the outermost bounds of the city of the dead, when a bison bounded bellowing across their way.

'Look!' Zeresh cried, 'the wild ox! He eats the grass of the earth, yet spurns the earth with his foot. Who can tame him? He tosses his head in his strength. He is the emblem of the unbridled spirit—what they of Ionia call '*atasthalia,*' the undisciplined soul.'

'Cease, hag!' the King cried.

Zeresh covered her mouth with her hand.

They had now come to the entrance to the tombs, when all at once both stopped as if struck to stone, the gold of the hag's face growing a ghastlier hue, a new terror weakening the King's knees.

---

[*] See Job

The Great King

A darkness had fallen upon the earth. The moon brooded a lurid ruby.

'Astarté veils her face!' rattled Zeresh's throat: 'there is wrath!'

But when the earth's shadow began to journey from the girdle of the satellite, the hag asked, 'Will the King advance?'

The King was leaning on a rock. His lips quivered, but could not speak.

'Let us proceed,' urged the witch, 'or the King's chance of seeing the vision may pass.' With effort he raised himself, to walk now with steps all inconsequent through rows of mausoleums, till Zeresh stopped before an open portal.

'If my lord has courage to enter; the revelation will not fail; all will be as I said—the odours, the music, the vision.'

'But the tomb is black as doom; I dare not pass through it!'

'The gloom is necessary,' Zeresh answered; 'there is nothing for my lord to dread.'

The King trembled through the portal into a passage, at the end of which, pushing aside a curtain, he entered the first chamber, lost in the darkness, hearing behind him, down the corridor, the coronachs of the breezes sighing. He waited stationary, that the promised fragrances might gratify him: his nostrils were assailed by the smell of death exhaled by the sarcophagi.

Uttering a grunt of disgust, he groped onward, and drawing aside a tapestry, descended three long steps to the second apartment.

Instantly he was aware of another presence in the apartment, a being rushing like the wind from end to end, which presently in brushing briskly past, touched him. A spirit riving in his pangs! So, too, had thought the maidens secreted there by Zeresh, who had fled with shrieks from the cave before the spectre, not knowing that Pul, since he had followed his mistress to the tombs, had become a denizen of their solitudes.

But the music! With all of sense that remained to him—with a despairing *hope*—the King listened, straining every dazed faculty to catch the strains, while to and fro swept the breath of Pul. And now, indeed, there came a sound—but loud, heart-madding—a sound of clash and clangour, like the crackling of glass, like the battering apart by the dead of the bars of the prison house of death.

The King's flesh crept, and with all sense of direction lost, casting up his arms, he ran. Thus he came to the third drapery, which parted before his flight.

And now at last there was light. The cauldron of Zeresh burning over a pan containing embers, sent up its pharos of vapour, in the midst of which the King's eye lighted on a form at whose horror his brain tottered: a form tall, wrapped from head to foot in the cerements of the grave, her arms outspread, her brow bound about with a napkin. He saw the straight nose—the bulging chin—the risen Nicotris! And, as he looked, the face-cloth, knotted loosely above the poll, slowly unravelled itself, and dropped; the gashed jaws, held together by a single ligament, dropped agape.

. . . From her throat there broke an outcry . . .

King Nebuchadnezzar stood with his eyes staring before him—the muscles of his face rigid—his thick lips parted. So passed a full minute. Then he drew his fingers across his forehead with a look of lunacy; but this, too, soon passed; and now he was calm, as his mouth sidled and settled into the smile of idiotcy.

And he was driven from men; and his dwelling was with the beasts of the field; and his hairs were grown like bird's feathers, as the eagle's; and his nails like bird's claws, as the bittern's; and he did eat grass as the wild ox.

And his body was wet with the dew of heaven.

THE BRIDE

'He shall not see the rivers, the floods,
the brooks of honey and butter.'—JOB

THEY met at Krupp and Mason's, musical-instrument-makers, of Little Britain, E.C., where Walter had been employed two years, and then came Annie to typewrite, and be serviceable. They began to 'go out' together after six o'clock; and when Mrs Evans, Annie's mamma, lost her lodger, Annie mentioned it, and Walter went to live with them at No. 13 Culford Road, N.; by which time Annie and Walter might almost be said to have been engaged. His salary, however, was only thirty shillings a week.

He was the thorough Cockney, Walter; a well-set-up person of thirty, strong-shouldered, with a square brow, a moustache, and black acne-specks in his nose and pale face.

It was on the night of his arrival at No. 13, that he for the first time saw Rachel, Annie's younger sister. Both girls, in fact, were named 'Rachel'—after a much-mourned mother of Mrs Evans'; but Annie Rachel was called 'Annie,' and Mary Rachel was called 'Rachel.' Rachel helped Walter at the handle of his box to the top-back room, and here, in the lamplight, he was able to see that she was a tallish girl, with hair almost black, and with a sprinkling of freckles on her very white, thin nose, on the tip of which stood collected, usually, some little sweats. She was thin-faced, and her top teeth projected a little so that her lips only closed with effort, she not so pretty as pink-and-white little Annie, though one could guess, at a glance, that she was a person more to be respected.

'What do you think of him?' said Annie, meeting Rachel as she came down.

'He seems a nice fellow,' Rachel said: 'rather good-looking. And strong in the back, you bet.'

Walter spent that evening with them in the area front-room, smoking a foul bulldog pipe, which slushed and gurgled to his suction; and at once Mrs Evans, a dark old lady without waist, all sighs and lack of breath, decided that he was 'a gentlemanly, decent fellow.' When bedtime came he made the proposal to lead them in prayer; and to this they submitted, Annie having forewarned them that he was 'a Christian'. As he climbed to his room, the devoted girl found an excuse to slip out after him, and in the passage of the first floor there was a little kiss.

'Only one,' she said, with an uplifted finger.

'And what about his little brother, then?' he chuckled a chuckle with which all his jokes were accompanied: a kind of guttural chuckle, which seemed to descend or stick straining in the throat, instead of rising to the lips.

'You go on,' she said playfully, tapped his cheek, and ran down. So Walter slept for the first night at Mrs Evans'. On the whole, as time passed, he had a good deal of the society of the women: for the theatre was a thing abominable to him, and in the evenings he stayed in the underground parlour, sharing the bread-and-cheese supper, and growing familiar with the sighs of Mrs Evans over her once estate in the world. Rachel, the silent, sewed; Annie, whose relation with Walter was still unannounced, though perhaps guessed, could play hymn-tunes on the old piano, and she played. Last of all, Walter laid down the inveterate wet pipe, led them in prayer, and went to bed. Most mornings he and Annie set out together for Little Britain.

There came a day when he confided to her his intention to ask for a rise of 'screw,' and when this was actually promised by His Terror, the Boss, there was joy in heaven, and radiance in futurity, and secret talks of rings, a wedding, 'a Home'. Annie felt herself not far from the kingdom of Hymen, and rejoiced. But nothing, as yet, was said at No. 13: for to Mrs Evans' past grandeurs thirty shillings a week was felt to be inappropriate.

The next Sunday, however, soon after dinner, this strangeness occurred: Rachel, the silent, disappeared. Mrs Evans called for her, Annie called, but it was found that she was not in the house, though the putting away of the dinner-things, her usual task, was only half accomplished. Not till tea-time did Rachel return. She was then cold, and somewhat sullen, and somewhat pale, her lips closing firmly over her projecting teeth. When timidly questioned —for her resentment was greatly feared—she replied that she had just been looking in upon Alice Soulsby, a few squares away, for a little chat: and this was the truth.

It was not, however, the whole truth; she had also looked in at the Church Lane Sunday School on her way: and this fact she guiltily concealed. For half an hour she had sat darkly at the end of the building in a corner, listening to the 'address'. This address was delivered by Walter. To this school every Sunday, after dinner, he put down the beloved pipe to go. He was, in fact, its 'superintendent.'

After this, the tone and temper of the little household rapidly changed, and a true element of hell was introduced into its platitude. It became, first of all, a question whether or not Rachel could be 'experiencing religion,' a thing which her mother and Annie had never dreamt of expecting of her. Praying people, and the Salvationist, had always been the contempt of her strong and callous mind. But on Sunday nights she was now observed to go out alone, and 'chapel' was the explanation which she coolly gave. *Which* chapel she did not specify: but, in reality, it was the Newton Street Hall, at which Walter frequently exhorted and 'prayed'. In the Church Lane school-room there was prayer-meeting on Thursday evenings; and twice within one month Rachel sallied forth on Thursday evening—soon after Walter. The secret disease which preyed upon the poor girl could hardly now be concealed. At first she suffered bitter, solitary shame; sobbed in a hundred paroxysms; hoped to draw a veil over her infirmity. But her gash was too glaring. In the long Sabbath evenings of summer he preached at street corners, and sometimes secretly, sometimes openly, Rachel would attend these meetings, singing meekly with the rest of the undivine hymns of the modern evangelist. In his presence, in the parlour, on other nights, she quietly sewed, hardly speaking. When, at seven p.m., she heard his key in the front door her heart darted toward its master; when in the morning he flew away to business her universe was cinders.

'It's a wonder to me what's coming to our Rachel lately,' said Annie in the train, coming home; 'you're doing her soul good, or something, aren't you?'

He chuckled, with slushy suction-sounds about the back of the tongue and molars.

'Oh, that be jiggered for a tale!' he said *'she's* all right.'

'I know her better than you, you see. She's quite changed—since you've come. Looks to me as if she's having a touch of the blues, or something.'

'Poor thing! She wants looking after, don't she?'

Annie laughed, too: but less brutally, more uneasily.

Walter said: 'But she *oughtn't* to have the blues, if she's giving her heart to the Lord! People seem to think a Christian must be this and that. A Christian, if it comes to that, ought to be the jolliest fellow going!'

This was on a Thursday, the night of the Church Lane prayer-meeting, and Walter had only time to rush in at No. 13, wash his face, snatch his Bible, and be off. Rachel, for her part, must verily now have been badly bitten with the rabies of love, or she would have felt that to follow tonight, for the third time lately, could not fail to incur remark. But this consideration never even entered a mind now completely blinded and entranced by the personality of Walter. Through the day her work about the house had been rushed forward with this very object, and at the moment when he banged the door after him she was before her glass, dressing in blanched, intense and trembling flurry, and casting, as she bent to give the last touches to her fringe, a look of bitterest hate at the projection of her lip above the teeth.

This night, for the first time, she waited in the chapel till the end of the service, and walked slowly homeward on the way which she knew that Walter would take; and he came striding presently, that morocco Bible in his hand, nearly every passage in which was neatly under-ruled in black and red inks.

'What, is that you?' he said, taking into his a hand cold with sweat.

'It is,' she answered, in a hard, formal tone.

'You don't mean to say you've been to the meeting?'

'I do.'

'Why, where were my eyes? *I* didn't see you.'

'It isn't likely that you would want to, Mr Teeger.'

'Go on—drop that! What do you take me for? I'm only too glad! And I tell you what it is, Miss Rachel, I say to you as the Lord

The Bride

Jesus said to the young man: "Thou art not far from the kingdom of heaven." '

She was *in* it!—near him, alone, in a darkling square, yet suffering, too, in the flames of a passion such as perhaps consumes only the strongest natures.

She caught for support at his unoffered arm; and when he bent his steps straight homeward, she said, trembling violently: 'I don't wish to go home as yet. I wish to have a little walk. Do you mind, Mr Teeger?'

'Mind, no. Come along, then,' and they went walking among an intricacy of streets and squares, he talking of 'the Work,' and of common subjects. After half an hour, she was saying: 'I often wish I was a man. A man can say and do what he likes; but with a girl it's different. There's you, now, Mr Teeger, always out and about, having people listening to you, and that. I often wish I was only a man.'

'Oh, well, it all depends how you look at it,' he said. 'And, look here, you may as well call me Walter and be done.'

'Oh, I shouldn't think of *that*,' she replied. 'Not till—'

Her hand trembled on his arm.

'Well, out with it, why don't you?'

'Till—till we know something more definite about you—and Annie.'

He chuckled slushily, she now leading him fleetly round and round a square.

'Ah, you girls again!' he cried, 'been blabbing again like all the girls! It takes a bright man to hide much from them, don't it?'

'But there isn't much to hide in this case, as far as I can see—*is* there?'

Always Walter laughed, straining deep in the throat. He said: 'Oh, come—that would be telling, wouldn't it?'

After a minute's stillness, this treacherous phrase came from Rachel: 'Annie doesn't care for anyone, Mr Teeger.'

'Oh, come—that's rather a tall order, *any* one. *She's* all right.'

'But she *doesn't*. Of course, most girls are silly, and that, and like to get married—'

'Well, that's only nature, ain't it?'

This was a joke; and downward the laugh strained in his throat, like struggling phlegm.

'Yes, but they don't understand what love is,' said Rachel. 'They haven't an idea. They like to be married women, and have a husband, and that. But they don't know what love is—believe me! The men don't either.'

How she trembled!—her body, her dying voice—she pressing heavily upon him, while the moon triumphed now through cloud glaring a moment white on the lunacy of her ghostly face.

'Well, I don't know—I think *I* understand, lass, what it is,' he said.

'You don't, Mr Teeger!'

'How's that, then?'

'Because, when it takes you, it makes you—'

'Well, let's have it. You seem to know all about it.'

Now Rachel commenced to tell him what 'it' was—in frenzied definitions, and a power of expression strange for her. *It* was a lunacy, its name was Legion, it was possession by the furies; it was a spasm in the throat, and a sickness of the limbs, and a yearning of the eye-whites, and a fire in the marrow; it was catalepsy, trance, apocalypse; it was high as the galaxy, it was addicted to the gutter; it was Vesuvius, borealis, the sunset; it was the rainbow in a cesspool, St John plus Heliogabalus, Beatrice plus Messalina; it was a transfiguration, and a leprosy, and a metempsychosis, and a neurosis; it was the dance of the maenads, and the bite of the tarantula, and baptism in a sun: out poured the wild definition in simple words, but with the strife of one fighting for life. And she had not half done when he understood her fully; and he had no sooner understood her, than he was subdued, and succumbed.

'You don't mean to say—' he faltered.

'Ah, Mr Teeger,' she answered, 'there's none so blind as those who will not see.'

His arm stole round her shuddering body.

Everyone is said to have his failing; and this man, Walter, in no respect a man of strong mind, was certainly on his amatory side, most sudden, promiscuous, and infirm. And this tendency was, if anything, heightened by the quite sincere strain of his mind in the direction of 'spiritual things': for, under sudden temptation, back rushed his being, with the greater rigour, into its natural channel. On the whole, had he not been a Puritan, he would have been a Don Juan.

The Bride

In an instant Rachel's weight was hanging upon his neck, he kissing her with passion.

After this she said to him: 'But you are only doing this out of pity, Walter. Tell the truth, you are in love with Annie?'

He, like Peter, tumbled at once into a fib. 'That's what *you* say!'

'You are,' she insisted, filled with the bliss of the fib.

'Bah! I'm not. Never was. You are the girl for me.'

When they went home, they entered the house at different times, she first, he waiting twenty minutes in the street.

The house was small, so the sisters slept together in the second-floor front room; Walter in the second-floor back; Mrs Evans in the first-floor back, the first-floor front being 'the drawing-room'. The girls, therefore, generally went to bed together: and that night, as they undressed, there was a row.

First, a long silence. Then Rachel, to say something, pointed to some new gloves of Annie's, asking: 'How much did you give for those?'

'Money and kind words,' replied Annie.

This was the beginning.

'Well, there's no need to be rude about it,' said Rachel. She was happy, in paradise, despised Annie that night.

'Still,' said Annie, after a silence of ten minutes before the glass, 'still, I should never run after a man like that. I'd die first.'

'I haven't the least idea what you're talking about,' replied Rachel.

'You have. I should be *ashamed* of myself, if I were you.'

'Talk away. You're a little fool.'

'It's *you*. Throwing yourself at the head of a man who doesn't care for you. What *can* you call yourself?'

Rachel laughed—happily, yet dangerously.

'Don't bother yourself, my girl,' she said.

'Think of going out every night to meet a man in that way: look here, it's too disgusting of you, girl!'

'Is it?

'You can't deny that you were with Mr Teeger tonight?'

'That I wasn't.'

'It's false! Anyone can see it by the joy in your face.'

'Well, suppose I was, what about it?'

'But a woman should be decent, I think; a woman should be able to command her feelings, and not expose herself like that. Believe me, it gives me the creeps all over to think of.'

'Never mind, don't be jealous, my girl.'

The gentle Annie flamed!

'Jealous! of you!'

'There isn't any need, you know—not *yet*.'

'But I'm *not!* There never *will* be need! Do you take Mr Teeger for a raving lunatic? I should go and have some false teeth put in first if I were you!'

Thus did Annie drop to the rock-bed of vulgarity; but she knew it to be necessary in order to touch Rachel, as with a white-hot wire, on her very nerve of anguish, and, in fact, at these words Rachel's face resembled white iron, while she cried out, 'Never mind my teeth! It isn't the teeth a man looks at! A man knows a finely built woman when he sees her—not like a little dumpy podge!'

'Thank you. You are very polite,' replied Annie, browbeaten by an intensity fiercer than her own. 'But still, it's nonsense, Rachel, to talk of my being jealous of *you*. I knew Mr Teeger six months before you. And you won't know him much longer either, for I don't want to have mother disgraced here, and this is no fit place for him to lodge in. I can easily make him leave it soon—'

At this thing Rachel flew, with minatory palm over Annie's cheek, ready to strike 'You *dare* do anything to make him go away! I'll tear your little—'

Annie winked, flinched, uttered a sob, no more fight left in her.

So for two weeks the situation lasted. Only, after that night, so intense grew the bitterness between the sisters, that Annie moved down to the first-floor back, sleeping now with Mrs Evans who dimly wondered. As for Walter, meanwhile, his heart was divided within him. He loved Annie; he was fascinated and mesmerised by Rachel. In another age and country he would have married both. Every day he came to a different resolve, not knowing what to do. One thing was evident—a wedding-ring would be necessary, and he purchased one, uncertain for which of the girls.

The Bride

'Look here, lass,' he said to Annie in the train, coming home, 'let us put a stop to this. The boss doesn't seem to be in a hurry about that rise of screw, so suppose we get spliced, and be done?'

'Privately?'

'Rather. Your ma and sister mustn't know—not just yet a while.'

'And you will still keep on living at the house?'

'Well, of course, for the time being.'

She looked up into his face and smiled. It was settled.

But two nights afterwards he met Rachel on his way home from prayer-meeting; at first was honest and distant; but then committed the incredible weakness of going with her for a walk among the squares, and, ended by winning from her an easily granted promise of marriage, on the same terms as those arranged with Annie.

When, the next day at lunch-time, he put his foot on the threshold of the Registrar's office to give notice, he was still in a state of agonised indecision as to the name which he should couple with his own.

When the official said, 'Now the name of the other party?' Walter hesitated, shuffled with his feet, then answered:

'Rachel Evans.'

Not till he was again in the street did he remember that Rachel was the name of both the girls, and that liberty of choice between them still remained to him.

Now, from the day of 'notice' to the day of wedlock an interval of twenty-one clear days must, by law, elapse, and Walter, though weak enough to inform both the sisters of the step he had taken, was careful to give them only a vague idea of the date fixed. His once clear conscience, meanwhile, was grievously troubled, his feet in a net; he feared to look within himself; he feared to speak to God; and went drifting like flotsam on the river of chance.

And chance alone it was which at last cast him upon the land. The fifth day before the marriage was a Bank Holiday, and he had arranged with Rachel to go out with her that day to Hyde Park, she to wait for him at an arranged spot at two o'clock. At two, then, at a street-corner, stood Rachel waiting, twirling her parasol, walking a little, returning. Walter, however, did not appear, and what could have happened was beyond her divination. Had he misunderstood or missed her? Though incredible, it was the only thing to think. To Hyde Park, at any rate, she went alone, feeling desolate and *ennuyée,* in the vague hope of there meeting him.

What had happened was this: Walter had been half-way toward the rendezvous with Rachel, when he was met in the street by Annie, who had gone to spend the day with a married friend at Stroud Green, but had returned, owing to the husband's illness. Seeing Walter, her face lit up with smiles.

'Harry's down with the influenza,' she said, 'so I couldn't stay and bore poor Ethel. Where are you going?'

For the first time since his 'conversion' twelve years before, Walter, with a high flush, now consciously lied.

'Only to the schoolroom,' he said, 'to hunt for something.'

'Well, I am open to be taken out, if any kind friend will be so kind,' she said fondly.

Now, he had that morning vowed to himself to wed Rachel; and by this vow he now again vowed to be bound. All the more reason why, for the last time, he should 'take out' Annie.

'Come along, then, old girl,' he gaily said: 'where shall we go?'

'Let us go to Hyde Park,' said Annie. And to Hyde Park they went, Walter, ever and anon, stabbed by the bitter memory of waiting Rachel.

At five o'clock the two were walking along the north bank of the Serpentine westward toward a two-arched bridge, which is also pierced by a third narrow arch over the bank: to this narrow arch, since it was drizzling, they were making for shelter, when Rachel, a person of the keenest vision, sighted them from the south bank. She was frantic at once. Annie, who was supposed to be at Stroud Green! *What treachery!* This, then, was why . . . She ran panting along the bank, toward the bridge, then over it, northward, and now heard the two under the arch, who stood there talking of the wedding. Unfortunately, just here is a block of masonry, which prevented Rachel from leaning directly over the arch to listen. Yet the necessity to hear was absolute: so she ran back clear of the masonry, and bent far over the parapet, outwards and sidewards toward the arch, straining neck, body, ears, and anyone looking into those staring eyes *then* would have comprehended the doctrine of the Ferine Soul. But she was at a disadvantage, heard

The Bride

only murmurs, and—was that a kiss? Further and further forth she strained. And now suddenly, with a cry, she is in the water, where it is shallow near the bank. In the fall her head struck upon a stone in the mud.

For three days she screamed continuously the name of Walter, filling the street with it, calling him hers only. On the third night, in the midst of a frightful crisis of cries, she suddenly died.

'Oh, Rachel, don't say you are dead!' cried Annie over her.

The death occurred two days before the marriage-day, and on the next, Walter, well wounded, said to Annie: 'This knocks our little affair on the head, of course.'

Annie was silent. Then, with a pout, she said: 'I don't see why. After all, it was her own fault entirely. Why should *we* suffer?'

For the feud between the sisters had become cruel as death; and it outlasted death: Annie, on the subject of Rachel and Walter, being no longer a gentle girl, but marble, without respect or pity.

And so, in spite of the trepidations and hesitancy of Walter, the marriage took place, even while Rachel lay stretched on the bed in the second-floor front of No. 13.

The ceremony did not, however, transpire without hitch and omen. It was necessary, first of all, for Walter to forewarn Annie that he had given notice of her to the Registrar by her second name of 'Rachel'—a mad-looking proceeding that was almost the cause of a rupture which nothing but Walter's most ardent pleadings could steer him clear of. At any rate it was to 'Rachel,' and not to 'Annie' that he was, as a matter of fact, after all married.

After the ceremony, performed in their lunch-time, they returned to business together in Little Britain.

At ten o'clock the same night, as he was going up to bed, she ran after him, and in the passage there was a long, furtive kiss—their last on earth.

'Twelve o'clock?' he whispered intensely.

She held up her forefinger. 'One!'

'Oh, say twelve!'

She did not answer, but drew her palm playfully across his cheek, meaning consent, for Mrs Evans was an inveterately heavy sleeper. He went up. And, careful to leave his door a little ajar, he extinguished his candle, and went to bed. In the apartment near by lay stark in the dark—with learned, eternal eyelids and drowsy brow—the dead.

Walter could not but think of this presence close at hand. 'Well, poor girl!' he sighed. 'Poor Rachel! Well, well. His way is in the sea, after all, and His path in the Great Deep, and His footsteps are not known.' Then he thought of Annie—the little wife! But instead of Annie, there was Rachel. The two women fought vehemently for his thought—and ever the dead was stronger than the living. . . . Instead of Annie there was Rachel—and again Rachel.

At last he could hear twelve strike from a steeple, and sat up in bed, listening eagerly for the door to open, or a footfall on the floor.

A little American clock ticked in the room; and in the flue of the chimney was a sough and chaunt just audible.

Suddenly she was intensely with him, filling the chamber—from nowhere. He had heard no footsteps, no opening of the door: yet certainly, she was with him *now*, all suddenly, close to him, over him, talking breathlessly to him.

His first sensation was a shuddering which strongly shook him from head to foot, like the shuddering of Russian cold. She held him down by the shoulders; was stretched at length on the bed, over him; and the room seemed full of a rustling and rushing, very strange, like starched muslins rushing out in stormy agitation. She was speaking, too, to him, in *breathless haste,* whimpering a secret gibberish which whimpered like a pup for passion—about love and its definition, and about the soul, and the worm, and Eternity, and the passion of death, and the nuptials of the tomb, and the lust and hollowness of the void. And he, too, was speaking, whispering through his pattering teeth, saying: 'Sh-h-h, Rachel—Annie, I mean—sh-h-h, my girl—your ma will hear! Rachel, don't—sh-h-h, now!' But even while he kept up this 'sh-h-h, dear—sh-h-h, now,' he was conscious of the invasion of a strange rage, of such a strength as if energy was being vehemently pumped into him from some behemoth omnipotence. The form above him he could hardly discern, the room was so dark, but he felt that her garment was flowing forth from her neck in a continuous flutter, with the rustling of the starch of a thousand shrouds, like the outflow of a pennant in wind; and the quivering gauze seemed now to swell and

The Bride

fill the chamber, and now to sink again to the size of woman. And ever the rhapsody of love and death went on, mixed with the chattered 'Sh-h-h, Rachel—Annie, I mean,' of Walter; till, suddenly, he was involved in an embrace so horrible, felt himself encompassed by a might so intolerable, that his soul fainted within him. He sank back; thought span and failed in darkness beneath the spell of that lullaby; he muttered, 'Receive my spirit. . . .'

After two days Walter, still unconscious, died. His disfigured body they placed in a grave not far from Rachel's.

THE END